DEATHLESS

SCOTT PRUSSING

Heather,

Enjoy!

Scott Prussing

This is a work of fiction. All the characters or events portrayed in this novel are either fictitious or used fictitiously.

DEATHLESS

Scott Prussing Publishing
1027 Felspar St.
Suite 2
San Diego, CA 92109

Cover design:
Theresa Jackson at Orchard View Color and Scott Prussing

ISBN: 0615533051
ISBN-13: 978-0615533056

GOLDEN CIRCLE

This page is a big THANK YOU to the biggest fans and supporters of BREATHLESS, Book One in the Blue Fire Saga. They bought multiple copies (or caused multiple copies to be bought) and/or supported BREATHLESS relentlessly on Facebook, Twitter and other places online.

I give you the members of the GOLDEN CIRCLE:

Cheryl Gillespie
Nichole Smith
Candice Conway Simpson
Marie Manalo
Angie Brennan
Cami Faith Brakhage
Kristin Maier
September Angel
Dan Flaherty
Alexia Purdy
Heather Hodapp
Dara-Janel Drilling
Renee C. Fountain
Johna Ferra
Jim Houle
Tamika Anderson
Natalie Lutz
Barbara Bright Wilder

Teri Kappes
Victoria Kennedy
Kristi Brolezi
Danielle Christian
Anne Wallace
Teresa McWhirter
Lisa Gisczinski
Bella Belikov Colella
Tannis Herron
Heather Devirgilio
Heather Smallwood
Rhonda Valverde
Ruby Groves
Wendy Lovetiggi Gonzalez
Andrea Hindbaugh
Ashley Kay
Angie Edmonds

To all the fans of Breathless, whose enthusiasm made this book necessary.

PROLOGUE

107 years ago

The volkaane Rave raced silently through the snow-filled woods. His long, dark copper hair streamed behind him as he flashed through the trees, his bronze skin seeming almost to glow in the gray twilight. Tiny blue flames flickered from his fingertips, the only outward manifestation of the magical fire blazing inside him.

Despite his speed, footing was not a problem—the heat from his inner fire melted the thin carpet of snow almost as soon as his moccasin covered feet touched it, leaving steaming ovals of rotting leaves in his wake. A trail of similar marks stretched ahead of him, left by his friend Helm. But no steam floated up from Helm's footprints, and Rave knew he was almost certainly too late to save his friend.

Helm's horrific screams still echoed in his ears. Only one thing could make a volkaane scream like that—the fangs of a vampire. And if a vampire had ripped into Helm's throat, then Helm was almost certainly dead by now. Still, Rave had to try. If he couldn't save Helm, Rave hoped he could at least avenge him.

Too often of late, he had heard similar screams, each one marking the death of a volkaane. It was the cursed *Destiratu*, he knew. Normally, volkaanes and vampires maintained a kind of balance, each hunting and slaying only the weak or the foolish. But

1

when magical energies in the earth and in the air combined to form the phenomenon known as *Destiratu,* everything changed. Somehow, in a way Rave did not fully understand and none of his elders could fully explain, *Destiratu* raised the killing ire in volkaane and vampire alike. Hunger and bloodlust raged, becoming uncontrollable for many. Fortunately, *Destiratu* arose less than once every hundred years.

Understanding the phenomenon was not important now— surviving it was all that mattered. Part of Rave knew he should be moving more carefully, that danger was likely near, but the magic had magnified his hunger—and his anger as well. So he raced through the trees, moving with a speed even a vampire could never match, hoping against hope Helm was not yet dead. Rave was still young—only ten years past the four decade mark that symbolized volkaane adulthood—and still foolish. He did not even consider that this same blinding hunger was behind Helm's demise.

Up ahead, he saw the sight he had dreaded to see. Helm's body lay crumpled on the ground in the center of a circle of still steaming leaves. Even in death, his inner fire had lingered, melting the snow around him. A few feet from his friend's body, Rave spied a long pile of gray and white ash. Despite his grief, he allowed himself a small smile. Helm had managed to kill one of his foes before being slain. Leading away from the circle, Rave saw two sets of widely spaced footprints that could only have been made by a pair of vampires. Helm had had the misfortune to run into three of the creatures. He never stood a chance.

Rave knelt at his dead friend's side. Helm's lifeless eyes stared skyward. His throat had been savagely ripped open, confirming what Rave already knew. There was no blood in the grisly wound or anywhere on the ground—no vampire would waste even a single drop of the glowing blue liquid, a treasure they tasted only rarely.

Tenderly, Rave closed his friend's eyes and then rested his palm Helm's forehead. Helm's skin was still warm, but the heat that was the essence of a volkaane was gone. Rave ignored the voice whispering in his head that the vampires might still be close, just as he ignored the training which taught him he should be directing his senses outward, letting his instincts feel any trace of vampire presence. Such was the effect of *Destiratu*, especially on the young and inexperienced. Rave was both.

Had he followed the tracks of the departed vampires, he would have seen they had taken to the trees less than a hundred yards from where he knelt. He would have been alert to any danger from above.

Instead, he was taken by surprise when two vampires thumped to the ground on either side of him. Despite his youth, Rave's magical inner fire ranked among the most powerful of his kind. Rare was the vampire who could match his power, but even he could not hope to defeat two of the creatures at once. Still, he was determined to take at least one of his foes with him, just as Helm had done.

The vampires probably expected him to flee. Perhaps he could have escaped even now, using his superior speed, but his *Destiratu* fueled hunger would not let him try. From his kneeling position, he lunged up at the vampire in front of him, wrapping his arms around its back and pressing his mouth toward the vampire's face, ready to let his magical fire suck the life breath from the creature.

Vampires were fast as well, though, and he felt the second creature fasten its powerful grip upon his shoulders from behind, ready to tear him from its brother. In a moment, its fangs would sink into Rave's flesh. There was little Rave could do to prevent it, so he forced his mouth closer to the vampire in his grasp.

Suddenly, he felt a blast of volkaane heat behind him, and the hold on his shoulders vanished. There was no time to wonder about it now—the vampire in his grip was trying to reach his neck with its fangs.

With no help from its companion, the vampire was no match for Rave. Rave pressed his mouth over the creature's nose and lips. The raging heat of his magical fire sucked the life force from the vampire, funneling it into Rave's lungs. The sensation was beyond exhilarating, and Rave relished every moment of it.

In less than a minute, it was over. He dropped the vampire's limp body to the ground. The heat from Rave's fire continued to consume the beast from the inside out. The vampire's pallid face slowly grew lighter, becoming almost translucent. With a sudden, barely audible crackling sound, the creature shimmered and crumpled to a pile of gray and white ash.

"Well done, young Rave," said a familiar voice behind him.

Rave turned and smiled at Balin, his friend and mentor. An identical pile of ash lay at Balin's feet. Balin had destroyed his vampire even before Rave had finished with his. Tiny blue flames flickered from Balin's fingertips. Rave glanced down at his own fingers. They, too, glowed brightly.

"Without your help," Rave said, "I fear the outcome would have been less pleasant."

"That's precisely why I followed you. You must be more careful, young Rave. *Destiratu* is a dangerous time for all, but it is especially so for the inexperienced."

"I'm sorry, Balin. You taught me better than this. But when I heard Helm scream, I could not stop myself."

"Such is the power of *Destiratu*," Balin said, "as well as the pull of anger." He draped his arm around Rave's shoulders. "I believe you are destined for great things, young Rave, but for that to happen, you must first survive."

1. NEW BEGINNINGS

Leesa Nyland was afraid to open her eyes. Not because she was scared she might see something frightening—though god knows she'd seen and experienced enough scary stuff her first few months at Weston College to last a lifetime—but because she was afraid if she opened her eyes she might discover she'd merely been dreaming all the *wonderful* things that had happened.

She had every right to be worried about that, she knew. She had seen and done things in the last three months—could it really have been only three months?—that few people would believe, or could even imagine. Maybe it all *was* just a dream. Maybe there were no vampires. Maybe she'd never allowed herself to be bitten by the enigmatic Stefan, in a bargain to save her brother Bradley from an imprisonment far more horrible than death. She almost reached for her throat, but pulled her fingers back. What if she found no twin scars there? That would mean it was only a dream, and that Bradley was still missing. And that her mom was probably still a recluse, refusing to leave the house during the day, claiming sunlight hurt her skin because she'd been bitten by a one-fanged vampire. Leesa did not want to return to that reality.

And she certainly did not want to discover that the comforting warmth she felt against her cheek was nothing more than her electric blanket. No, she much preferred believing the magical heat radiated from her amazing volkaane boyfriend Rave. She snuggled her face more tightly against the warm cloth and sighed.

She could feel the hard muscles of Rave's chest working beneath the material. This was no dream—no blanket or pillow would move like that. She opened her eyes and confirmed it, staring at Rave's brown and purple flannel shirt, not her blanket. She looked up into his handsome face and smiled.

He carried her effortlessly, racing through the woods along old game paths at speeds that should have been impossible, his gait so smooth she felt almost as if they were flying. She loved it when Rave carried her like this, cradled snug in his arms. It more than made up for his people not using cars or any form of transportation other than their feet.

Volkaanes did not use any electrical or battery operated devices. They couldn't. The energy from their magical inner heat simply shorted out any kind of appliance. Leesa had learned that the hard way, when she'd tried to use her cell phone while holding Rave's hand. Even the indirect contact had destroyed her cell, frying the chips and the battery. And since Rave could not use phones, she had no way to contact him when she wanted to see him or even to talk to him. All she could do was wait for him to show up. While she wished that weren't the case, it served to make any time they spent together extra special.

Rave's magical fire had one other drawback—a major, major drawback. If he lost control for even a moment when they kissed, it could kill her, burning the life out of her from the inside out. And that really sucked, because that same inner heat made his kisses beyond amazing. Most girls were merely waxing poetic when they said they "melted" at their boyfriend's kisses, but with Rave it was almost literally true. So far, she and Rave had been able to share only the briefest of kisses, under the watchful eye of Rave's mentor Balin, who could sense even the slightest changes in Rave's heat. Balin and Rave were working on technique for controlling Rave's fire that few volkaanes dared attempt, but it was still far too dangerous for Leesa to kiss Rave in the manner she longed to.

She had given in fully to his kiss only once, when she thought Stefan had made her a vampire and Rave had come to kill her as he'd promised. Luckily, Rave had learned enough control by then and broke the kiss before she was harmed. But she still remembered how amazing that near fatal kiss felt, and how she thought what a wonderful way to die it would have been. She longed for the day when they could kiss without danger, without fear. Still, she was certain their brief kisses were far beyond anything other girls could even imagine, no matter how in love they might be.

As if Rave was reading her mind, he bent his head and kissed her lightly on the cheek. She thrilled as the familiar warmth flowed through her. Kisses anywhere other than on her mouth were safe, though they would leave a mark if he let his lips linger too long.

Rave carried her for another few minutes before setting her gently to the ground. Leesa sighed, wishing the journey was a longer one—a much longer one. But they were just going to her aunt and uncle's house for Thanksgiving dinner, and they were almost there. With no more trees to hide their passage, they would walk the rest of the way. Leesa rose up on her toes and kissed Rave on the cheek.

"Thanks for the lift," she said, smiling.

"Anytime, beautiful."

Leesa fluffed her fingers through her long blond hair, trying to work out the tangles caused by her "ride."

"This is far and away my favorite way to travel," she said, "but it sure does a number on my hair."

Rave laughed and plucked a few pieces of forest debris from Leesa's heavy dark blue sweatshirt. "I imagine it must be a bit like riding in a car with your head stuck out the window—not that I've ever had the pleasure."

"Ha! Exactly," Leesa said, grinning. "Only this is a lot more fun."

"Does that mean you no longer mind having a boyfriend without a car?"

"Well, I wish you could at least ride in one now and then, but no,

I don't mind at all. I do wish you volkaanes would figure out some way you could use a cell phone, though."

"Maybe Balin and I could figure something out. But we would have to stop working on the kissing thing while we did."

"Ha! Never mind. Number one priority: the kissing thing. Number two priority: the kissing thing. Number three priority:...."

"Let me guess. The kissing thing?"

Leesa laughed. "How'd you guess?"

Rave grinned. "Just a wild hunch."

Leesa grabbed his bicep in both her hands and snuggled against him. "Mmmm, strong *and* smart. What more could a girl want?"

She felt her stomach quietly rumble, reminding her she was hungry. Wanting to save plenty of room for Thanksgiving dinner, she had eaten only half a bowl of cereal for breakfast.

"Hungry?" Rave asked.

Leesa blushed. She couldn't believe he had heard that, but Rave's hearing was far more acute than any human. She shook her head—there were more than a few downsides to having a supernatural boyfriend, for sure. She wondered if he could hear her heartbeat, too.

"Yeah. I didn't have much breakfast. Aunt Janet's a great cook, so I wanted to make sure I left plenty of room for dinner. And for Uncle Roger's pies, too. They're to die for."

"Well, what are we waiting for, then? Let's get to your aunt and uncle's so we can get some food into you."

"I'm down with that, for sure," Leesa said. She let go of his arm and began limping toward the street. Rave fell into step beside her.

Leesa had been born missing a small piece of bone in her lower leg and had limped all her life. It didn't hurt, and she proudly maintained she could walk as fast and far as almost anyone—anyone who was not a volkaane, that is. She seldom even thought about her limp, unless someone asked her about it, or sometimes when she was with Rave and noticed how noisily she walked compared to him. But everyone walked noisily compared to Rave, who seemed to be able to walk over any surface, even dead crinkly leaves, and scarcely make a sound.

She reached out and took his hand. As always, the warmth of his skin thrilled her. She smiled, thinking back to the first few times they'd held hands, before he'd revealed his magical nature. Rave had kept his gloves on, so she wouldn't notice his unnatural warmth. She'd made the mistake of telling her friends about it, and they had teased her endlessly. Thankfully, the days of gloves were long gone.

Nobody else in her life knew Rave was not human, and that was how she intended to keep it, for awhile, at least. Her mother and brother had suffered enough from supernatural creatures—they didn't need to know she was in love with one, even one who was a sworn enemy of vampires. Rave could control his heat well enough now that something like a quick handshake would not give him away, so she expected no problems keeping his secret.

When they reached her aunt and uncle's house, a pale yellow Colonial set back from the street behind a wide yard dominated by four leafless maple trees, Rave gently grabbled Leesa's arm and drew her to a stop.

"I think you should bring their dog outside to meet me before I go in."

Leesa looked at him with a puzzled expression.

"How come? Max is a really great dog. He likes everybody." A sudden thought flashed through her brain. "Uh, oh. Don't tell me dogs don't like volkaanes."

"No, it's not that. They like us just fine. Better than fine, in fact. Volkaanes have a special relationship with many animals, especially dogs. But Max may act a bit strange until I introduce myself to him, and I do not think we want your family to see that."

"Oh… okay. But what am I going to tell everyone when I show up at the door without you?"

Rave thought for a moment. "Just tell them I am admiring their beautiful neighborhood for a few minutes."

"Okay. They may think that's a little weird, though."

"Trust me, it's better than what they might think if Max meets me inside."

Leesa did trust him, implicitly. She kissed him on the cheek.

"Back in minute," she said.

She turned and headed for the door. Max came rushing to greet her before she even got the door open. He was a four-year-old golden retriever with seemingly endless energy and the friendly demeanor common to his breed. Leesa stepped inside the house and gave him a quick but vigorous chest rub, one of his favorite things.

Bradley and Uncle Roger were sitting on the couch, watching a football game on the widescreen. Uncle Roger was wearing the blue and red number twelve Patriots jersey he always wore when he watched football, whether his team was playing or not. Bradley wasn't sporting any team colors, but he was an avid Jets fan, the result of living in New Jersey for the first ten years of his life. Leesa wasn't much of a football fan herself, but she knew those two teams hated each other, and that Bradley and Uncle Roger would be in for some animated afternoons when their teams met. She thought how wonderful it was to be thinking of her brother arguing about football, rather than about the ordeal he had suffered for the last two years, when no one knew what had happened to him.

She didn't see her mom or Aunt Janet, and guessed they were still busy cooking. The delicious smells emanating from the kitchen made her stomach rumble again. She smiled, wondering if Rave could hear it from outside. She hoped his hearing wasn't *that* good.

Bradley popped up from the couch to greet her.

"Hey, pumpkin," he said as gave her a warm hug.

Leesa thought her brother looked great. Especially for someone who had been kept captive for almost two years by a female vampire as a "feeder"—a kind of human blood bank. When Stefan brought Bradley to her that fateful night she'd bargained for his freedom, her brother had been paler even than Stefan, and was so thin and weak he couldn't stand on up his own. Now, his color was back to normal, and he had gained some much needed weight. He could still use another ten pounds, but Leesa expected Thanksgiving dinner should be good for a few pounds, at least.

Uncle Roger followed Bradley's hug with one of his own. As she wrapped her arms around his ample form, she wished she had some magic powers of her own, so she could magically transfer a few of Uncle Roger's extra pounds to her brother. She was certain they would both go for that.

"Is that my beautiful daughter I hear?" Judy Nyland, hurrying out of the kitchen.

Leesa smiled. "Hi, mom."

They embraced each other tightly. Leesa couldn't believe how much her mom had changed. Her pallid complexion finally had some color to it, and there was barely a trace left of the anxious, timid woman Leesa had grown up with. She'd spent her entire childhood thinking her mom was crazy, with that insane story about having been bitten by a one-fanged vampire. But the story turned out to be true. One of Leesa's professors had cured her mom, by injecting her with the blood of a one fanged-vampire Rave had captured for them. Her mom was becoming more and more normal every day.

"Where's Rave, honey?" Judy asked when they finally ended their embrace.

"He's outside, enjoying the neighborhood. I'm going to take Max out for a couple minutes, and then we'll all be back in." She looked at her uncle. "Is that okay, Uncle Roger?"

Uncle Roger grinned. He had the widest smile Leesa had ever seen.

"Sure is. And I'm pretty sure you won't get any argument from Max."

"Do I need his leash?"

"Not as long as you're staying in the yard. He won't go anywhere."

"Okay. I'll let you guys get back to your game. We'll be back in a few minutes."

Leesa held the door open, and Max raced outside. She pulled the door closed and watched as Max bounded down the stairs and galloped toward Rave. She had never seen Max this excited. She didn't know what was going to happen next, but was glad she had closed the door so no one else could see, just in case.

Rave held out his hand, palm out, and Max skidded to a halt five feet in front of him. Rave turned his palm down and lowered his hand. Max sank obediently to his belly on the grass.

Leesa was amazed. Max was an obedient dog, but he had never met Rave. She wasn't sure even Uncle Roger could have gotten Max to stop that quickly.

She moved closer, watching as Rave walked over to Max and knelt beside him. He seemed to whisper something into Max's ear, and then petted him on top of his head. When he stood up, Max got to his feet and stood next to him, waiting. They looked like they'd known each other forever.

Rave smiled at Leesa. "It's all good now. Max and I are buddies. We can go inside. He will behave normally."

"Wow. That was something," Leesa said. "Max always has a lot of energy, but I've never seen him quite that amped up. I'm glad you thought to meet him outside. I'm not sure the house could have withstood that much Max."

They went inside. Rave had already met everyone, so no introductions were necessary, just hellos. Leesa watched as Rave moved easily about the room. He moved with such fluid grace you wouldn't notice unless you were watching closely for it, but he took care to remain a safe distance from anything electrical—the television, stereo, even lamps.

This time, Aunt Janet was able to pull herself away from the kitchen, so she and Leesa exchanged a warm embrace. Aunt Janet was four years older than her sister, but Leesa thought the two looked remarkably similar, now that her mom had lost the haunted look she had borne for so many years. The matching blue and white checked aprons both wore over their dresses did not hurt the similarity.

Aunt Janet was fifteen or twenty pounds heavier than Leesa's mom, but from the neck up no one could fail to see they were sisters. Both wore their dark blond hair medium short, styled casually with loose curls framing their faces. Aunt Janet had obviously taken her sister to visit her hair stylist. The most striking feature of each woman was a pair of bright blue eyes almost identical to the ones Leesa saw reflected in her mirror every day.

"Dinner will be ready in ten or fifteen minutes," Aunt Janet said.

"Then it's time for some of my special appetizers," Uncle Roger said, hurrying toward the kitchen with a big smile on his face.

Leesa smiled, too, knowing what was coming. Uncle Roger owned a bakery famous for its pies. His favorite saying was "life is short, eat dessert first."

Sure enough, Uncle Roger emerged from the kitchen carrying a platter filled with bite-sized squares of steaming apple pie. Toothpicks topped by red or blue foil streamers protruded from the center of each piece, making them easy to eat. Leave it to Uncle Roger to figure out how to turn pie into hors d'oeurves. He offered the platter to Leesa first.

The cinnamon-laced aroma of baked apples made her stomach rumble again. She grabbed a piece with each hand and plopped one into her mouth. The pie tasted even better than it smelled. The chunks of apple were soft and tangy, and the buttery crust simply melted in her mouth. Dessert first was definitely not a bad idea!

Dinner was just as delicious as Uncle Roger's appetizers. The turkey was moist and tender, and Aunt Janet's gravy was to die for. Side dishes included mashed potatoes, tender green beans sautéed with shallots and pine nuts, buttery sweet potatoes, cranberries and homemade stuffing made with raisins, almonds, celery and tiny bits of sausage.

Leesa ate healthy quantities of everything. Her hunger had long since been satisfied, and she was rapidly approaching the point of being stuffed. Reluctantly, she put down her fork, determined to save room for dessert.

She was glad to see Bradley reaching for a third helping of turkey—the more food her brother ate, the better. Uncle Roger was still eating with his usual gusto, and Rave did not seem to have slowed down, either. She could only imagine what his metabolism must be like, with all that inner heat.

She noticed her mom staring down at her plate, slowly pushing a piece of turkey around with her fork, but making no move to eat it. Her face seemed strangely sad.

"What's the matter, Mom?"

Judy looked up. "Oh, nothing, honey. I was just thinking how happy you and your brother look. I'm sorry I never made a dinner like this for you two."

"Mom, we've been over this. It wasn't your fault."

"We're the ones who are sorry, Mom," Bradley added. "Sorry we didn't believe your story. Maybe we could have done something differently if we had."

"Thankfully, all that's in the past," Aunt Janet said. "This year we have so much to be thankful for. Let's remember that."

"Amen to that," Uncle Roger said as he reached for another helping of turkey.

"I can't imagine anything better than this," Leesa said. "Being here with all of you, eating this delicious food… and with dessert still to come!"

Everyone laughed, but it was her mom's laughter that warmed Leesa's heart the most. She truly had never been happier.

Now if only that *Destiratu* thing Rave had told her about didn't mess everything up.

2. THROWING STONES

"This must be the place," Leesa said.

She stood with Rave and Max at the top of a long asphalt driveway above Black Pond State Park. Below them, the waters of a large lake sparkled in the sunshine. Leesa was wearing her heavy blue sweatshirt over a long sleeve pullover shirt and black leggings. Rave had on a dark brown, long sleeve waffle-knit shirt and jeans. With their inner heat, volkaanes didn't require much in the way of clothes, but Rave made sure always to wear something somewhat appropriate for the weather, to avoid drawing unnecessary attention or questions.

Uncle Roger had suggested Black Pond as a good place for a hike, since it was less than a fifteen minute walk from the house. Leesa almost wished it had been farther, so she could have enjoyed another ride in Rave's arms. But she wanted to get some exercise, and as wonderful as it felt to have Rave carry her, it did not qualify as exercise—even though it certainly got her heart rate up!

Max waited patiently in front of them, his side pressed up against Rave's leg. His tail wagged excitedly as he looked down toward the park, but he made no move to head down the driveway without them. Rave carried Max's leash in his hand—he had unfastened it as soon as they were out of sight of the house. Leesa had looked at him worriedly when he undid the leash, but Rave assured her there was nothing to worry about. He had knelt and whispered a few words into Max's ear, and Max had not strayed more than a few feet from them the whole way here. Leesa was amazed; every time she'd walked Max he was constantly pulling on his leash, wanting to smell or chase something. But not today. Not with Rave here.

It was just past ten o'clock on Saturday morning. The day promised to be a nice one, especially considering the season. The temperature had already topped forty degrees and the few puffy white clouds in the sky betrayed no hint of any coming bad weather. Perfect hiking weather, so that's what Leesa and Rave had decided to do.

Thanksgiving weekend was going great. Leesa was staying at her aunt and uncle's house, sharing a room with her mom. Since Bradley still lived there as well, they were all together for the first time in years. They had done some shopping and gone to a movie at the mall on Friday, then enjoyed Thanksgiving leftovers that evening. Rave had gone home Thursday night, but he had returned this morning.

A nice long hike gave them the perfect excuse for some alone time. Holding hands, they walked down the driveway toward the lake. Below them, a half-dozen boats and canoes floated lazily out on the water. All but one had at least one fishing pole hanging over the side. Leesa wondered what kind of fish lived in the lake.

The eastern shore was steep and rocky, plummeting into the lake at a sharp angle, so they turned west at the bottom of the ramp and followed a dirt trail into the mostly leafless trees. The path was flat and well-maintained, making walking easy. Max led the way, his tail wagging happily as he bounded along the trail. Despite his exuberance, he never got farther than twenty feet or so ahead of them, not even when they heard small animals rustling their way through the underbrush nearby.

"How are you doing this?" Leesa asked Rave when a rabbit streaked across the trail less than ten feet in front of Max and he made no move to chase it. "Dogs love to chase rabbits. I know Max does—I've seen him. But you've got him behaving like he's on an invisible leash."

Rave smiled. "It's no big deal. I just told him to be a good dog and stay near us."

Leesa looked at him skeptically. "That's it? You just told him to be a good dog?"

"I told you, volkaanes and dogs have a special affinity for each other."

"A special affinity?" Leesa said, frowning. "There's got to be more to it than that."

Rave shrugged. "I'm not sure I can explain it any better than that. It goes back ages, when volkaanes and werewolves forged an alliance against vampires, who were dominant back then. Wolves and dogs are closely related, so I guess some of that spilled over somehow."

Leesa stopped abruptly and grabbed Rave's arm. "Werewolves?" she asked. "Don't tell me werewolves are real, too."

"Of course they are. Or, at least they were. Something, or someone, wiped them out centuries ago."

"Vampires?" Leesa asked.

"No one really knows, at least not that I'm aware of. But I do not think vampires were behind it. We would know if vampires had done it, I think. It could simply have been a disease of some kind—or it could have been something more sinister."

Leesa's head felt like it was spinning. She had asked a simple question about Max—well, maybe not all that simple—and all of a sudden they were talking about werewolves. She wanted to know more, but decided she'd heard enough for now. She had to admit, dating a volkaane was never dull.

They hiked for another twenty-five minutes, and Leesa loved every bit of it. Sometimes the path carried them within a few feet of the water, other times it meandered farther back into the trees. Part way along, she began to grow warm, so she peeled off her sweatshirt and tied it around her waist. Max continued to resist all temptations to leave the trail. Finally, they reached the far side of the lake. The trail continued on, but it turned away from the lake and led off into the hills, so they stopped at a small dirt beach. It was a peaceful, pretty spot, and they had it all to themselves.

Leesa stooped and dug a small flat stone out of the soft dirt. Max rushed over and sniffed the rock, hoping Leesa had discovered some sort of treasure. He moved away after only a moment, clearly disappointed. Rave watched with interest as Leesa hefted the stone in her hand and studied it like it was something special. It looked like an ordinary rock to him.

"Watch this," Leesa said.

She bent slightly at the waist and whipped the stone out over the water with an underhand, sidearm motion. The stone skipped four or five times atop the lake's surface before sinking out of sight. Max began to run after the rock, thinking it was a game of fetch, but he stopped before his paws were barely wet.

"Hey, that's pretty good," Rave said.

"Pretty good, yeah," Leesa said, smiling. "But not good enough. Bradley used to tell me that if I could skip one six times, I could make a wish that would come true. I only got five that time."

Rave bent and picked up a rock. "Let me try."

Before he could throw it, Leesa laid her hand on his forearm to stop him. He had obviously never done this. With all the stuff he knew and all the amazing things he could do, it always surprised her when he was clueless about something as simple as skipping a stone on the water. Somehow, it made him seem more human.

She took the stone from his hand. "You have to use a flat one. This one's way too round. No way you could get it to skip."

She tossed it underhand into the water and squatted to find him a better rock. When she found one she liked, she pried it out of the ground and brushed the dirt off it.

"Try this one." She wrapped her thumb and index finger around the edge of the stone, like a backwards C. "Hold it like this."

She gave the rock to Rave and he gripped it the way she showed him. Trying to mimic her motion, he winged it out onto the lake. The rock flew so fast Leesa could barely follow it. It hit the water with a loud splash and sank without bouncing even once. Rave looked at her sheepishly.

"No wishes for me, I guess."

"It takes practice."

Leesa picked up another stone and hurled it out across the water. This time it skipped so many times she lost count. It was definitely more than six, though. She closed her eyes and tilted her head tilted upward, making a wish.

"That was great," Rave said when Leesa opened her eyes. "Nine skips."

Leesa looked at him skeptically. The tiny little skips at the end were almost impossible to count.

"You could count even all those little ones at the end?"

"Sure. No problem. Volkaanes have very keen eyesight. What did you wish for?"

Leesa smiled and shook her head. "If I tell you, it won't come true," she said. And she very badly wanted this wish to come true. "It's like blowing out the candles on a birthday cake. If you reveal the wish, you lose it."

Rave looked at her with a puzzled expression on his face.

"I guess volkaanes don't have birthday cakes, huh?" Leesa said. She grinned as she pictured Rave bent over a big chocolate birthday cake. Instead of blowing the candles out, he was blowing on unlit candles and igniting them with his magical fire. Naturally, the candles all burned blue.

Rave smiled. "We do not even have birthdays."

"Oh. Well, don't worry about it. Just know that if you tell your wish, you lose it. And I don't want to lose this one."

"I want a wish, too. Let me try one more."

He picked up a flat, round stone and threw it, mimicking Leesa's form. This time, it skipped off the surface and flew several hundred feet before it skipped again. By the time it finished skipping, it had flown almost clear across the lake. Even Max seemed mesmerized by Rave's throw.

"Holy crap!" Leesa said. "I forgot how strong you are. Good thing you didn't hit one of those boats—you'd have sunk the thing for sure." She swiveled her head back and forth, checking to see if anyone had witnessed Rave's throw. "I hope no one saw that. I'm not sure how we'd explain it."

"Was it good enough for a wish?"

Leesa grinned. "Yeah, it was. I'd say it was good for one gigantic wish." She grabbed his hand and pulled him away from the shoreline. "Let's get out of here, though, just in case someone happened to see."

They retraced their steps back the way they had come. Every time Leesa thought of Rave's throw, she grinned. She wondered if she'd ever stop being surprised by the things he could do. But then her thoughts turned more somber. She worried if Rave would one day grow tired of how normal she was. He had already told her that he'd never been attracted to a human—there was probably a good reason for that. So why should she think she could hold his attention for any real length of time?

"What's the matter, Leesa?" Rave asked. "You look so glum all of a sudden."

His question caught her by surprise. "Oh... I'm sorry. I was just thinking."

He stopped walking and turned to face her. "About?"

Leesa stared out at the lake. "About us," she admitted.

"I don't understand. Why does thinking about us make you sad? I always feel so good when I think about us."

"I usually do, too, Rave. Really, I do. But that throw of yours back there got me worrying."

Rave looked perplexed. "I don't understand. Why did that make you worry?"

"Oh, it's just a girl thing, I guess. I started wondering if you were going to get tired of me one of these days. I'm so ordinary. So human. And you're a volkaane." She was afraid to meet his eyes, so she looked down at her feet instead.

Rave put his hands on her shoulders. His wonderful warmth immediately flowed into her.

"You are anything but ordinary, Leesa, believe me. You have managed to make a volkaane fall in love with you, and to make a vampire want you for his consort. No ordinary girl could have done either of those things."

Leesa looked up at him and smiled. "Well, there is that, I guess."

"And don't forget," Rave continued, "you've got some of that *grafhym* blood in you, too."

Leesa's smile widened. *Grafhym* was the name given to one-fanged vampires, like the one who had bitten her mom while she was pregnant with Leesa. It was the taint of *grafhym* blood inside her that had prevented Stefan from turning her vampire, when she had agreed to his deal to save her brother.

"Ha! That's right. I'd forgotten about that. I guess I do have a bit of the supernatural in me after all."

Rave smiled back at her. "Yes, you do. And you know how much vampire blood turns me on." He didn't tell her he wasn't certain the taint of *grafhym* blood in her veins was enough to explain the strength of the pull between them. It was enough that she understood nothing was ever going to change the way he felt toward her.

3. AN UNEXPECTED CALL

Leesa and Rave walked back up the entrance drive of Black Pond Park. Halfway up the hill, her phone buzzed. She didn't know why, but a sense of impending trouble stole over her as she unzipped her small fanny pack and grabbed the cell. She automatically stepped away from Rave, taking no chances his energy would zap her phone. He grinned at her in understanding. Max just looked on curiously.

The screen showed the call was from an unknown caller. Leesa breathed a bit easier. At least the call wasn't from her mom or her brother. Still, she could not shake the feeling that this call meant trouble.

"Hello?" she said.

"Is this Leesa Nyland?" asked an unfamiliar male voice on the other end.

"Yes, it is."

"The Leesa Nyland who was born eighteen years ago in Springfield, New Jersey?"

The alarm bells in Leesa's head really started clanging now. What was this all about? Her fingers began twirling in hair, an unconscious habit she lapsed into when she was nervous.

"Yeah, that's me," she said cautiously. "Who is this, please?"

Leesa thought she heard a sigh of relief through the phone.

"Leesa, you don't know how glad I am to hear your voice. I've been trying to find you for quite some time. Where do you live now?"

Leesa wasn't sure she should answer that. The caller still had not identified himself. She glanced at Rave and saw he was watching her intently, a concerned look on his face. With his volkaane hearing, she knew he'd probably heard every word the guy had spoken.

"Who is this?" she asked again, more forcefully this time.

Never in a million years would she have guessed the words she heard next.

"It's your father, Leesa."

Leesa's jaw dropped. Was it possible? Her father had abandoned her family when she was only seven years old. She had not heard from him or of him since. Her fingers danced more rapidly in her hair.

"Dad?"

There was a brief hesitation before the man answered. "No, not him, Leesa. This is your *real* father."

The phone slipped from Leesa's suddenly lifeless fingers. Max barked once as Rave instinctively reached out to catch it. With his speed, he could have caught it easily, but at the last second he pulled his hand back. If he touched the phone, its circuits would be fried, so he let it crash to the pavement. At least there was a chance the phone would survive the fall. It banged onto the asphalt and bounced into a small puddle beside the drive.

Leesa bent to pick up it up. She felt like she was moving in slow motion, as if the air had magically developed the viscosity of water. Finally, her fingers closed around the phone and she picked it up. A narrow crack zigzagged through the plastic casing. She wiped the phone on her sweatshirt and then held it to her ear. The cell phone was dead.

Her knees began to feel weak and her head felt like it was spinning. She might have collapsed, but Rave had already enfolded her in his arms. She buried her head against his chest, unsure what to think or do. She barely felt Max rubbing his furry body against the back of her legs.

The man on the other end of the call was named Dominic, though he

23

could not remember the last time anyone had called him that. He stared at the now silent phone in his hand and cursed himself. He should have been less abrupt with his message, should have told her to prepare herself for some shocking news, and to please listen to what he had to say. Instead, he'd been so excited he had bulled ahead with no finesse and taken her by complete surprise, telling her the man she thought was her father was not really her dad, and that he, Dominic, was her real father. That was true in some ways, in others it was not. She would have difficulty understanding even if he was standing right in front of her trying to explain it—how could he have expected her to comprehend it through an unexpected phone call? He hadn't even gotten the chance to tell her his name. He had heard a noise before the connection was broken. He didn't know if Leesa had simply hung up on him, or if something had happened to her.

He slammed the phone down into its cradle, and then looked quickly around to see if anyone had noticed his outburst. The last thing he wanted was to draw attention. Dominic was tall and slender, with dark hair speckled with gray that hung fashionably over the collar of a black polo shirt. His neatly trimmed goatee was slightly lighter in color than his hair and came to a sharp point beneath his chin. He appeared to be in his late forties or early fifties, but he was far older than that. Far, far older.

He stood in the lobby of the Springfield Public Library, in front of a bank of three pay phones. It was getting more and more difficult to find working public phones these days, but Dominic had no choice. To say he was "off the grid" would have been putting it far too mildly. He had never been on the grid in the first place. He had no permanent residence, owned no phone and no car, had never possessed a credit card or bank account, or even a driver's license. He had no social security number and paid no taxes. As far as the ordinary world was concerned, Dominic did not exist.

His enemies knew he existed, though, and they were undoubtedly searching for him with as much diligence as he was searching for Leesa. Those enemies were deadly, and they would never quit. So Dominic needed to remain invisible, even though it compounded the difficulty in finding Leesa. At some point, he might need to risk his anonymity, but not yet. No, not yet.

He was certain his foes had no idea Leesa even existed, and he was going to do all he could to keep it that way. That was why he had disappeared before she was born, and why he stayed far away all these years, resisting the impulse even to check up on her. Staying away completely was the only way he knew to insure her safety, and her safety was more important than anyone could know. She hadn't needed him to be around—not then.

She was going to need him now, though. He had to find her. He had been searching for almost a year, starting a few months before her eighteenth birthday. Things were going to start happening to her— puzzling, frightening things—that she would not understand. That she could not understand. Indeed, they may already have started happening. He needed to explain those things to her, and train her how to control them. Especially with the rise of *Destiratu*.

Destiratu forming at the same time Leesa turned eighteen was something he could never have expected, could never have planned for. The magical phenomenon was so rare the chance of the two events happening at the same time had never occurred to him. He was not sure exactly how *Destiratu* might interact with Leesa's coming of age, but it was another thing he would have to deal with.

He had not expected finding her to be so difficult. The bond between them should have allowed him to sense her location within a hundred miles, but for some reason, he could not. He wondered if *Destiratu* had anything to with it, or if it was something else entirely. There was no way for him to know. He had spent months systematically crisscrossing the country, stopping every hundred miles or so and casting his senses outward, seeking her unique vibration, the one that should have resonated with his own, but had felt nothing. He had grown worried something might have happened to her, some stupid random accident perhaps, and maybe she was dead. At least now he knew she was alive. That was something, at least. Now all he had to do was find her.

But something was preventing his magic from connecting to her. Maybe he needed to be closer than he thought. There was just one problem—how do you get closer to someone when you have no idea where they are?

He inserted another bunch of coins into the phone and dialed her number again, holding his breath while it rang.

Please pick up, he implored silently. *Please, please pick up.*

The phone rang twice, and then went to a recorded message: "The number you are trying to reach is presently unavailable. Please try again later."

This time, he controlled his frustration and dropped the phone into its cradle more gently. He would do as the voice instructed and try again later, but not from here. Waiting was not in his nature, and there was precious little time to waste. He needed to be on the move, seeking Leesa and avoiding his enemies. The area code for her cell phone was from San Diego. He knew people often kept the same cell number when they moved, so there was no guarantee she still lived in San Diego, but it was all he had to go on. He hurried from the library and boarded a bus that would take him to the train station.

Dominic had no way of knowing he was heading almost three thousand miles in the wrong direction.

4. QUESTIONS

Leesa lingered in Rave's embrace for several minutes, her mind a whirling kaleidoscope of unanswered questions and unfinished thoughts. With all she had gone through the past three months, she thought nothing could ever surprise her like this. When you've discovered your mom had truly been bitten by a one-fanged vampire, and that your boyfriend is a supernatural vampire hunter, and a guy at school who liked you is a real-life vampire, it's hard to believe anything could shock you to this degree. But this one simple phone call had knocked her for a loop, for sure.

The man's message just could not be true—it challenged everything she had believed about her childhood. How could the man she had called Dad until she was seven years old not be her father? It did not make sense.

Finally, she eased back from Rave's embrace. Max backed away and looked up at them, his eyes wide and seemingly sympathetic, as if he understood what was going on in her head. Rave's brown eyes were also filled with sympathy and understanding.

"You heard all that, of course?" she asked.

Rave nodded. "Yeah, I did."

She looked down at the broken phone she still held in her hand and cursed herself for dropping it. Its memory held the number the man had called from, but the cell was useless. Now that she had recovered a bit, she wanted to call him back, to question him, to find out why he would make such a ridiculous claim, but she could not. He might even be trying to call her again right now. What would he think when he received no answer? What would he do next? She had no way of knowing.

"I don't know how or why, but I felt like it was trouble as soon as my phone rang," she said. "But I never expected anything like this. Not in a million years. How could he claim to be my father? That's ridiculous. My father lived with us until I was seven. What could this guy want?"

Rave shook his head. "I do not know. I wish I could help, but I don't even know who my father is. It's not the volkaane way."

Leesa remembered Rave telling her about a volkaane mating ritual, when each female paired up with a male during a special festival held only every few decades. Any children that resulted were raised communally, not by their parents. Rave's mentor Balin was the closest thing he had to a father. Leesa had met the old volkaane several times and liked him a lot.

"I know," Leesa said. "But I'm still glad you were here when it happened."

"Do you think there is any chance it could be true?"

Leesa thought for a moment. "A chance? I guess there's always a chance. Maybe I was adopted—not all parents tell their adopted kids about it. Maybe mine didn't tell me." She did not really believe that, though.

"No, I do not think so," Rave said. "If that were true, how would you explain the taint of *grafhym* in your blood?"

Leesa had forgotten about that. Rave was right—her mom had to be her real mother. The chances of some other woman being bitten by a one-fang and giving a child up for adoption were too small to even be considered.

"You're right," she said. "I guess that leaves only two possibilities. Either my mom had an affair, or the guy on the phone is lying." She shook her head. "I just can't see my mom having an affair, but I guess all kids probably think that about their moms. Who knows what she might have been like before the *grafhym* bit her? I've only known her as the timid, reclusive woman who kept insisting she was bitten by a one-fanged vampire."

"A story that turned out to be true, of course." Rave took Leesa's hands in his. "So, what are you going to do?"

"I don't know. I don't see how I could possibly ask my mom about this, not after everything she's been through." Leesa shook her head and sighed. She was growing up fast, but this was not something she could imagine doing, not unless this thing turned out to be way more important than it seemed right now. The call had been troubling, sure, but it wasn't worth risking her mom's all too recent recovery.

"What would I do, anyhow?" she said, more to herself than to Rave. "Say to her 'by the way, Mom, did you sleep with someone besides Dad before you got pregnant with me?' No way I could do that."

A sudden thought hit her like a blow. Could that be the reason her father found it so easy to leave his family, because his wife had cheated on him and he knew he wasn't Leesa's real father? Heck, maybe he wasn't Bradley's father, either. She would have to ask the caller about that, too, if she ever spoke to him again.

"If the guy on the phone was lying," Rave said, "that means he wants something from you."

Leesa had already considered that. But what could he want? That had been one of the thousand or so questions whirling around inside her head a few minutes ago.

"Yeah, but what? I don't have anything anybody would want." She thought about all the motives that drove people in stories she had read. "It's not like I have any old manuscripts or magical jewelry lying around. I'm just an ordinary kid."

Rave smiled. "We have already established you are far from ordinary, remember? Maybe it's not about something you own, but something *about* you."

Leesa had not considered that. "What could he want from me?

My *grafhym* blood? Do you think he needs to keep a vampire away or something?"

"I doubt that. The guy sounded like he's been looking for you for awhile. If he wants something from you, I do not think it has anything to do with the *grafhym*."

"What, then? The *grafhym* blood is the only thing special about me."

Rave wasn't too certain about that, but he had nothing specific or concrete to offer, so he remained silent about it. "I do not know," was all he said.

Leesa's head was beginning to hurt. There was just not enough to go on. She certainly wasn't going to risk upsetting her mother or Bradley by talking to them about it. They had both been through more than enough.

The guy on the phone had asked where she lived, which meant he had no idea where she was. She decided to try to keep it that way. When she got a new phone, she would get a new number as well. It wouldn't be much of an inconvenience—only about a dozen people had her number anyhow. And now there would be one less.

"Well, I'm not going to worry about it any longer. He doesn't know where I live, and that's how I like it." Leesa looped her arms around Rave's elbow and grinned. "And if he does find me, I've got a big strong boyfriend to protect me."

Max barked, once. His big brown eyes were looking up at her.

Leesa smiled. "Okay, a big strong boyfriend and a really smart dog to protect me as well."

Rave kissed her forehead. Of course he would protect her, with his life if need be, but what about when he wasn't around? He wished they knew more about the caller and what he wanted. But they didn't, and there was nothing he could do about it.

Having made up her mind, Leesa felt better. She did not have to worry about the guy for a while. All he had to go on was a phone number that no longer worked and was registered in San Diego. Maybe she wouldn't even get another cell for awhile. After all, it wasn't like she could call or text her boyfriend, like most girls could. And if her family needed to reach her when she was back at school, they could call the dorm.

Leesa smiled, pleased with the idea. No cell phone. She would just pretend she was a volkaane for awhile.

She had no way of knowing the consequences of the decision she had just made.

5. EDWINA

Leesa was not the only one making an important decision. Thirty-some miles to the south and west, in a gigantic underground grotto that was home to a coven of more than three score vampires, a tall, slender female vampire named Edwina had also reached a decision.

For hundreds of years, the vampires have used the perpetual night of this deep cavern to avoid the hated sun and to remain hidden from the ever-growing human population as well. Cut eons ago under the tree-covered hills on the eastern side of the Connecticut River by a now vanished underground waterway, the cavern was the perfect hideaway. Thousands of hours of labor had gone into shaping the various chambers to suit the vampires' needs—but what were hours, or even years, to the undead, who have eternity?

Until recently, Edwina had kept a captive feeder in the caverns, using him to slake her thirst for blood whenever she desired. Bradley had been taken from her by Stefan, however, to use as a bargaining chip in an unsuccessful attempt to make Leesa his consort. Edwina still seethed over the loss, especially with the growing *Destiratu* inflaming her thirst. Stefan was a member of the High Council, and she had been powerless to stop him. She burned to get back at him, but knew she must move carefully.

Stefan was powerful, and he was a favorite of Ricard, Lord of the High Council, as well.

Edwina was one of the youngest vampires in the coven, and so among the more susceptible to the pull of *Destiratu*. But she also possessed a steely discipline that enabled her to resist the pull. She had been turned early in the Civil War, barely one hundred and fifty years ago. Those had been heady days—with so much death and carnage everywhere, vampires had been able to feed without worry, for what mattered a few more corpses among the thousands strewn about the land? She had hunted the hills and woods of Virginia with Vanina, the vampire who had turned her, learning from her and thrilling to her own newfound powers and the exquisite taste of fresh, hot blood. But Vanina had fallen to an angry mob—beheaded by a soldier's sword—shortly after the war's end. Without her mentor and companion, Edwina drifted north. Still too new a vampire to turn a victim, she left a trail of bloodless bodies behind her.

As the years passed and the human population grew, she learned to become more careful, for even a vampire could fall prey to a large enough mob, especially as the weapons of the humans became more deadly. Eventually, she had reached Connecticut and fallen in with her present coven.

Among the entire coven, Edwina was the one who blended in most easily among the humans. Her complexion was darker than those of her brethren, courtesy of her maternal grandmother, who had been a plantation slave. While her pale skinned fellows needed to masquerade as goths or emos to mingle openly with humans, Edwinas's darker skin let her dress and act more or less as she wished. Her features were exotic—again, courtesy of her grandmother—but nothing that hinted at her true nature. She wore her long, straight black hair parted in the middle, letting it hang against her cheeks and down over her small but shapely breasts. Since she had been only twenty when she was turned, she fit in easily on college campuses. That was where she had met Bradley.

Edwina was different from most of her brethren in another way—she liked to play with her victims before taking them. Maybe it was because she fit in so easily among the humans, maybe it was just a quirk of her nature, but she enjoyed getting to know them and stoking their desire for her before finally claiming them. With Bradley, she had acted as his girlfriend for months, slowly drawing him away from his family and friends before turning him into her feeder.

The desire to "play" again was growing along with her thirst. She needed to venture out, despite the orders of the Council, which had decreed no member of the coven could leave the caverns alone without special permission. She thought a return to the Weston College campus was in order. She wanted to seek out Leesa, to see what was so special about this human to make Stefan want her so badly. And to see if there was some way she could use Stefan's interest in the girl to exact some much desired revenge. A sinister smile crept over her lips as she began formulating her plan.

6. COLD AND HOT

Leesa's first week back at school flew by. Final exams were only three weeks away, and her professors were cramming as much material into their classes and homework as they could. Physics was especially tough—it had been Leesa's most difficult class by far all semester. She wished she could magically transport herself through time to the end of finals and to the start of Christmas break, but she was pretty sure something in her physics curriculum said time travel was impossible. Leave it to physics to suck all the joy out of life, she thought, in more ways than one. Instead, all she could do was buckle down and do her best.

The busy week had one benefit, at least—it kept her from thinking too much about the phone call from the guy who claimed to be her father. She had canceled her cell service, but she'd still been on edge the first few days, constantly looking over her shoulder to see if anyone might be watching or following her, especially anyone old enough to be her father. But as each day passed, she worried about it less and less.

She had only seen Rave once so far this week—he had come by Tuesday night to make sure she was doing okay—but that was about to change. He should be here anytime now, to take her to visit Balin. Leesa smiled at the thought. Visiting Balin was a double bonus. First, she would get another long ride nestled in

Rave's arms, and then, once they were there, she would get to kiss him. It had been well over a week since she had gotten anything more than a peck on her cheek or forehead. She couldn't wait!

She stood outside her dorm with her best friend Cali, waiting for Rave to show. Cali's real name was Kelly, but everyone called her Cali, because of a small port-wine stain on her right cheek that was shaped remarkably like the state of California. Cali was anything but shy about it, saying it helped her stand out. And Cali loved to stand out, which made her the complete opposite of Leesa. That was one of the things Leesa liked about Cali—she drew attention away from her. Cali even streaked her shoulder length black hair with burgundy highlights that matched the color of the birthmark almost exactly. As did her lipstick. She had added a couple of narrow blue streaks to her hair over Thanksgiving.

Leesa suspected the blue streaks were the reason Cali was wearing a pair of furry black earmuffs instead of a hat—so she wouldn't have to cover up her newly decorated hair. Because it was certainly cold enough out for a hat, that was for sure. The sun hung low in a clear blue sky as the afternoon ebbed to a close, and a stiff northerly breeze made the thirty degree temperature feel much colder.

Leesa had pulled her dark blue ski cap down over her ears, and even though she was wearing a pair of black leather gloves, she had her hands tucked deep into the pockets of her bright blue down parka. A pair of tan Ugg boots kept her feet warm. Her cheeks tingled in the cold, and she could see her breath floating up in front of her face in a misty white cloud.

Cali was wearing a heavy dark brown leather jacket with a fluffy light brown fleece color. Her jeans were tucked into a pair of knee high black leather boots, which, from the way she was bouncing back and forth on her feet, were not doing nearly as good a job keeping her feet as warm as Leesa's Uggs.

"This ain't like San Diego, huh?" Cali said, blowing out a long stream of steamy breath.

"Ha! Not even close."

"I bet on days like this, you wish Rave had a car."

Cali did not know anything about Rave's magical heat, but she knew he was a member of a clan called the Mastons, who, like the Amish, did not use any modern devices or appliances. So there was no way she could know that walking arm in arm with Rave was more than enough to keep Leesa warm, and that once they reached the other side of the river, she would be cradled in his arms as he carried her, making her even warmer.

"Yeah, that'd be nice," Leesa said. "But there's nothing I can do about it—except dress warm." She kept few secrets from Cali, but had not told her about Rave's true nature. That information was not hers to share. As far as Leesa knew, Cali had never even heard of a volkaane. Leesa had pointed Stefan out to Cali and told her he was a vampire, so Cali did know vampires were real. Cali being Cali, she thought that was really cool.

"You're gonna be in for a *long* winter, girl," Cali said, grinning. She puffed out another big cloud of steamy breath. "Ol' Man Winter is barely getting started."

Leesa pulled her gloved hands out of her pocket. "Heck, it's not like I lived in San Diego my whole life," she said, a bit defensively. "I grew up in New Jersey, remember?"

"Yeah, but only until you were seven, right? That was a long time ago. I bet your blood has thinned a lot by now."

Leesa wondered what Cali would think if she knew about the *grafhym* blood in her veins. Knowing Cali, she would probably think it was way cool. When Leesa told Cali Stefan was a vampire, she'd asked if he had any vampire friends he could fix her up with. She had been joking, of course. At least, Leesa hoped she had been joking. Besides, Cali had already had a boyfriend, a cute frat guy named Andy, who she really liked.

"So, tell me again why we're waiting out here in the cold for

Rave?" Cali asked. "Instead of waiting inside, where it's nice and warm."

"Because I can't wait to see him, that's why. Don't tell me that thick New England blood of yours can't handle it?"

"Rule forty-three," Cali said. "Never let yourself seem too eager where a guy is concerned—even one as hot and nice as Rave."

Leesa grinned. Cali had a "rule" for seemingly every situation. She had finally admitted she made most of them up on the spot to suit whatever point she was trying to make. But she did have a few real ones. Indeed, that's how she and Leesa had first met, at Freshman Orientation the first day of school. Cali had come up to Leesa and told her she was cute. Leesa wasn't sure how to handle the comment, especially since she had never thought of herself as all that cute. Cali had followed her statement with "rule seventeen: always make friends with a cute girl, because there will be plenty of extra guys around."

Leesa brought her mind back to the present. "I'll try to remember that in the future, oh wise one."

Rave's arrival ended their banter. He strode rapidly up the sidewalk toward them, a big smile on his face. He was wearing a black and white checked flannel shirt, with no hat and no gloves. He looked great, as always.

"I do see why you're so eager, though," Cali whispered. "Rave is definitely smokin'."

Leesa smiled. Cali was more right than she knew. And she was pretty sure Rave had heard what Cali said, though she knew he would never let on.

"Hi, Leesa. Hi Cali," Rave said when he reached them. He gave Leesa a quick kiss on the cheek. The cold disappeared immediately from her skin.

Cali looked at Rave suspiciously. "How come you wore gloves back when you first started dating Leesa, but don't have any today, on one of the coldest days of the year?" She was referring to the story Leesa had told her and two other friends, Stacie and Caitlin, about how Rave kept his gloves on when he held her hand on a not so cold day early in the fall. Leesa had suffered quite a bit of teasing about it.

Rave grinned. "I guess I wasn't in love back then. Love keeps me warm now."

Leesa blushed, but she loved hearing him say that.

"Very smooth, Rave," Cali said, smiling. "Very smooth." She turned to Leesa. "Are there any more like him at home?"

"Ha! Should I tell Andy you asked?" Leesa asked.

Cali's smile widened. "Never mind. So, where are you two lovebirds off to?"

If only you knew, Leesa thought. But she was not about to tell her that first Rave would carry her fifteen miles in his arms—in little more than an hour—and then they would very carefully kiss under the watchful eye of Balin, to make sure Rave didn't lose control and accidentally burn the life out of her. Not that Cali wouldn't totally get into a story like that, Leesa knew. Especially if she described how amazing Rave's kisses were.

"We're just going for a long walk, maybe stop for a pizza," Leesa said. "Nothing fancy. What about you? What do you and Andy have going on tonight?"

"We're gonna check out a place over in Meriden. Test out my new fake ID."

Cali was eighteen, just like Leesa, but that didn't stop her from drinking. Andy was twenty-one, so he was legal.

"Have fun, but be careful," Leesa said. She almost never drank, though she'd had a glass of wine with Cali twice. And she'd had a bit of Balin's homemade mead once, too.

"Yes, Mom," Cali said, grinning. She stamped her feet a couple of times. "It's freakin' cold out here. I'm going back inside. Try not to freeze, you two."

"See you later," Leesa said as Cali turned back toward the dorm's entrance.

Leesa snuggled up against Rave's side, soaking in his warmth. There was no way she would freeze.

"Let's get going," she said.

Time did strange things whenever Rave carried Leesa in his arms. Their journeys seemed to last forever, a joyous eternity of bliss. But when he put her down, she always felt cheated, as if the trip had barely begun. She did not understand how something could seem endless, yet be all too short at the same time. She bet nothing in her physics class could explain that.

Rave set her down gently on the rutted dirt road in front of Balin's ancient cabin—road being a kind description of what was really nothing more than a wide dirt path. Rave's people preferred it this way, to keep outsiders from wandering into their settlement by accident. No driver in his right mind would try to negotiate the narrow, pitted roadway in any vehicle without off-road capabilities. A stout wooden gate a half mile from the highway kept even these away.

To the outside world, the Mastons were simply a strange clan—some even called them a cult—who had forsworn the trappings of the modern age. When Leesa first told her friends she had met a Maston, Cali tried to warn her off, recounting stories about strange noises, blue fires and even rumors of human sacrifice. The noises were real—they were called the Moodus Noises, named after the nearby Moodus River. The unexplained underground rumblings and tremors had been occurring in the area for centuries and were a well-known piece of Connecticut lore. They had nothing to do with the Mastons, though. Blue fires were also real, of course, though the volkaanes took care to shield any displays of their magical fire. As for human sacrifices, that was nonsense cooked up by overactive imaginations trying to deal with a group of people they did not understand.

Leesa had been to Balin's home several times before with Rave. The small, one-room cabin was the oldest in the Maston settlement, built by Balin himself over three hundred years ago. Constructed from trees hewn from the local woods, the logs were cracked and weathered, and the mud between them was black with age. Two tiny windows winked from the front wall—glass had not been an option when the cabin was built, so deer hide had hung over the openings back then. Glass had been added later. A thin ribbon of smoke curled upward a few feet from a stone chimney before being blown away by the stiff breeze. The whole area was wonderfully quiet.

Farther up the road, before it curved into the woods, Leesa could see another old cabin and a couple of crude wooden houses. Each home had a small field cleared beside it—more of a garden, really. They were bare and fallow this time of year, but in the spring, the gardens would brim with vegetables and herbs. Across the road, an apple orchard covered a low hillside. The gnarled gray branches were bare of leaves, but she had seen the trees when they were full of delicious fruit. The Mastons were very self-sufficient. Balin even brewed his own homemade mead.

Rave led Leesa up the short dirt pathway to the cabin door and knocked twice.

A moment later, the door swung open. Balin stood in the doorway, smiling. The old volkaane was even taller than Rave, with a lean body only slightly bent from more than five hundred years of living. He wore handmade buckskin clothes, the same as he had worn when he was younger—unlike many of his folk, he had never switched to more modern garb. His long hair was dark gray, the color of lead, with streaks of the characteristic Maston copper still visible in places.

"Greetings, young Rave," he said. "And Leesa, it is always a pleasure to see you, my dear." He stepped back from the doorway. "Come in, come in."

Leesa still had not gotten used to hearing Rave called "young Rave," since he was more than a century and a half old, but that's how Balin always referred to him. Balin had been

Rave's teacher when Rave was a child, and the "young Rave" appellation had remained with him all these years.

The inside of the cabin was Spartan. The entire place was one room, six paces wide and ten paces long, furnished with simple, handmade wooden furniture. A rectangular dining table with a split log bench on either side filled most of one end of the cabin, and a buckskin sleeping mat stuffed with straw lay upon the plank floor at the other end. In the middle of the room lay a brown bearskin rug so old the fur had worn away down to the skin in several places. Naturally, there was no television, radio, or refrigerator anywhere to be seen.

A small fire popped and crackled in a stone fireplace built into the far wall, adding its flickering light to the illumination cast by four tallow candles high on the walls. Volkaanes did not need fireplaces for warmth—their inner fire kept them warm no matter what the temperature—but they often used fires for cooking and light. If necessary, their inner heat could even be used for cooking, but it was usually simpler and more efficient to put something over the fire. A black metal cooking pot hung over the fire right now and Leesa could smell a stew of some kind bubbling inside it. Four crude wooden chairs formed a half circle in front of the fireplace—volkaanes enjoyed watching any kind of fire flicker and burn.

"Sit down, please," Balin said. "Can I get you something to drink? Water? Mead?"

Leesa remembered how good Balin's mead tasted, but the stuff was really strong, so she opted for water. Besides, Balin got his water from a natural spring out back and it was pretty tasty in its own right. Rave also asked for water, so Balin crossed to the table and poured two pewter mugs of water from a big ceramic jug.

While Balin was getting their water, Leesa pulled off her hat and gloves and shoved them into the pockets of her parka, then peeled off her jacket and handed it to Rave, who hung it on a wooden peg in the wall by the door. She settled into one of the chairs in front of the fire. This close to the flames, the smell of Balin's stew was even more delicious.

Balin handed a mug of water to Leesa and one to Rave. Rave took the chair on her left, and Balin sat down to her right. With the fire in front of her and a volkaane on either side, Leesa could not imagine any better place to be on a cold winter evening. And what would be coming soon would warm her up even better—and she wasn't thinking about the stew....

7. A CLOSE CALL

"So, what would you two like to do first?" Balin asked. "Do you want some dinner, or would you rather get right to Rave's practice with *Rammugul?*"

Rammugul was an almost forgotten volkaane technique for temporarily extinguishing their inner fire. Balin had seen it used once when he was much younger to save the life of a pregnant volkaane when something had gone awry during childbirth . When Leesa and Rave had come to him and asked if there was some way they could safely kiss, Balin had remembered the incident. He had searched through old volkaane lore until he discovered instructions on the technique. With Balin's help, Rave had been practicing *Rammugul* for more than a month now.

Balin insisted they go very slowly and very carefully, because although the mother had managed to extinguish her fire and save her baby, she had never been able to bring her fire back. Because of that, *Rammugul* had not been practiced in the Maston clan since. Rave said he was willing to risk losing his fire for Leesa, but there was no way she would let him even consider it. The inner fire was the essence of a volkaane—she was adamant he do nothing to endanger it. So Rave and Balin had been working long and hard on Rave's control over his heat, but so far, Balin had not let Rave get even close to dousing his fire completely.

With the control Rave had already learned, he and Leesa were able to kiss briefly, but only under Balin's watchful eye. The old volkaane could sense even the minutest changes in Rave's heat. If Rave showed the slightest sign of extinguishing his fire, or worse, losing control and putting Leesa in danger, Balin would pull them apart. So far, their longest kiss had been almost fifteen seconds—fifteen amazing seconds that seemed like long, delicious hours to Leesa.

"I'm pretty hungry," Leesa said. "But I vote for *Rammugul*."

Rave grinned. "Now why does that not surprise me?" he said jokingly.

"Ha! You like it as much as I do, Rave," Leesa said, smiling.

Rave's grin widened. "That I do," he said. "That I do."

"Well, I guess that settles it, then," Balin said. "Let us get to it. Stand up, young Rave."

Rave and Balin both stood up. Leesa remained seated, watching.

"Away from the fire," Balin instructed Rave. "I need to be able to sense your heat without any interference."

Rave took a couple of steps away from the fireplace, until he was near the edge of the straw-filled sleeping mat on the floor. Balin followed behind him.

"Close your eyes, young Rave. Begin the breathing."

Balin placed his fingers lightly on Rave's cheek. Leesa watched as Rave began a series of long, slow breaths through his nose. With each breath, the inhale and exhale grew slightly longer. When each seemed to Leesa to last an impossibly long time, Rave began to shorten his breaths, just as gradually as he had lengthened them.

The breathing exercise lasted for several minutes. Finally, Balin removed his fingers from Rave's cheek. He motioned for Leesa to join them.

"Very good, young Rave," Balin said. "Very good indeed. Open your eyes."

Rave opened his eyes. "This is the part of practice I like the best," he said as Leesa moved close in front of him.

Leesa's heart fluttered as Rave laid his hands softly on her shoulders and leaned his head toward her, his beautiful eyes locked onto hers. She could smell his warm breath as his mouth inched closer. Just before their lips met, she closed her eyes and parted her lips.

He kissed her gently, in no hurry now with Balin watching, keeping them safe. The tips of their tongues met, and Leesa felt the familiar heat surge through her. His tongue began to dance inside her mouth, and she let hers dance with it as the heat spread, filling every inch of her body. She was floating, flying, falling, spinning, tumbling, twirling. She felt like a thousand tiny mouths were kissing every inch of her body, like her skin was wrapped in the most delicious chocolate and every pore could taste it.

The heat continued to grow, beyond anything she had felt in any of their previous kisses, threatening to consume her. Her last thought before she lost all ability to think was there could no way back from this—but why would anyone *want* to come back from something so wonderful? She willingly gave herself to Rave's heat as it began to devour her.

Suddenly, the heat diminished as Balin yanked Rave away from Leesa. She thought she heard Balin yell Rave's name, but the sound seemed to issue from somewhere far away, like she was standing at the end of a long, dark tunnel.

The strength seemed to drain from her body. She sagged to her knees, as if her legs had suddenly melted from Rave's heat. Her whole body felt hot, feverish. She struggled to open her eyes, but her eyelids felt like they were fashioned of stone. Finally, she managed to force them open. She looked up. Through a fog, she could see Balin shaking Rave gently by the shoulders and repeating his name over and over, softer now, no longer yelling. Leesa could not be sure, but she thought Rave's eyes looked glassy. She tried to stand, but her legs betrayed her and she fell back to her knees.

The life reappeared in Rave's eyes, as if a light had suddenly been turned on.

"What happened?" he asked Balin, shaking his head to try to clear his mind. His gaze alighted on Leesa.

"Oh, no," he moaned, dropping to one knee beside her and wrapping his arm around her back. "Are you all right?"

The pain on Rave's face pierced Leesa like a knife. She forced herself to smile.

"Yeah. I think so. I'm just having a little trouble standing, that's all. That was quite a kiss."

Rave lifted her effortlessly to her feet and guided her to one of the chairs. Balin handed her a glass of water. She gulped greedily of the cool liquid. Rave sat beside her and draped his arm around her shoulders and held her close.

"What happened?" Rave asked Balin again.

"I was going to ask you the same question. You were doing fine, and then your fire suddenly exploded. I barely got you two apart in time."

Rave pulled his arm from around Leesa's shoulders and leaned away from her, aghast at what he had almost done. Leesa grabbed his hand.

"I'm fine, Rave," she said, squeezing his hand. "Really. I'm fine."

Rave stood up, gently disengaging his hand from Leesa's. He paced a few steps away, then turned back, his face still a mask of anguish.

"I do not understand it. Everything was working. I felt like I was in total control, and then... I don't know. Suddenly, my mind went blank."

"You lost control, young Rave," Balin said. "I do not know why, but I felt it the instant it happened."

Rave looked at Leesa. "I could have killed you," he said. "I almost did."

Leesa could not bear the look of guilt and anguish on Rave's face. She tried to lighten the mood.

"It felt really good, Rave," she said, smiling. "Really, really, really good. If that's how it feels to a vampire when you take it, I'm surprised they're not lined up, waiting their turn."

Rave smiled back at her, but it was a half-hearted effort, she could see.

"It's okay, Rave," she said. "I'm tougher than you think."

Balin sat down beside her and studied her closely.

"I thought I might be too late," he said. "But you do look fine. I think perhaps you are stronger than either of us thought."

"That does not change what happened," Rave said. "I nearly killed her. We have to figure out why."

Balin stood up. "Your control has been excellent up to now, young Rave. I am afraid this may be an effect of *Destiratu*. It's growing stronger by the day. The solstice is but a few weeks away, and I fear its arrival is magnifying the magic. We need to let the Council of Elders know about this—sooner rather than later."

Balin put his hand on Rave's forehead, checking his heat. "Trying to practice precision control at a time when the magical energies are heightening our hungers was unwise. I should have known better—I have felt the forces beginning to pull at me. *Rammugul* and *Destiratu* do not seem to be a good mix. At least not for this."

Disappointment welled up in Leesa. If what Balin said was true, then *Rammugul* was useless. This was the end of any kissing for her and Rave, at least while this stupid *Destiratu* thing was around. She could not bear the thought of not being able to kiss him, not after all the tastes she'd had of it. She wondered how long the phenomenon usually lasted.

"You're right," Rave said to Balin. "I cannot risk this happening again. No more *Rammugul* for me. Not now."

Balin laid a hand on Rave's shoulder. "Not so fast, young

Rave. I said using *Rammugul* for kissing was too dangerous during *Destiratu*. But I do not think you should give up on your practice of the technique itself. Indeed, practicing under these conditions may increase your control in the long run."

Balin winked at Leesa. "And when *Destiratu* ends, young Rave, as it one day must, perhaps you will have mastered *Rammugul* enough to kiss this beautiful young lady to your heart's content."

Leesa smiled. That was the best thing she had heard all day.

8. WALKING DEAD

A few nights later, Leesa lay awake in the darkness. The glowing blue numbers on her digital clock told her it was 3:42am. The soft blue glow reminded her of Rave's fingertips when he let his fire show. The thought of Rave was comforting, but she could still feel her heart beating in her chest, faster than normal for someone who had just been sleeping. She did not want to be awake, didn't need to be awake, but something had dragged her from her sleep. She had no idea what it might have been.

Lying on her back, she looked and listened, straining to penetrate the darkness for any sign something was amiss, but found nothing. Her room was certainly dark enough to invite sleep. Thin starlight outlined her windows and leaked into the room, not bright enough to show more than the barest outlines of her furniture. The night was peacefully quiet—she had seen movies where a nervous character would say it was *too* quiet, right before disaster struck—but such scenes always took place during the day or earlier in the evening, never at this hour. Such silence was normal for this time of night. Nor could it be the temperature affecting her sleep. It might be freezing outside, but she was comfortably warm under her down comforter and electric blanket. No, everything was fine. She could find no good reason not to be soundly sleeping.

So why was she lying here awake in the middle of the night? More importantly, why was her heart racing?

She wondered if she had been dreaming, if perhaps a nightmare of some kind had snatched her from the arms of sleep. A bad dream would account for her elevated heart rate. But if that were true, she could not recall what is was.

This was not the first night she had found herself lying awake. Her sleep had been increasingly restless for some time now, but she did not know why. Rave losing control of his fire could not be it—that had happened only a few days ago. Nor could it be the phone call from the man who claimed to be her father. Her trouble sleeping predated that as well. She wondered if it had anything to do with Stefan's bite. He had withdrawn his fangs at the first taste of her *grafhym*-tainted blood, but maybe a bit of his vampire essence had seeped into her, causing a part of her to want to roam the darkness, rather than sleeping soundly through the night.

The idea seemed far-fetched, but was it any more unbelievable than being bitten by a vampire in the first place? She could ask Rave about it, maybe he would have some idea whether it could be true. And maybe she could ask Dr. Clerval, her Vampire Science professor. He knew more about vampires than any human she knew. It had been Professor Clerval who had come up with the way to cure her mother, and who had driven her to her meeting with Stefan the night she'd gone to him to fulfill her bargain. If she ever saw Stefan again, she could ask him, too. Who would know more about this than a vampire?

The tossing and turning was a self-perpetuating thing, she knew. Something woke her up, and then she fretted about what it might have been, which kept her from falling back asleep. It was a vicious cycle. Not being able to sleep might be a blessing in disguise next week, when she'd be studying for finals, but not now. She needed to shut off her thoughts.

Bradley had taught her a breathing technique to help her

sleep when she was younger and troubled by her mother's increasingly strange behavior. Rave used a similar breathing thing to learn to control his fire. She didn't know if it would work here, but she had nothing to lose.

She closed her eyes and inhaled deeply through her nose, holding the breath for just a moment before slowly exhaling. She counted each breath on the exhale, starting with one hundred and counting backwards. Ninety-nine...ninety-eight...ninety-seven.... She remembered getting to seventy-three, but no further. By then, sleep had claimed her again.

She was walking through a patch of unfamiliar woods. The night was dark, with a quarter moon providing barely enough pale illumination to see where she was stepping. Dead leaves crackled under her feet, but with less noise than she expected, especially given the silence of the night. The twisted black limbs of the leafless trees seemed to be reaching for her, but whenever she looked directly at any of them, she saw only stillness.

The air was cold against her cheeks, but not uncomfortably so. She was in no hurry; nor was she sneaking through the woods. Her pace was normal walking speed. She had no sense of where she was heading in this unknown place, but for some reason, the lack of a specific destination did not bother her. Up ahead, the remains of one of the old stone walls so common to New England snaked through the trees. As she drew nearer, she saw the wall bordered an old cemetery overgrown with tall, stringy weeds. Crumbling gray headstones stood sentinel above the graves, which were scattered throughout the yard in no apparent pattern, the way they often were in old graveyards.

Something told her to stop here. Whether it was a warning to stay out of this ancient graveyard or a sense that she should wait and watch, she did not know. She found a flat rock atop one of the taller remaining sections of wall and sat down, facing inside the cemetery. Her feet dangled inches above the packed dirt below the wall. She wondered idly why the weeds did not grow right up to the stones.

After a few minutes, she became aware of a faint sound breaking the silence. She realized it was the first noise of any kind she'd heard since she stopped walking. The sound was difficult to describe, a kind of rustling, or scratching. Not the rustling of leaves in the wind—the branches were barren of leaves and there was no hint of a breeze. Nor was it the sound of footsteps. She strained to see through the darkness, trying to find a source for the noise, but saw nothing.

Slowly, the sounds grew louder. They definitely emanated from somewhere in front of her—within the cemetery, she was certain—but still she saw nothing. Even so, she was not alarmed. She simply sat and watched, waiting.

At last, the sounds became loud and clear enough for her to recognize. They were the sounds of digging. Something or someone was scraping and digging at the ground in front of her. It was unmistakable. There was just one problem, though—the graveyard was empty!

She had a brief thought that perhaps whoever was digging might somehow be invisible to her, but even that failed to explain what she heard. Not only was she alone—but there were no holes appearing anywhere in the ground. Still, the digging persisted, growing louder by the moment. She was certain now the sounds came from more than one spot in the cemetery.

Finally, a tiny movement off to her right caught her eye, but by the time she turned toward it, she saw nothing. If only it were not quite so dark. She kept her eyes fastened on the spot. A few moments later, she saw it. A tiny bit of soil popped a few inches up from the ground, like a miniature geyser of dirt. She smiled. No one was digging atop the ground—the digging was happening beneath the surface. She wondered if it could be gophers. But how was it she could hear gophers burrowing inside the earth?

She continued watching. More earth pushed upward, in

several scattered places now. She kept her gaze fixed on the largest of the growing piles of dirt. There! She was certain she saw something push up above the surface. She squinted, trying to see more clearly, and gasped. This most certainly was not a gopher, nor any other burrowing animal. Reaching up out of the earth was the unmistakable shape of a human hand!

More hands pushed up from the ground, a half-dozen now. Soon, entire arms appeared...and then heads. Heads that were part flesh and part bone. A few were wrapped in rotting cloth; one wore what could only be the remains of an old-fashioned tri-cornered hat.

Leesa watched, frozen to her spot atop the wall, as six corpses climbed out of their graves. They moved awkwardly, clumsily, but moved nonetheless. They looked at each other and walked in circles, almost as if they were waiting for direction. They didn't seem to notice her.

Suddenly, all six collapsed to the ground, like marionettes whose strings had been cut.

Leesa awoke again, the image of the corpses falling to the ground clear and sharp in her mind. Her room was lighter now, with the first gray light of dawn spilling in through the windows. She could hear muted sounds from elsewhere in her dorm—music playing softly, a door closing—as some early risers prepared to start their day. Outside, a truck beeped annoyingly as it backed up to unload its cargo somewhere nearby.

She seemed to be dreaming more and more frequently of late, but she could not remember one staying with her so clearly after she woke up. While the rotting, reanimated bodies were not a pleasant image, the dream had not really been frightening, and she much preferred it to what she had experienced earlier that night, waking up with her heart racing and not being able to recall why.

9. VIDEO CONFIRMATION

Leesa sat hunched over her desk, slogging through her physics book, struggling to understand Heisenberg's Uncertainty Principle. Her room had grown dark while she was studying, but her desk lamp provided a small island of light. Adele's "Rolling in the Deep" was playing in the background. Leesa loved the young British singer's voice, so powerful and full of raw emotion. It was hard to believe she wasn't even twenty-five years old yet. Leesa let her mind drift for a moment, escaping into the lyrics. She particularly liked the part about a fire starting in her heart. That was definitely a good description of how Rave made her feel—in more ways than one!

As the song wound down, she turned back to her physics book. "Uncertainty" was a fitting word for her right now, she thought. Not only was she uncertain about this whole Heisenberg Principle, but she was uncertain about so many other things going on in her life as well. Just when things were finally becoming normal with her mom and her brother, all this other stuff kept cropping up. Rave losing control of his fire, the strange phone call, her difficulty sleeping and her weird dream—all that was way more than any one person should have to deal with.

There didn't seem to be anything she could do about those things, though, so she forced her mind back to physics. Final exams were only two weeks away. They were something under her control, at least. She just had to concentrate.

Suddenly, something gripped her tightly by the shoulders. She almost jumped out of her skin as adrenaline shot through her system. She whipped her head around to see Cali grinning down at her.

"Sorry," Cali said. "Your door was open and I just couldn't resist. You were totally lost in that book. I didn't know physics was so enthralling."

"You almost gave me a heart attack," Leesa said, her heart still racing.

Cali plopped down on the edge of Leesa's bed. She was wearing ripped jeans with tiny red sequins outlining the front pockets and a dark brown T-shirt with a gold tic-tac-toe game etched on the front. Instead of O's, the designer had used shiny gold hearts. Three hearts formed a diagonal row from the bottom left square to the top right, with an arrow drawn through them to show hearts had won the game.

"I really am sorry, Lees. Rule ninety-four: sneaking up on someone who hangs out with vampires is *not* a good idea."

Leesa smiled, her body beginning to recover from the adrenaline jolt. "I don't 'hang out' with them. I just happen to know one. And if I never see Stefan again, that will be just fine with me."

"Speaking of things that go bump in the night, did you hear about that thing in the graveyard over in Higganum?"

Leesa's heart rate spiked again as the images from her dream came rushing back to her. Higganum was a small rural community less than ten miles south of Weston College. She hoped Cali wasn't going to say what she thought she was going to say.

"Graveyard?" she asked. "No, I didn't hear anything." She was almost afraid to ask about it, but she had to know. "What happened?"

"It's really freaky. Someone dug up a bunch of bodies, and then left 'em lying right there on the ground."

Leesa closed her eyes for a moment. She could see the images from her dream as clearly as if she were dreaming it right now.

She opened her eyes. "How do they know someone dug them up?"

Cali's brow knit in puzzlement as she stared at Leesa. "How else would they have gotten there, silly? They sure didn't climb up out of the graves themselves."

I hope not, Leesa thought. I really and truly hope not.

Cali saw the concern on Leesa's face. "Oh, no...you're not going to tell me zombies are real, too, are you?"

"No, of course not," Leesa said. "At least not as far as I know, anyway. It's just that I had this weird dream last night. Some bodies pushed themselves up out of the ground in an old cemetery."

"Really? That's definitely freaky, especially with this story today."

It was much too freaky, Leesa thought. But if vampires existed, and volkaanes, why not zombies? She was definitely going to have to ask Rave about it.

"In your dream, what did they do?" Cali asked. "Once they got out of their graves, I mean?"

"Nothing, really. They stumbled around in circles for a few minutes, then fell to the ground. That's when I woke up."

"It's six-thirty. Turn on the TV. Maybe we can catch something about it on the news."

Leesa grabbed her remote and switched on the television. The local news was just coming on. They had to sit through a boring story about some possible corruption in the state house, but then a jumpy video of an old graveyard, probably taken from a helicopter, filled the screen. It was still light out in the video, so it had obviously been taken earlier in the day.

"There's a strange story coming out of Higganum today," the neatly coiffed, gray-haired anchorman began. "Police are investigating an unusual act of vandalism in one of the town's old cemeteries."

The picture switched to a live shot of a reporter on the scene. Bright klieg lights lit up the graveyard behind her. A green knit ski cap pulled down over her blond hair showed how cold it was outside. Her foggy breath was visible on the television as she spoke. Still, she looked remarkably fresh and perky.

"Here's what we know so far," she said. "Sometime last night, someone dug up six bodies here at the old cemetery. Police aren't sure if this was simply a thoughtless act of vandalism, or perhaps the work of grave robbers searching for valuables. All the graves here are well over one hundred years old, so it's doubtful thieves could have found much of value."

The camera panned over her shoulder to the graveyard, focusing on several very old headstones. Leesa looked closely, but no bodies were visible from this angle. The news director had probably decided that a pile of rotting corpses was not proper dinnertime fare. Either that, or the authorities had already covered them up.

The reporter continued speaking. "Police are puzzled by several strange aspects to all this. Earlier, I spoke with Detective Dave Sanderson."

The picture reverted to a daylight shot again, and the mustachioed face of a good-looking man in his late thirties or early forties filled the screen.

"We have no real leads at this time," he said. "We're asking for the public's help. If you know anything about this brazen, disrespectful act, please call the number on the bottom of your screen. There are no signs of any heavy equipment having been in the cemetery, so we know the perpetrators had to be here a long time to dig up so many graves by hand. This is a pretty out of the way spot, but we're hoping someone driving by saw something unusual here last night."

A live shot of the reporter replaced the detective's face. "There's another troubling aspect about this incident that no one will talk about on camera," the reporter said. "But I've been told by a member of the forensics crew that not only was there no evidence of heavy equipment, but they've been unable to find any sign of any digging equipment at all. 'There aren't even any shovel marks,' he told me. 'It doesn't make any sense, but it looks like somebody dug the bodies up by hand.'"

"Holy crap!" Cali said, turning to Leesa. "Did you hear that?"

Leesa's head was spinning. What the heck was going on here? Her fingers began twirling in her hair.

"Shhh. I want to hear the rest of this."

The reporter flashed a cheerleader smile. "Now there's a mystery wrapped up inside a puzzle," she said. "Who or what would dig up a half-dozen dead bodies without even using a shovel? And why go to all that trouble, and then just leave the bodies lying there?"

The picture returned to the earlier helicopter shot. "That's all we have for now," the reporter said as the camera zoomed in on the graveyard. Leesa leaned closer to the television. A ragged circle of dark lumps was barely visible now. They had to be the unearthed bodies. From this distance, she couldn't tell if they were covered by anything or not.

She shuddered. Even though the view was still too far to see clearly, she was struck by how similar the circle of bodies looked to the one she had seen in her dream. She switched off the television.

"Wow, that's freakin' crazy," Cali said. "Do you think your vampire friends could have done it?"

"I keep telling you, they're not my friends." Leesa stood up and took a few aimless steps around the room. "But no, I doubt vampires had anything to do with it. What would they want with

59

dead bodies? They only like live ones, filled with lots of warm blood."

"Oh, yeah, I guess you're right. I definitely need to take that Vampire Science class you're always talking about next semester."

Cali looked at Leesa more closely and saw the worry etched on her face. She reached over and gently pulled Leesa's hand from her hair. "So, how close was that to what you dreamed?"

"I'm not sure. It was hard to see. I wish they'd zoomed in closer, but I guess it's not the kind of thing they're going to show on TV." Leesa took a deep breath. "But from what I could see, it looked *way* too similar."

"There were a bunch of people watching from outside the cemetery," Cali said as an idea popped into her head. "I bet someone took pictures or video with their cell." She grabbed Leesa's laptop from the desk. "Let's check YouTube."

Cali sat back down on the edge of the bed and opened the computer on her lap. Leesa came over and sat beside her, unsure whether she wanted Cali to find anything or not.

Cali's fingers pecked rapidly at the keyboard, opening the YouTube home page and then typing in her search.

"I knew it," she said excitedly. "Look. Someone posted a clip from the cemetery. Gotta love all those smartphones out there."

Leesa leaned in more closely as Cali started the video. At first, the picture was grainy and jumpy—barely recognizable as a graveyard. The phone's owner was behind the police crime scene tape, well over one hundred feet from whatever was in the center of cemetery. As he or she zoomed in and found the proper focus, the image began to grow clearer.

Leesa found herself holding her breath. She forced herself to exhale, but kept her eyes glued to the screen. Finally, the details became sharp enough to recognize the bodies for what they were. And they were not covered, at least not when the video was taken.

The low angle of the shot prevented her from being able to see all the corpses, but she could see most of the closest body and parts of two others. She looked more closely at one of the farther bodies, whose head and shoulders jutted out from behind the first one. She blinked, unable—or unwilling—to believe her eyes. She was pretty sure the corpse was wearing the remains of a tri-cornered hat....

10. MILLION DOLLAR QUESTION

"So, what do you think?" Cali asked when the video ended. "Did it look anything like your dream?"

"The video wasn't that clear," Leesa said, "but yeah, it definitely seemed similar."

Cali pecked at the keyboard again, searching for another video, one that might show things more clearly, but there were none.

"That was the only video," she said, closing the laptop. "You got any idea what the heck is going on?"

Leesa thought for a moment. That was the million dollar question. What the heck did this all mean? She closed her eyes and tried to bring back the images from her dream, but she kept seeing the pictures in the video. She wondered if she was making the two more similar than they really were, if her brain was taking the fresher images and making them part of her memory. Even if that was true, how had she managed to dream about corpses rising from their graves the night before real bodies were found in a graveyard—a graveyard less than ten miles away, no less. That in itself was strange enough, regardless how similar or not the actual images were. And she was pretty sure there'd been a tri-cornered hat in her dream. Her brain wasn't making that detail up.

"I don't know," she said finally. "I really don't have a clue."

Cali could see how disturbed Leesa was by all this. She draped her arm around Leesa's shoulder.

"Maybe it's just one of those freaky coincidences. Like déjà vu or something, only in reverse. Has anything like this ever happened to you before?"

Leesa shook her head. "No, never. My sleep's been kinda messed up the last week or two, but that's about it. This is the first weird dream I remember."

"Well, if anyone has a reason to have a few sleepless nights or some weird dreams, it would be you, with all you've been through recently. Your mom and the one-fang, the thing with Stefan to get your brother back—I'd be having nightmares, for sure."

"Yeah, I guess." Leesa grabbed a bottle of water from atop her mini-fridge and took a drink. "But I wasn't having any dreams while all that was happening. Not that I can remember, anyhow. So why now?"

Cali shrugged. "There are more things in heaven and earth than are dreamt of in your philosophy," she quoted.

Leesa grinned. "Now I'm *really* amazed. Since when did you start quoting Shakespeare?"

Cali smiled back. "That's one of the few things I remember from high school. Never thought I'd actually get a chance to use it, though. Are you impressed?"

"Totally." Leesa took another swallow of water, then asked, "Got any more words of wisdom for me from ol' Will?"

"Just this: 'To be or not to be.' But damned if I know how that applies here, though."

Leesa laughed. Cali was always so good at cheering her up.

"Too bad there won't be any of that on my English Lit final," Cali continued.

"Speaking of finals, I'd better get back to my physics homework, or that's one final that will kick my ass."

"I'm glad I don't have physics," Cali said as she got up off the bed. "Algebra is hard enough for me. Why'd you take that class, anyhow?"

Leesa smiled. "To quote a very wise person of my acquaintance, 'damned if I know.'"

Cali cracked up. "Good one, Lees," she said when she finished laughing. She turned and headed for the door. "Have fun with your physics."

"Yeah, sure," Leesa said as she sat down at her desk.

"Oh, and one more thing," Cali said.

Leesa turned and saw that Cali was halfway out the door, but had grabbed the doorframe and twisted around to face back into the room.

"What's that?" Leesa asked.

Cali grinned. "Sweet dreams tonight."

Leesa picked up a pen from her desk and threw it toward the door, but Cali spun out of the way before the pen could hit her.

"Thanks a lot," Leesa said, laughing. She could hear Cali laughing as well as she headed down the hall.

11. SPECIAL PERMISSION

Edwina prowled the dark caverns of the vampire lair. She had formulated the beginnings of a plan, and now she needed to find Stefan so she could start to put it into motion. She'd seen him earlier, conversing with Ricard, but for what she wanted, she had to get Stefan alone. Only then could she pressure and persuade him to give her what she needed.

She finally came upon him in one of the tunnels leading from the Council chamber. She pasted a sweet smile upon her face.

"Stefan, I've been looking for you. I need to speak to you."

Stefan's black eyes were wary. He had forced Edwina to give up her feeder, with no recompense for her, which was no small thing. He did not trust her friendly manner, not even a little. And he certainly did not trust her smile.

"What is it, Edwina?" he asked, keeping his voice neutral.

"I want to go outside."

Stefan folded his arms across his chest. "So? Why tell me?"

Edwina stepped closer, cutting the distance between them by half.

"Because I want to go out alone," she said in a near whisper.

Stefan studied her face, but Edwina's expression gave away nothing. "You know the Council's decree. As long as the

Destiratu continues to strengthen, only Council members may go out alone. If you want to go, you must find two others to go with you. It's for your protection, as well as for the coven's."

"I don't need protection," Edwina said evenly.

"Perhaps not, Edwina. But *Destiratu* can fan your blood thirst when you least expect it. Without companions to restrain you, you might act foolishly. You know we cannot risk attention being brought upon our kind. Hence the Council's decree."

"But the decree also states that a Council member may grant permission. You are a Council member, Stefan. *You* can give me permission."

Stefan stroked the black soul patch on his chin. He was the newest and youngest member of the High Council—it had been less than four hundred years since that glorious day Ricard turned him—but he had the same rights and powers as the others.

"And why would I do that?"

Edwina's expression grew hard. "Because you owe me, Stefan. You took my feeder from me, for your own selfish purposes. Needlessly, it turned out, I might add."

Stefan winced inside. He had made a bargain with the human girl Leesa. She had agreed to become his consort in return for her brother's freedom. But at the first taste of her blood, he realized he could not turn her. Still, he kept his part of the bargain and allowed Bradley to remain free. Despite his failure to turn Leesa vampire, she still maintained a pull on him he had been unable to break—or even to fully understand.

"What will you do if I give you the permission you seek?"

Edwina smiled again. She had him now, she knew.

"Why, look for another feeder, of course. That's all. Find a human to replace the one you took from me."

Stefan did not trust her smile one bit. Still, he did owe her. He could not deny it, even to himself.

"And this has nothing to with Leesa or her brother?" he asked.

Edwina gave him a look that was all innocence.

No wonder she so easily plays with humans, Stefan thought. No one would ever suspect her true nature.

"No, of course not. That's ancient history. I desire new blood."

"I am serious, Edwina," Stefan said sternly. "I do not want you going anywhere near Leesa or her family. Understood?"

Edwina ran her finger softly down Stefan's cheek, scraping his smooth skin lightly with her fingernail. "Why, Stefan! Don't tell me you still have feelings for that girl."

Stefan did not know what to make of his feelings for Leesa, but he certainly wasn't about to try to explain them to Edwina. He took hold of her wrist and pulled her hand away from his face.

"It is for your safety as much as hers," he said, keeping a tight grip on her wrist. "She has a volkaane friend—a very powerful volkaane friend. You would stand no chance against him."

Stefan thought back to his own confrontation with Rave. The volkaane's power was undeniable, among the strongest Stefan had ever sensed. Stefan was powerful among vampires, but even he was not sure who would have prevailed had Leesa not stepped between them and stopped their fight before it began.

He felt the hunger rising inside him. The desire to test his strength against the volkaane was a palpable thing he could feel in his chest. He forced the feeling down. *Destiratu* was stoking his hunger, he knew. He would not give in to it.

"A volkaane friend, huh?" Edwina said, thinking. This was important information. She would have to be very careful if she were to go near the girl. "Thank you for the warning, Stefan. And for your concern. But like I said, my plans have nothing to do with her."

Stefan fastened his eyes onto hers. "See that your plans remain that way, then." He let go of her wrist. "You have my permission to go out alone, Edwina. See that you do not abuse it."

Edwina smiled and gave him a slight bow. It wouldn't hurt to show a little gratitude and deference. "Thank you, Stefan. You do not have to worry about me, I promise."

Stefan looked at her for another moment, then turned and strode away without saying anything more. As he disappeared, the smile on Edwina's face turned into a full-fledged grin. Step one of her plan had been achieved—she had permission to come and go as she pleased. And as a bonus, Stefan had given her some very important information about the girl having a volkaane friend.

The volkaane's presence meant Edwina had to give up a few of the possibilities she had been considering. Still, she was confident she would be able to come up with something suitable that did not endanger her at the hands of this powerful hunter, something that would still give her the revenge she sought.

12. STATUE WITH A HAT

Leesa stood behind the top row of the amphitheatre style classroom, surveying the seats below. The room was about half full right now, and more kids were steadily filtering in through the doorway behind her. She wanted an aisle seat, as close to the front as possible. Aisle seats were always in demand, though, and the best one she saw was on the left aisle, only about one-third of the way down from the top. She limped quickly toward the left stairs before someone else nabbed the seat.

She needed to be on the aisle so she could get down to the stage as swiftly as possible when class ended, to talk to Dr. Clerval about her strange dream. The professor was always surrounded by students wanting to talk to him after class, so it was best to get down there quickly. With their shared history, she knew he would make time for her in any case, but she didn't want to have to wait while he answered questions from other kids.

She settled into the seat she had eyed from the back, pleased to be on the aisle. The two seats next to her were empty, and then came three girls sitting together. From the way the three of them were chattering, they obviously knew each other. Leesa heard one of the girls gush, "to die for," and guessed they were talking about a guy one of them had just met. She knew the feeling.

Movement in the front of the room caught her eye, and she turned to see Dr. Clerval appear at the right side of the stage.

Class did not start for another two minutes, so he stopped to talk to his teaching assistant, who always sat near the edge of the stage, out of the way, but ready to lend any assistance the professor required. Leesa couldn't remember the guy's real name, because Professor Clerval always called him Renfield, after Dracula's assistant.

Dr. Clerval looked the same at every class. His thin frame was slightly stooped with age, but he moved with surprising ease, given his frail appearance. Long white hair hung limply from his head onto his shoulders, the color a sharp contrast to the rumpled black suit he always wore. Leesa still didn't know whether it was the same suit each time, or whether the professor had a collection of them. As usual, he had black Converse hi-top sneakers on his feet. The sneakers with a suit look might have been hip on a college kid, but it was decidedly out of place for a man in his sixties. Dr. Clerval had confided to Leesa that the sneakers were the most comfortable shoes he owned, and he'd long since given up fashion for comfort. As Leesa had gotten to know him better, she had learned it was just one of many unconventional things about him.

Done with whatever business he had with Renfield, Dr. Clerval shuffled toward the lectern in the middle of the stage. The room began to slowly quiet as more and more students saw him draw near the lectern.

Leesa suddenly became aware of a presence beside her. She turned and found herself looking up into Rave's smiling face. He looked great, as usual, dressed in dark jeans and a plain, faded red T-shirt worn over a dark crimson long sleeve shirt. The tight shirts showed off his athletic form and the pale red set off his bronze complexion and dark copper hair.

"You saving that seat for someone?" he asked, nodding toward the seat next to her.

"Rave!" she exclaimed in a loud whisper. "What are you doing here?"

She regretted the question the instant it left her mouth. He was here to see her, of course. Why else would he be here? And as always, she was thrilled to see him. She hoped he didn't take her stupid question to indicate otherwise.

"Sit, please," she said. "Of course I'm not saving it for anyone. It's great to see you. This is a wonderful surprise."

It was wonderful, and it was a surprise. For it was in this very room that she had first laid eyes on Rave, way back in September. He had not been back to this class since.

Leesa remembered the day as if it were yesterday. She had been sitting in the middle of the top row, totally enjoying Dr. Clerval's unique presentation and outlook about vampires. At the end of class, when Renfield climbed the steps to pass out the reading assignment lists, she had turned toward the aisle, watching him. Rave was sitting at the end of her row, partially hidden by the kids seated between them. Something about him caught her attention, and she'd leaned forward to get a better look. She had been stunned by how gorgeous he was.

As if sensing her gaze, Rave had turned to look at her. When their eyes met, she thought she saw the barest flicker of surprise crease his handsome features, but it was gone before she could be sure. He'd smiled, his eyes holding hers for the briefest of moments, but then he turned his head and rose from his seat, disappearing swiftly out the back of the room.

Leesa had sat paralyzed for a moment, her heart hammering. She remembered the strange warmth she had felt radiating through her body. She had never experienced anything like the pull she had immediately felt toward him. Guys just did *not* make her feel that way, ever. She remembered wondering why he'd left so abruptly.

She had rushed out the back door to find him, but somehow, he had disappeared. She hadn't known then he was a volkaane, and how incredibly fast he could move. Unable to see him anywhere on the big grass courtyard outside the building, she had almost thought she had imagined him—a gorgeous stranger conjured up by all the talk of vampires during class.

She had looked for him at the next class, but he was nowhere to be found. It turned out he had been as puzzled as she was by the unexpected pull between them, but of course she hadn't known that at the time. She also hadn't known he had been secretly watching her. It wasn't until Rave saw her talking to Stefan at a frat party that he decided he had to act. He waited until Stefan left, then introduced himself and warned her to stay away from Stefan because he was a vampire.

Leesa brought her mind back to the present as Rave squeezed past her and settled down beside her. Behind him, she could see the three girls a few seats down staring at him, but Rave didn't notice. This was another of the thousand or so things Leesa loved about him—he seemed unaware of the effect he had on most human women. When he took her hand, Leesa saw the nearest of the girls frown in disappointment. If you only knew, Leesa thought as his delicious heat soaked into her—you'd *really* be jealous.

Rave's presence erased Leesa's need to talk to Dr. Clerval after class. She could ask Rave about her dream instead and see if he knew anything about zombies or the dead coming back to life. If there was anything to it, she thought Rave would be more likely to know than the professor.

For the first time all semester, Vampire Science class seemed to drag. Leesa was sure Dr. Clerval was probably as interesting as ever, but she was having trouble focusing on what he was saying. She wanted class to be over, so she could get Rave outside and begin questioning him. She glanced over at him. His eyes were fixed on Professor Clerval, but he seemed to sense her look. He turned his head and smiled.

Finally, class ended. Dr. Clerval reminded them about the term paper they had due next week in lieu of a final exam, then walked out from behind the lectern. Students from the first few rows were already hurrying toward the stage to talk to him.

Leesa grabbed Rave's hand and stood up.

"C'mon," she said. "I need to talk to you."

Rave's eyes widened in surprise at the urgency of her tone. "Is something wrong?" he asked concernedly as he rose to his feet.

"No," Leesa reassured him. "I don't think so. At least, I hope not."

It was cold and dark outside, but with Rave close beside her, neither mattered to Leesa. This section of campus was well lit by streetlights resembling old-fashioned gas lamps, but she knew she would be safe with Rave even in the darkest of places. And snuggled close against him with his arm around her back, there was no such thing as cold.

Rave led her part way across the courtyard, away from the students streaming out of the building, then stopped and turned to face her. He looped his hands loosely around behind her waist, keeping his protective warmth flowing into her.

"So, what's going on?"

"Can we go sit somewhere? This might take longer than a minute or two."

"Sure, whatever you want. Where would you like to go?"

"How about over there?" Leesa pointed to the center of the courtyard where several stone benches surrounded a tall statue of a Revolutionary War soldier. The man's tri-corned hat reminded Leesa of her dream. With the evening so cold, the plaza was empty. Privacy would not be a problem.

"Sure. Let's go," Rave said.

They walked across the grass to the nearest of the benches. Before she could sit, Rave grabbed her elbow.

"Wait a second." He sat down for a moment, then got up and offered the spot to Leesa. "Sit here."

As soon as she sat, Leesa understood what Rave had done. The stone underneath her was as warm as if it had been baking in the summer sun all day. She smiled at him as he sat beside her.

"Have I ever told you how useful you are to have around?"

Rave grinned. "Yeah, you've mentioned it once or twice, I think."

"Well, it's true, for sure."

Rave took her hand. "So, what's on your mind, sweetheart?"

Leesa hesitated. Now that she was about to talk about the dream with Rave and had made a bit of a big deal about it, she felt a little foolish. Still, she needed to learn whatever she could, and Rave was definitely her best link to the supernatural world.

"It's about a dream I had last week," she said. "I dreamed some dead bodies dug themselves up out of the ground in an old cemetery and walked around the graveyard like a bunch of zombies or something."

"Why does that trouble you? You were probably just remembering part of some movie or TV show you saw. I hear zombies are all the rage right now."

"That's what I thought at first, even though the dream seemed so real. It's what happened the next day that kinda freaked me out."

Rave's face grew serious. "What happened?"

"There was a story on the news about someone digging up bodies in a graveyard over in Higganum." Leesa's fingers began playing in her hair. "Cali found a video of the place on YouTube. The bodies on the ground looked a lot like the ones in my dream." She took her hand out of her hair and pointed to the statue in front of them. "One of them was wearing a hat just like that one. So was one of the bodies in my dream."

Rave studied the statue for a moment, then turned back to Leesa. "No wonder you're upset. Has anything like this ever happened to you before?"

"No, never." She thought about telling Rave about her recent trouble sleeping, but didn't want to cloud the real issue, which was her dream seeming to show up on the news.

"Any idea what it means?" Rave asked.

"I'm not sure. Maybe it was just a weird coincidence or something. But I was wondering if you knew anything about zombies. Do they exist? Are they as real, like vampires and volkaanes?"

Rave pursed his lips, thinking. "I really do not know," he said after a moment. "My people have stories of the dead coming back to life and feasting on human flesh, but I have never seen it or talked to anyone who has. I've never really paid much attention to it."

Leesa wasn't sure whether she was relieved by Rave's answer or not. "So you think that's all they are then, just stories?"

"I don't know. Most of our lore is based on things my people have encountered in the past. It would not surprise me if zombies, or something like them, existed sometime in the past. But if they had been anywhere around here in the last hundred years, I think I would know about it."

Leesa thought about it for a few moments, digesting what Rave had said.

"I guess you're right. Your people would know." She stood up and walked over to the statue. Placing her hand on one of the soldier's cold stone thighs, she stared up at his hat. That one detail troubled her more than anything, because such hats were not something she'd expect to see. So why had she conjured up something so unusual in her dream? And why was one of the bodies in the cemetery wearing a similar one?

Out of range of Rave's warmth, the cold slowly seeped into her, especially into her exposed hands. She tucked them into her pockets and stared at the statue for another moment. If she expected the soldier to give her any answers, she was sorely disappointed. But heck, would a talking statue be any stranger than dead bodies coming back to life? She wondered idly whether zombies could talk. Turning away from the statue, she limped back to the bench and sat beside Rave. The cold immediately vanished.

"I can't get past that stupid hat," she said. "It doesn't make any sense."

"Why does the hat bother you so much?" Rave grinned, trying to lighten her mood. "You don't think it is part of some kind of official zombie uniform, do you?"

Leesa smiled and punched him playfully on the arm. "No, of course not. I think they probably just wear whatever they were buried in—if they exist at all, that is. I just think it's strange I'd imagine a hat like that in the first place, and then find one in the video, too. It's not like I see kids walking around campus wearing those things."

"What about the Halloween party? There were lots of pirates wearing hats like that."

Leesa's eyes lit up. "That's right! I'd forgotten." She had gone to the party dressed up as a pirate herself, but with a red bandana around her head instead of a hat. She felt extra warm inside all of a sudden, and it had nothing to do with Rave's magical heat. The Halloween party had been the first time she and Rave had slow danced together, and she still remembered how awesome it felt.

"Maybe that's where the hat came from," she said. She paused, her brow knitted in thought. "That might explain the hat in my dream, but it's still a little weird there would be one in the video, too."

Rave shrugged. "We may never be able to explain that. I'm sorry I have not been more help."

Leesa wrapped her arms around Rave's arm. "You've helped, for sure. The pirate costume thing, for one. And you've pretty much reassured me there aren't any zombies around right now, even if they may have been here in the past."

"But that does not mean they couldn't come back," Rave said. "Just to be safe, I'll go over to Higganum later and see if I can detect any magical energy."

"Can you do that?" Leesa asked excitedly. "Detect that kind of energy?"

"I'm not sure. I can sense when vampires are nearby—maybe I'll feel something similar if there are zombies around."

"That would be awesome."

"It's a long shot. If there was any kind of magic associated with the bodies from the cemetery, it may have dissipated by now. But I will see what I can find."

"Thanks. Have I mentioned that I love you?"

Rave smiled. "Not nearly enough."

Leesa kissed his cheek. "Well, I do. But I'd better be getting back to the dorm." She hated to say that, because she didn't know when she would see him next. "Finals are next week—I need to do some studying."

Rave stood up. "I'll walk you back, then."

Leesa snuggled against him as they headed back toward her dorm. She had no way of knowing Rave had come to class tonight because there was something he wanted to talk to her about, but after he'd seen how bothered she was about her dream, he had decided it could wait. He didn't want to add to her stress, especially with her finals around the corner.

Edwina watched from the blackness between two buildings almost a hundred yards from where Leesa sat with her volkaane friend. The guy was more than just a friend—that was obvious from the way they interacted. They held hands, they snuggled close, and they exchanged brief kisses. There had been no long, passionate kisses, of course—such a kiss would burn the girl to ashes in seconds. Edwina shivered momentarily at the thought of the volkaane's fire burning her own life breath from her. She wondered what kind of relationship the human girl and the volkaane expected to have, when his very kiss would kill her. Her lips curved into a sinister smile as she recalled some of her own relationships with humans over the years. She was pretty sure most of them would have preferred her to have killed them right away.

She wished she could have gotten closer, to hear what Leesa and the volkaane were saying, but she was taking no chances he might sense her presence, especially if he was as powerful as Stefan claimed.

She was fortunate Stefan had warned her about him. She had guessed Leesa would be taking that silly Vampire Science class—her brother Bradley had loved it—and Edwina's first thought had been to go inside the classroom and watch Leesa from somewhere in the room. Had she done that, the volkaane would have sensed her for sure.

Instead, she had found a spot suitably far from the door and settled in to wait. Her patience was rewarded when the two of them left the building together and made their way to the center of the courtyard. She was surprised to see the girl walked with a noticeable limp and wondered if she had injured herself.

When they finally got up and began walking away, Edwina followed silently behind, taking care to maintain her distance. She watched the volkaane give the girl a lingering kiss on the forehead in front of one of the dormitories. He remained outside the door for several moments after she went inside, his eyes roaming the darkness. Edwina was glad she had remained so far back.

A smile curved her lips as she disappeared into the darkness. She now knew where Leesa lived.

13. SEEING THINGS

Near midnight on Friday night, Leesa sat at her desk, pouring over her biology book. Avril Lavigne's "Goodbye Lullaby" CD was playing softly in the background for the third or fourth time. Leesa had been too consumed with her studying to bother changing it, but this time the raucous sounds of "What the Hell" pulled her attention away from the book. The parts about needing time to play and needing to be a bit crazy sure sounded like a good idea to her right now.

There were a million things she would rather be doing than studying tonight, but finals started on Monday, so it was time to buckle down. She would rather be doing something with Rave, of course, or hanging out with Cali, Stacie and Caitlin playing Guitar Hero, or even bowling on Caitlin's Wii. Or watching a movie, or reading a good book, or.... Her mouth stretched open into a big yawn. Sleeping wouldn't be a bad choice, either.

A week had passed since her graveyard dream, and she was still having trouble getting a full night's sleep. She had not experienced any other weird dreams that she could remember, but she woke up a couple of times almost every night and wasn't always able to fall right back to sleep. She had hoped her talk with Rave yesterday might help, but last night had been as restless as the others. Oh, well, she thought, sleep wasn't going to be much of a priority for the next week anyhow.

At least she had drawn a pretty good exam schedule. Biology would be her second toughest test, and she'd be getting it out of the way first thing Monday morning. The rest of her exams were spread out one per day, which was nice. Cali had two finals on Tuesday and Caitlin had two on Wednesday, but Leesa had gotten lucky and avoided any doubles. The other nice thing about her schedule was physics would be her final final, on Thursday. She giggled at the phrase, "final final." It wasn't really all that funny—she was definitely getting punch drunk. But it was great to have her toughest test last. She could pull an all-nighter for it if need be and then crash after the exam, knowing her studying was over.

That was a week away, though, so she turned her attention back to biology. She planned on doing another hour or so of work tonight, then to spend most of Saturday on physics, with some reviewing of English and psychology, and then return to biology on Sunday.

She yawned again. If she was this tired already, she thought, when her studying had barely begun, what was she going to be like next week? She would be a basket case for sure. She reached for the open can of Red Bull—a college kid's best friend during exams—that sat on the corner of her desk. Another boost of energy was definitely in order. Her hand was a couple of inches from the can when her tired eyes popped open and a gasp escaped her throat. Had she just seen what she thought she had seen? She couldn't have.

She stared at the Red Bull, now grasped firmly in her right hand. She could swear the can had just slid the final few inches across the desk into her hand. But that was impossible, right? She must be even more tired than she thought. Her mind was playing tricks on her. It had to be. She had probably just zoned out for an instant, and didn't see her hand cover those last couple inches. Yeah, that was the ticket. She had just zoned out.

What other explanation could there be? Even Rave couldn't move quickly enough to be invisible, and he wouldn't play that kind of trick on her even if he could. Maybe it was the work of a ghost, she thought, though she didn't really believe in ghosts. Of course, she hadn't believed in vampires either, until a few months ago. And now she was entertaining the idea that the dead could climb out of their graves, so why not ghosts, too? What the heck—the more the merrier. Ghosts, goblins, witches…lions and tigers and bears, oh my! She shook her head at her silliness as the famous refrain from the "Wizard of Oz" echoed in her head. Even if ghosts did exist, why would one push a can of Red Bull into her hand? She doubted any ghost would be interested enough in her studying to help her out by moving the energy drink for her.

Maybe it had been an earthquake that moved it, or a sudden shift of the earth's axis or magnetic field. She found herself looking around the room to see if anything else had moved, and then chastised herself for her foolishness. No, her mind was simply playing tricks on her. She was overly tired, and that was it.

She gulped down an extra couple swallows of Red Bull and got back to work.

14. DOMINIC'S FRUSTRATION

Dominic was frustrated. He sat hunched forward on a diamond-shaped cement block in front of the Pacific Beach branch of the San Diego Library. There were plenty of people around, some browsing though used books at an outdoor book sale, others who were obviously homeless and taking advantage of the public facilities offered by the library. One guy in a brightly colored tie dye T-shirt was banging on a pair of bongo drums with surprisingly good rhythm. His tangled black dreadlocks bounced on his shoulders as he bobbed his head to the driving beat.

Dominic had been in San Diego for two weeks now, but with precious little to show for it. The city was beautiful, but he had scarcely noticed the palm trees, blue skies and all the brightly colored flowers that had no business blooming in December. Likewise, he paid little attention to the pleasantly warm days and the nights that could barely be described as cool. Back in his home country it would be cold and dreary right now, and the only colors would be dismal shades of brown and gray.

He had spent his first couple of days here riding the city's three trolley lines, getting off the train at every stop and trying to sense Leesa's vibration. When he failed, he hopped back onto the next trolley that came along and repeated the process all over again at the next stop. The trolley provided excellent coverage of central San Diego and the southern coastal strip of the county, but his search produced no results. Next, he risked a small bit of his anonymity by spending a week crisscrossing the rest of the county in a series of taxis, stopping every mile or two and getting out of the car to try to sense Leesa. He changed taxis every few hours to prevent any of the drivers from wondering in more than an idle fashion what their strange passenger was doing.

His was certain his painstakingly thorough search had taken him within a mile or two of every residential section in the sprawling San Diego area, with no luck. Either Leesa was not in San Diego, or he was completely unable to sense her. He wasn't sure which he hoped was true.

Next, he had visited several public libraries to use their computer systems. Distrustful of the cyber grid and unsure who might be monitoring entries and searches, he seldom used computers and so was not very skilled with the machines. He was loath to enter Leesa's name or phone number lest it somehow attract attention in the system, but it was a risk he felt he had to take. He tried to minimize the danger by changing computers and libraries frequently. After lots of searching, he had finally located a few people search sites that seemed promising, but none of them would provide any detailed information without first receiving payment via a credit card. That, of course, left him out.

So now he had to make a decision. He had come outside to think about his choices. He could ask someone in the library to help him. Maybe one of the young people who seemed so skilled and comfortable with computers would know a way to locate Leesa without a fee, or, failing that, perhaps he could entice the person to use their own credit card in exchange for a cash payment. But such a request would be at least a bit unusual and was likely to provoke some curiosity. His other choice would be to hire a professional investigator—which was how he had learned Leesa's phone number in the first place—and rely on professional discretion.

Dominic wasn't comfortable with either choice, but he had hit another in a long series of dead ends and had to do something. Speed was beginning to become increasingly more important than caution.

15. STUDYING

Finals were way worse than midterms, Leesa quickly discovered. Not only was there twice as much material to study and remember, but the exams counted as a much bigger portion of the final grade, making the pressure that much greater. Everyone in the dorm was feeling it—everyone but Stacie, that was. Stacie was a brainiac who never studied past eleven o'clock and still got nothing but A's. She was always smiling and energetic, when glassy stares and dragging gaits had become the norm.

If Leesa had the time, she was sure she could make some decent money simply by recycling the piles of energy drink cans that kept the big trash bin outside the dorm overflowing. She could make a few bucks just from the cans she and Cali were going through.

But, alas, there was little time for anything but studying, eating and sleeping—and little enough for the latter two. She couldn't believe she would have to go through this hell seven more times before she graduated. She sure hoped it got easier with experience.

She did most of her studying in her room, but went to the library for an hour or two every day, just for a break in the routine. The library was also a great place to be reminded that lots of kids were even more stressed out about finals than she was. Some looked like they hadn't slept—or showered—in days.

Leesa took a couple of short walk breaks every day to clear her head and stretch her muscles. Sometimes she dragged Cali, Stacie or Caitlin along, other times she went alone. She seldom went far, usually just wandering about the area near the dorm. The weather remained cold, but luckily it was clear. She wasn't sure how she would handle it if it snowed or sleeted. Her walk breaks were pretty much the only thing keeping her sane.

She was fairly sure she had done well on her first three finals, but the dreaded physics exam was looming tomorrow. It promised to be the toughest by far, so she wasn't planning on getting much sleep tonight, if any. Complex equations and theorems flitted around inside her head like bees buzzing around a hive. She just hoped she would be able to tame the little pests when she sat down to take the test.

She wasn't the only one feeling the stress. Girls wandered the halls of the dorm like lost souls, wearing no makeup, their eyes swollen and bloodshot. If zombies truly did exist, Leesa thought, they could hide out pretty well in any dorm on campus during finals week. She was scared to look in a mirror, afraid she would see something very similar staring back at her.

Yellow light leaked under doors and soft music filtered through the walls at all hours of the night as many kids pull all-nighters. Leesa had been up until the early hours twice already this week—but tonight was going to make those nights seem like nothing. It was nearly two o'clock now, and she was still at her desk, pouring over her physics textbook. With plenty more still to go.

Three empty cans of Red Bull filled the straw wastebasket beside her bed, with another half-full can waiting on the corner of her desk. She wasn't in love with the taste of the drink, but she had been downing a couple of cans every night all week and was beginning to worry she might be getting addicted to the stuff. Still, there was nothing like an energy drink for staying awake, except maybe for some of the illicit drugs she was sure some of the other girls in the dorm were using. Leesa would never allow herself to go that route, no matter how tired she got. Red Bull was more than enough for her. If she couldn't stay awake drinking Red Bull, then she had no business being awake in the first place.

Her head was beginning to feel heavy and the numbers on the pages were starting to blur, so she reached for her Red Bull. Pink's "Greatest Hits...So Far" CD was playing softly in the background, and the singer was crooning something about not wanting to be a four o'clock in the morning girl. Leesa was pretty sure four o'clock would find her right where she was now, still studying and probably reaching for another can of Red Bull.

As she had already done several times this week, she paused her hand a few inches from the can and waited to see if might magically slide over into her hand. Once again, the can just sat there, mocking her. And once again, Leesa felt foolish. She was thankful nobody was watching.

Just for the heck of it, she closed her eyes and concentrated hard, trying to picture the Red Bull sliding across the desk into her grip. After a few seconds, she opened her eyes. Had the can moved a fraction? She couldn't be sure. She looked closer, but there was no way to tell. It was probably just wishful thinking, some instinctive rebellion by her brain against the complex laws of physics that had been tormenting her all night. She was wasting valuable studying time, she knew, but this was more fun. Besides, she didn't think a little break now and then would hurt. In fact, it was probably good for her.

She picked up her pencil and drew a light arc on the desk along the bottom of the can, marking its position. She squeezed her eyes shut again and tried to picture the can sliding into her hand, waiting at least fifteen to twenty seconds this time. When she opened her eyes, the can was right where it started, behind the pencil mark. Oh, well, she thought, so much for that.

She grabbed the can and chugged the liquid down, resisting the temptation to hold her nose while she drank. When she had emptied the can, she tossed it into the wastebasket. It landed with a clang atop its comrades and stayed right where it landed. What was she expecting, she thought? That it was going to jump out of the basket and start dancing on the floor?

She shook her head. Break time was over. Back to the fun and games of physics.

16. SAD NEWS

Leesa closed her Blue Book and exhaled deeply, stretching her arms out in front of her and enjoying what felt like her first real breath in almost two hours. A glance at the sweeping second hand on the old-fashioned clock on the classroom wall showed she had a whole thirty seconds left before time was up. She had barely made it, but finished was finished—and boy, did she feel finished.

The exam had been a beast, but she thought she had done okay. A couple of science geeks had turned in their booklets early, but most of her classmates were still frantically scribbling, trying to solve one last problem. Leesa was confident she had gotten at least a C, and maybe even a B. Definitely good enough for physics, for sure. All her studying had paid off. She'd been up until six that morning, grabbed two hours of sleep, and then snuck in some last minute cramming before the exam. Now she just wanted to go home and crash.

She grabbed her parka from the back of her chair and walked her booklet up to the front. She dropped it on top of the three or four already there just as the professor, a preppy blond guy in his late thirties, called an end to the exam. He nodded at her and favored her with a small smile—her reward, she guessed, for finishing thirty seconds early. Leesa smiled back before turning and heading for the door. She felt like skipping. No more physics! Ever!

Her mood grew brighter still when she saw Rave smiling up at her from the bottom of the stairs. He was wearing his purple and brown flannel shirt and black jeans. The noon sun made his dark copper hair almost shine. Seeing him there melted away some of her fatigue as she limped down the steps.

"What a nice surprise," she said.

Rave kissed her on the forehead. A little more of her tiredness vanished.

"How did you do?"

"Good enough, I think."

"I bet you're glad to be done, huh?"

"Ha! 'Glad' doesn't even begin to cover it. I'm beat. I only got about two hours sleep last night. But I think it was worth it."

"And yet somehow, you still look beautiful," Rave said, smiling. "What's your secret?"

Leesa blushed. Her fingers reached for her hair, but she had clipped it up into a tight bun this morning, so there was nowhere for her hand to go.

"And here I thought volkaanes had good eyesight," she said, grinning. "But I'm glad you think so."

"I do," Rave said. His face turned serious. "Can you put off going home to sleep for a bit? I need to talk to you."

Leesa was struck by a sense of déjà vu, but this time knew she wasn't imagining it. Rave had surprised her by meeting her here after her physics midterm and had told her he needed to talk to her that day, too. She would never forget that morning—how could she? That was the day he had revealed his true nature to her and let her see the blue flames flicker from his fingertips to demonstrate his inner fire. And she had kissed him for the first time that afternoon, a quick peck on his lips so brief it barely counted as a kiss, yet had filled her with a feeling beyond anything she had ever imagined. It seemed like such a long time ago, but it was only two months.

Now he needed to talk to her again. She wondered what it could be about.

"Of course I can," she replied. She gently wrapped her fingers around his forearm. "Do you remember the last time you said that to me here?"

Rave smiled. "Yeah, I do. We went to lunch. I especially remember dessert. It was delicious. It left me wanting more— much more."

Leesa squeezed his arm lovingly. She knew he was talking about their kiss.

"So, what is it? Don't tell me you have more strange secrets to share."

"No, no secrets this time." Rave's eyes drifted down to the ground for a moment. "You're not going to like it, though. I know I don't."

"Uh, oh," Leesa said. She certainly did not like the sound of that.

Just then, a thick cloud drifted in front of the sun, dimming the day. She hoped it was not an omen. She sat down on the edge of the steps, barely noticing how cold the stone was.

"Go ahead, tell me," she said. "May as well get it over with."

Rave sat down next to her.

"Before I get to that, I wanted to let you know I went out to the cemetery in Higganum after we talked."

Leesa was surprised. With finals and everything else going on, she had forgotten Rave's promise to go take a look at the place. Now the images from her dream flashed back into her head, as clear as the night she dreamt them.

"What did you find?" she asked, not sure whether she wanted him to have found something or not.

"Not much. Nothing specific, anyway. But something felt just a little bit off. I cannot explain it any better than that, or make any guesses what it was. I just had a sense that something was wrong." He shrugged. "I know it's not much help, but I wanted you to know."

Leesa sighed. She should have suspected it would turn out something like this, with no clear cut answer in either direction. That seemed to be way things were going lately.

"Well, at least you tried," she said. "Thanks for going. And for letting me know."

"Have you had any more dreams like that?"

She shook her head. "No, thank goodness." She considered telling him about imagining the Red Bull can moving, but decided against it. That was probably just her overtired brain—no need to concern him with that. Besides, he said he needed to talk to her. She wanted to give him his chance.

"So, what did you want to talk to me about," she asked.

Rave took her hand in both of his. "I have to go away for a little while."

Leesa's heart sank. She had definitely not expected anything like this.

"What? Why?"

"It's the solstice," Rave explained. "The Council of Elders is afraid it may magnify the pull of *Destiratu*, so they have decided we should leave. We are too close to the vampire lair here. It is too dangerous under these circumstances. For everyone."

Leesa tried to process what Rave was saying. It was all so complicated. She barely understood *Destiratu*, and now he was saying something about the solstice. Balin had mentioned something about the solstice, too, she remembered now.

"Where will you go? For how long?"

"Up north. To some hidden caves in the mountains of New Hampshire. There are no vampires anywhere around there."

That's so far, Leesa wanted to say, but she held back the words. Rave was clearly troubled by having to leave, and she did not want to add to his anguish.

"How long will you be gone?" she asked instead.

"A couple of weeks, at least. Until we are sure the effects of the solstice are gone."

"When are you leaving?" Leesa knew it would be soon—the winter solstice was just four days away.

Rave put his arms around her shoulders and pulled her close. "This afternoon."

He felt Leesa stiffen in his embrace. She obviously had not expected it would be today.

"You could come," Rave said. "I have already gotten permission for you to join us, if you wish." He did not expect her to accept, but he had to offer.

Leesa snuggled against him. She wanted nothing more than to go away with him, especially since there would be no school for almost three weeks. But she knew she couldn't. Not now.

"Oh, Rave, I wish I could. But I can't leave my mom and Bradley. Not this soon."

"I know."

Rave eased Leesa away from his chest and looked directly into her eyes. She wanted nothing more than to disappear into his beautiful eyes.

"Promise me you'll all be careful," Rave said. "The vampires are going to be extra hungry, especially on the solstice and the few days after. They will not want to draw attention, so they will be hunting in secluded places, where people are alone or in very small numbers. Populated areas should be safe. Stay out the woods and avoid empty areas, especially at night."

"We will, Rave. I promise. Don't worry about us." She forced a smile onto her face. "This is one time I really wish you had a cell phone, though," she said, forgetting for the moment she didn't have one right now, either.

"If you need me," Rave said, "just tell Max. I can be here in a couple of hours."

Tell Max? What the heck was he talking about? "I don't understand," Leesa said. "What's Max going to do, go racing off to New Hampshire like Lassie to fetch you?"

Rave smiled. He had no idea who Lassie was, but he got the idea.

"No, that won't be necessary. Max and I have established a bond. I cannot explain it exactly, but the bond gives us a connection. If you tell him you need me, I will be able to sense it through his thoughts."

"Really? You're not kidding?"

"Yes, really."

"That's so cool." Leesa grinned, struck by a new thought. "What if I told Max I loved you? Would you hear that, too?"

Rave laughed. "I would, yes." He enfolded Leesa in his arms once again. "But I don't need Max to know that."

17. BONFIRE

Leesa and Rave walked arm in arm back to her dorm. For the most part, they walked in silence. Exhaustion had caught up with Leesa, and there was little more to say, anyhow. She knew Rave loved her, and she also knew he had to leave. She would miss him, of course, miss him terribly. But he would be back, and she hoped it would be sooner rather than later.

She would have plenty to keep her busy over the holiday break. Her family was going to have a real Christmas for the first time in years—maybe even a white one, she hoped, if the weatherman cooperated. Also, she would be helping her mom and Bradley find an apartment. Her mom had decided she was well enough to take care of herself and Bradley, and felt they had imposed on Aunt Janet and Uncle Roger's hospitality long enough. It was time to get their own place, and Leesa was more than happy to help.

Rave usually said his goodbyes outside the dorm, but today he accompanied Leesa up to her room. The Red Bull Leesa guzzled for breakfast had worn off and her lack of sleep was weighing on her heavily. She could barely keep her eyes open as she fumbled with her keys, trying unsuccessfully to get the right key into the lock. Rave gently took the keys from her hand and opened the door. She managed a small smile for him as she stepped inside.

She shrugged off her parka and let if fall to the floor, too tired to bother hanging it up in the closet. Rave picked it up and draped it over the desk chair as she limped across the room and collapsed onto her bed. She looked up and saw Rave watching her, his beautiful eyes filled with tenderness.

"Will you lie down here with me until I fall asleep, please?" she asked. She did not want to have to say good-bye to him, and knew it would be easier if he left while she was asleep.

"Of course," Rave replied.

He lay down beside her and wrapped his arms around her. Leesa nestled her cheek against his chest and quickly fell fast asleep.

A loud bang woke her. She opened her eyes to darkness, her heart racing once again. At least it wasn't from a dream this time. Her mouth felt parched and her eyes were gritty and burning. For a long, panicked moment, she was confused about where she was and what time it was. Why was she on top of her covers, fully dressed? And what the heck was that explosion?

Slowly, things began to come back to her. She remembered her talk with Rave after her exam and falling asleep in his arms. She had obviously slept for hours—it had barely been noon when she went to sleep, and now it was dark. Rave was probably half way to New Hampshire by now. The thought made her sad. She turned her head and checked the clock. The blue digits read 6:35. Six hours of exhausted sleep. No wonder she felt like she did. She was probably having Red Bull withdrawal on top of everything else.

That still left the bang that had awakened her unexplained. Another one exploded, close by. She could tell it came from outside, maybe from the courtyard behind the dorm. She listened more closely and heard the muffled shouts of a crowd outside. What the heck was going on out there?

She swung her legs over the edge of the bed and rubbed her eyes, not quite ready to attempt to make it to the window. She could not believe how wiped out she felt. No more all-nighters for her, she vowed.

Three knocks sounded at her door. She pushed herself to her feet and limped across the room. When she opened the door, she found Cali, Stacie and Caitlin looking in at her. They were all wearing coats and carrying hats.

"Wow, you look like crap," Cali said, grinning.

"Thanks a lot," Leesa replied, stepping aside and letting her friends into the room. "I just woke up. I crashed after my physics final."

She reached behind her head and let her bun out. Her hair fell across her shoulders in a tangled mess. She tried to fix it with her fingers, but with little luck. This job was going to need a brush, at least.

Another bang sounded outside.

"What's going on out there?" she asked.

"They're having a bonfire out in the courtyard, to celebrate the end of finals," Stacie said. "It's getting crazy out there. Kids are burning books, even some furniture."

"And someone brought fireworks," Caitlin said. "Sounds like a couple of M-80's to me. My dad used to let me set some off on the Fourth of July."

"C'mon, Lees, get dressed," Cali said. "We're going to join the party."

"Give me a minute," Leesa said. "I'm still waking up."

She bent over the sink and splashed cold water on her face. That helped some. She toweled off and wrapped her hair back into a bun. If she was going outside, she would need a hat, so it didn't matter what her hair looked like.

She grabbed a clean flannel shirt from her closet, leaving the same jeans on. While she dressed, her friends gathered at her back window and checked out the action below.

"Wow, that thing is really blazing," Caitlin said. "This is gonna be fun."

"I'm not burning any books," Leesa said as she grabbed her parka from the back of her chair. "Those things are too damn expensive. I can sell 'em back to the bookstore."

"Don't worry," Cali said. "We're not burning any books, either. We'll let the crazy kids do that. We're just gonna join the fun."

They rode down the elevator with two other girls from Leesa's floor, Cheryl and Ashley. Cheryl had a canvass shopping bag filled with paperback books slung over her shoulder. The ones Leesa could see looked pretty old and worn.

"Fuel for the fire," Cheryl said, grinning. "I've been meaning to get rid of these for awhile now. This looks like the perfect opportunity. And it will be a great excuse to buy some new books!"

"Cool," Cali said.

"Burn, baby, burn," Caitlin added.

They let Cheryl with her load of books step out of the elevator first, and then followed the two girls across the lobby. Cali pushed the door open for them.

Outside, the cold hit Leesa immediately, waking her up even better than the water she had splashed on her face. She put her blue ski cap on her head, tugging it down over her ears, and grabbed her gloves from her pockets. Her friends similarly fortified themselves against the chill. Cali's hat was a funky brown fur thing, complete with a chin strap and a pair of ears sticking up from the top that resembled wolf ears. The edges of both ears were torn ragged, making it look like some wild animal had gnawed on them. Leesa could barely keep from laughing.

"What the heck is that thing?" she asked.

"Pretty cool, huh?" Cali said. "I found it at a garage sale last year. Just because I need to be warm doesn't mean I can't make a statement at the same time."

"Yeah, and your statement is 'I'm one very weird chick,'" Leesa said, laughing.

"You know what they say," Stacie added. "There's no accounting for taste—or lack of it."

They all laughed.

"You're all just jealous," Cali said, "because I have *style*." She flipped one of the ears ostentatiously with her hand. "C'mon, let's go join the party."

Leesa guessed there were close to a hundred people already circled around the fire, with more streaming in by the minute as word of the impromptu party spread across campus. The driving beat of a hip-hop song she didn't recognize blasted from the open window of a nearby room. Kids were dancing, singing and throwing things into the blaze—anything to blow off the accumulated stresses of final exams. The flames snapped and crackled, leaping at least fifteen feet into the air. Leesa could see the charred outlines of two wooden desk chairs and a square table outlined inside the dancing flames. She shuddered to think what else might be burning in there.

A string of fire crackers exploded from within the fire, their staccato bangs sounding like a series of gunshots, and a loud cheer erupted from the crowd. Leesa and her friends moved to within twenty feet from the fire—even from here she could feel its heat. She pulled off her gloves and rolled her cap up above her ears.

Another loud cheer burst from the revelers, and she watched as the crowd parted for two bare-chested guys wearing only jeans and sneakers running toward the fire carrying a small, very ugly couch.

"Go! Go! Go!" the onlookers chanted as the two guys used the momentum from their run to toss the couch into the center of the fire. Golden sparks shot upward into the night as the upholstery ignited. The guys bowed happily as the crowd applauded. Leesa suspected they would rue the loss of their couch in the morning—she hoped it belonged to them, and not to someone who had neglected to lock his or her door—but the two guys were certainly having fun tonight. One of them took a long chug from a bottle of Tequila, and then handed it to his friend, who did the same. The crowd cheered again, and the bare-chested pair launched into a crazy, alcohol fueled dance. They bounced up and down, sometimes linking arms and spinning around in a circle, throwing their other arm wildly into the air without apparent rhyme or reason. It reminded Leesa of a scene from one of The Lord of the Rings movies, when two of the hobbits— Merry and Pippin, she thought—were drinking and dancing wildly atop a table.

Something about the fire made her miss Rave. It was stupid, she knew. He had only been gone a few hours, and she was used to going days without seeing him, sometimes even longer. This time was different, though. She knew she wouldn't be seeing him for some time, and that caused an empty space inside her.

She glanced over at her friends. They were all watching the fire and the dancing guys. Cali and Caitlin bobbed their heads to the music, while Stacie seemed to be studying the whole scene, like she was going to write a term paper or something on it later.

Someone passed Cali a red and brown bota bag of wine. She lifted it up in front of her face and shot a stream of red liquid into her mouth. She noticed Leesa watching and offered the bota to her. Leesa shook her head. She wasn't much of a drinker, and alcohol was the last thing she needed right now, with the way she felt.

Cali gave it to Caitlin instead, who took a long drink before passing it on.

"Pretty fun, huh," Cali said to Leesa.

"It's wild, alright."

Cali looked at Leesa more closely. She sensed something was not right.

"What's wrong, Lees? You don't look like you're having as

much fun as the rest of us. You still feeling wiped out?"

"A little, but that's not it. It's Rave. I miss him."

Cali grinned. "So, what else is new? I told you not to get involved with a guy without a phone or car."

"I've gotten used to that. This is different. He's gone for a couple of weeks, at least. They're all gone."

Cali linked her arm around Leesa's, a concerned look on her face. "What do you mean he's gone? That they're all gone?"

Leesa hesitated, trying to think of something she could tell Cali that would not reveal Rave's nature. "All the Mastons are gone," she said after a moment. "They left today. Went up north somewhere."

"All of them? The whole clan? Why?"

"It's some sort of pilgrimage thing. It has something to do with the winter solstice. I don't really understand it," she added, to keep from having to explain any further.

"Pilgrimage, huh?" Cali said. She grinned. "Are you sure it's not for some secret human sacrifice ceremony?"

Leesa smiled back. When she had first told Cali she had met one of the Mastons, Cali said there were stories they performed human sacrifices.

"I'm pretty sure it has nothing to do with any sacrifices, human or otherwise," Leesa said.

"They've always been strange and reclusive," Cali mused, "but I don't remember all of them disappearing at once. The solstice happens every year. I'm sure we would have noticed."

Cali had grown up in East Hampton, which was one of the closest towns to the Maston's isolated settlement. She would know this was something different, so Leesa decided she could safely tell her friend a little bit more.

"Yeah, I know. But there's something special about this solstice. Rave said it happens less than once every hundred years. Like I said, I don't understand exactly it."

That seemed to satisfy Cali.

"And he didn't say when he would be back?" she asked.

"No. He said he didn't know. It's not up to him. It's up to the elders."

Cali grimaced. "That sucks. But at least he's coming back eventually, right?"

"Yeah, he is," Leesa said. "I hope."

Cali squeezed Leesa's arm. "He'll be back, don't worry. I've seen the way he looks at you. There's no way he won't be back."

Leesa smiled. She had seen it, too, of course. But she did not know if it would be up to him.

18. A NEW HOME

Leesa was sitting on her bed reading when her mom and Bradley walked in through the open door. She had gotten a good night's sleep after the bonfire and was feeling pretty rested this morning. Smiling, she bounced up off the bed and gave her mom a big hug. When she was done, she moved into Bradley's arms.

"Hi, pumpkin," he said, squeezing her tightly.

"How are you feeling, big brother?" she asked when she stepped out of his embrace.

"I feel great."

In truth, he did look great, a far cry from the gaunt, glassy-eyed apparition Stefan had led out of the darkness when he had come to fulfill his side of his bargain with Leesa. Bradley's blue eyes were bright and clear, and he seemed to have put on another pound or two since she had seen him a week or so ago. But the best thing about him was his wide smile, a smile that had helped Leesa through so many difficult days during her childhood.

Her mom looked great too, but she'd had much more time to recover than Bradley. They were here to drive Leesa back to Aunt Janet's house, where they would all be staying for the holidays, at least until they found an apartment of their own to move into. Leesa could have remained on campus, but she would have had to move into another dorm, one the college left open for students who could not go home over the break for one reason or another. It would be a bit crowded at Aunt Janet's, but a lot more fun. Besides, Cali, Caitlin and Stacie were all going home for break, so Leesa would have been pretty much alone if she remained on campus.

Her suitcase was already packed so she grabbed her parka from the closet and was ready to go. Bradley beat her to her suitcase, so she let him wheel it out to the elevator. For a split second she thought of protesting, but realized the small gesture was his way of trying to restore their normal big brother/little sister relationship. He had spent most of his childhood taking care of her, and she sensed that he wanted to get back to his role of caretaker, even though they both realized she didn't need it any more. She didn't mind—she kind of liked the idea of having a big brother again.

The elevator stopped on the third floor on the way down. The door slid open to reveal Caitlin standing there, along with a slightly older girl who looked so much like Caitlin she had to be her sister. None of the others had met each other, so Leesa and Caitlin made the necessary introductions. Leesa was glad her mom got to meet Caitlin for the first time when Caitlin was wearing a coat, rather the one of the risqué T-shirts she liked to wear during the warmer weather. First impressions counted, and Leesa did not want her mom to get the wrong idea about her friend, who was much more talk than action.

Since Caitlin lived in New Jersey, Leesa would not be seeing her again until school started up in January. They hugged each other good-bye outside the dorm, and then Leesa limped over to Aunt Janet's blue Ford Taurus.

"Can I drive, Mom?" Leesa asked. "It seems like forever since I've had a chance." She had borrowed her aunt's car once to drive to see Rave, but other than that, she hadn't driven since summer.

"Of course, dear," Judy said, handing Leesa the keys.

Leesa got behind the wheel. Her mom slid in next to her and Bradley climbed into the back seat. A moment later, they were on their way.

"We need to make one stop, honey," Judy said when they pulled out of the main Weston College gate onto Washington Street. "It's right on the way."

Leesa guessed they would probably be stopping at a store to pick up something to bring back to Aunt Janet or Uncle Roger, so she was surprised when her mom told her to turn into the driveway of a large apartment complex three miles from campus. She swung the Taurus into the driveway. She had ridden past this complex many times, but had never been inside the grounds.

"Take the second right, and then the first left," Judy said.

Leesa did as instructed, winding her way among a series of two-story apartments constructed mostly of grey wood. Narrow lawns fronted the buildings and small bare trees filled the spaces between them. The place had a weathered, lived-in look, but both the buildings and the grounds appeared to be well-maintained. Strips of bare dirt lined the front of each building, and Leesa could imagine them filled with flowers in the spring and summer.

"Park over there, in space forty-seven," Judy told her.

Leesa pulled into the parking space. She switched off the engine and turned to her mom.

"What are we doing here, Mom? Do you know someone who lives here?" She did not see how her mother could know someone outside her family well enough to be visiting like this, but could not think of any other explanation.

"I have a surprise for you, honey. C'mon, let's get out."

Leesa looked back to Bradley, who was smiling. Clearly, he was in on the secret, but he wasn't telling.

They got out of the car and her mom led them toward one of the apartments, number twenty-four. The door was painted a dark blue.

"This is our new home," Judy said proudly. "At least it will be, right after Christmas."

Leesa looked at the door, then back at her mom and Bradley, thoroughly confused.

"I don't understand," she said. "I thought we were going apartment hunting next week. How'd you get a place already?"

"I found it on the internet," Bradley said. "On Craigslist."

"We looked at it in person the other day," Judy added, "and we both agreed it would be perfect. It's got two bedrooms and a loft. You can use the loft as your room, honey, during the summer or any other time you want to come visit. And I can't believe how much cheaper apartments are here compared to San Diego."

"Wow, Mom, that's great," Leesa said. "It's awesome you found a place already. I'm proud of both of you."

She really was glad to see her mom and Bradley were well enough to go out and find an apartment by themselves, and it seemed like they had chosen a nice one. Best of all, the place was only three miles from campus, easy walking distance for her. She was mildly disappointed they had found it without her—she had hoped apartment hunting would help keep her mind off missing Rave.

"We don't have it officially until January 1st," Judy explained, "but the manager said we could move in any time after Christmas. I wish I had the keys right now, so I could show it to you. I know you're going to love it."

"Tell her your other news, Mom," Bradley said.

Leesa looked at her mom, who was positively beaming.

"I've got a job," Judy said proudly. "Can you believe it?"

In truth, Leesa could not believe it. Her mom had never held a job, at least not as far back as Leesa could remember. How could she, when she had refused to leave the house for more than ten years?

"Mom, that's totally awesome! Where are you working?"

"At the bakery, for your uncle Ralph. He's always extra busy during the holidays. I started last Saturday. I'm having so much fun, meeting so many people."

Leesa gave her mom a quick hug. "Mom, I am sooo happy for you."

"After New Years," Judy continued, "I'll start looking for a real job. Your uncle said he'll be my reference, and he'll tell anyone who asks that I worked for him for a year. Isn't that exciting?"

"It sure is," Leesa said, amazed at how quickly things were starting to become normal for her family. And normal was definitely not something they had much experience with.

Perhaps that explained her feeling that somewhere, somehow, another shoe was about to drop. She prayed it wasn't going to drop on any of them.

19. SOLSTICE

Leesa sat on the front steps of her aunt's house, arms resting on her thighs, gazing off to the west. The sun hung low in a cloudless sky, a pale yellow orb that seemed almost to balance atop the rolling hills on the far horizon. No wonder it was so cold out here, she thought—the barely glowing disc seemed incapable of providing any real warmth.

She had bundled up against the cold, adding a black wool scarf around her neck to her usual winter garb of ski cap, parka, leather gloves and Ugg boots. She had been sitting out here for almost half an hour, thinking and watching the sun slowly sink lower and lower. Max was running around the front yard, occasionally coming back to the steps for a few moments of petting before racing out onto the lawn again and resuming his fun.

Today was the twenty-first of December—the winter solstice. The reason Rave was gone. Leesa was watching to see if she might notice anything different about the sun today, some slight change that could account for the volkaanes retreating to their New Hampshire sanctuary. If there was anything different, she could not detect it. It seemed like any other winter afternoon to her.

She had read up on the solstice on the internet. Today was

the day the sun reached its farthest point south in the sky. Tomorrow it would begin its slow trip north. Today was also one of the shortest days of the year. She wondered if one of those two things had the power to influence *Destiratu*, or any other magical phenomenon, for that matter. Perhaps it was something else entirely, something unaccounted for in the astronomical models she had found in her research.

She knew she was being foolish, but she couldn't help herself. Rave had said even the eldest and wisest among the volkaanes did not clearly understand the effects of the solstice on the supernatural world. They just knew it was potentially dangerous and had opted for caution. Still, it made her feel a little closer to Rave, watching the sinking sun and wondering what kind of pull it might be exerting on him.

Max bounded up on the steps again, and this time she grabbed his neck and gave him a vigorous chest rub. His tongue hung out and his tail wagged furiously as he reveled in the attention and affection. When she was done, Leesa pulled his head close to her face. What the heck, she thought.

"I love you, Rave," she whispered into Max's furry ear.

Max gave three short barks and bobbed his head up and down. Leesa almost believed Max understood her words and was somehow sending her message across the miles to Rave. No, check that. She didn't *almost* believe—she did believe. Suddenly she felt a little warmer, almost as if Rave were now sitting right beside her. A smile crept onto her face.

She waited outside another few minutes, until the sun disappeared and darkness began stealing across the sky. Finally, she got to her feet and turned toward the door.

"C'mon, Max. Time to go inside."

That night, Leesa dreamed again.

She stood in front of a dark, narrow opening cut into a rugged gray stone cliff. How she had come to be here, she had no idea. Cold, fetid air seeped from the cavern, assailing her nostrils and forcing her back a step. There was nothing here to draw her forward—indeed, the opening seemed to reek of danger. Yet something kept her from doing what she knew she should be doing—leaving this place as quickly as her feet could carry her. The sensible part of her brain screamed "get away!" but another part of her whispered "you must go on." Strangely, the whisper felt more powerful than the scream.

She stepped into the narrow tunnel.

Goosebumps rose on her arms as the cold air wrapped itself around her, seeming to enfold her in its clutches. To minimize the dank, rotting stench, she forced herself to breathe through her mouth, hoping she was not inhaling anything that might turn out to be harmful. The walls of the cavern were rough, but the floor was strangely smooth and worn. Again, the sensible part of her brain told her this meant something, something she should be worried about, but the whisper drew her onward.

No light filtered into the deeper reaches of the cavern, yet somehow she could still see. Not clearly, but well enough to make out the stone walls a few feet from her face, allowing her to follow the winding passage without crashing into the rock when the tunnel turned.

I'm dreaming, *she told herself.* That's why I can see in the dark. None of this is real. *She pressed her palm against the rough stone. It sure felt real.*

Subtly, the whisper that enticed her to keep going changed. No longer was it an abstract feeling pulling her in—it now had the flavor of "help me, please." She could almost hear the voice, but not quite. It was still a feeling in her head, not a voice coming to her ears.

She pressed on. Time seemed to have no meaning here. It's just a dream, *she reminded herself, puzzled that she could somehow know she was dreaming within the dream. Time does* not matter.

The plea for help grew steadily louder in her head.

Without noticing the change, she suddenly found herself standing in a large cavern. The smell was stronger here. It was the smell of death, she realized, but a kind of death she had never encountered before—a rotting, lingering death that promised no end. She stopped and slowly surveyed the chamber. Deep inside the mountain, where there should have been no light, she could still see. Dreams sure can be strange, *she thought.*

As her eyes swept slowly across the cavern, she almost missed it. She had to bring her gaze back a few feet to the left, directly opposite from where she stood, to make sure she hadn't imagined the shadowy presence. But she had not. A pair of pale yellow eyes glowed faintly in the blackness, watching her. The sense of danger grew. She had to get out of here—get out of here now. She was about to turn when she heard it again. "Help me. Please, help me." The voice sounded hauntingly familiar, but it took her a moment to recognize it. Bradley! *The tone was so weak and tortured she could barely recognize her brother's voice.*

She forced herself slowly across the chamber. I'm not limping, *she thought out of nowhere.* What's that about? *She'd never had a dream where she hadn't limped.*

The pale eyes remained fixed on her, but otherwise there was no movement in the cavern but hers. As Leesa drew closer, she became aware of a second presence, pressed against the wall, behind the first. She knew this one was Bradley, chained to the wall. But who, or what, was the other?

"The human is mine," a female voice said. "You cannot save it."

Leesa still could not see anything except the two yellow eyes, and perhaps a slight deepening of the blackness surrounding them. Somehow, she knew this apparition could not harm her—not here in her dream, at least—so she kept walking.

Suddenly, laughter cackled from the darkness. Below the eyes, Leesa could now see a pair of gleaming fangs. With no source of light here, the fangs should not have gleamed, but they did, almost as if they carried their own illumination inside them.

The shock of the laughter and the sudden appearance of the fangs stopped Leesa in her tracks. The blackness lessened slightly, enough for her to see that the figure against the wall was not her brother. She had been deceived. The captive was not even male. It was female. But who?

Leesa strained to pierce the darkness. She was certain she would recognize the girl, if she could just see a bit more clearly.

"You cannot stop it," the voice said. "You do not have the power."

Leesa ignored the voice, concentrating on the captive instead. There was something distressingly familiar about her. Something much too familiar. Almost as if it was....

Leesa awoke with a start, fully alert. She cursed silently. She had been but an instant from recognizing the girl chained against the cavern wall when she woke. For some reason, this dream felt eerily similar to her zombie dream. Somehow, she sensed they both held important information, but she had no idea what or why. She closed her eyes and struggled to bring back the image of the girl in the cavern. She could picture everything clearly right up until the instant she awoke. Unfortunately, that was not enough. The girl's identity still eluded her. And this time, she was pretty sure there would be no YouTube video to help her.

20. HUNGRY VAMPIRES

Kristi Brolen was glad to be home. This past semester, the first of her junior year at UConn, had been her most difficult by far. Upper level courses were much tougher than those she had taken her freshman and sophomore years. She had done okay, but it had required a lot of work. All she wanted to do now, at the beginning of her three week holiday break, was relax.

So that was exactly what she was doing, sitting and reading in the backyard of her parents' Ledyard home. She had dragged one of the heavy, dark green Adirondack chairs close to the edge of the yard—not an easy task for the five-foot five-inch, blue-eyed brunette—onto a small cement patio her dad had built a few years back to hold their propane gas grill and a wooden picnic table. She could have read at the table, but the Adirondack was so much more comfortable.

She loved it back here. Every breath she drew was tinged with fresh pine fragrance from a row of slender Blue Spruce a few feet behind her. The trees separated the yard from the woods and hills that stretched for almost a mile behind the house. The yard was quiet and peaceful, especially compared to the inside of the house, where her nine-year old twin brothers romped and raced about the place with little regard for the sanity of the other members of the family.

Sure, it was cold out here, and growing steadily colder now that the sun had set, but her purple L.L Bean jacket and matching ski cap pulled down over her ears shielded her from the chill. A pair of gray knit gloves kept her hands warm, yet still allowed her to turn the pages of her book without trouble. The dark was not a problem, either. Kristi's dad had run an electric cable to the patio last year so they could use it after dark. The covered brass lamp attached to a wooden pole behind her provided plenty of light to read by.

Kristi's attention was riveted upon her book. She loved to read, but had spent so much time studying and doing homework the last few months she'd had almost no chance to read just for pure, mindless fun. Over the next few weeks, she planned to make up for that. *Breathless* had her off to a great start.

She had sworn off vampire books—they were all starting to feel too much the same—but her best friend had recommended this one so she had decided to give it a try. She was glad she had. *Breathless* was proving to be a fast-paced read with lots of new and interesting twists—and plenty of romance, too. She found it easy to escape into the story, which was exactly what she wanted after the long, difficult semester.

She was so immersed in the book that she almost missed the soft sound from behind the spruce trees the first time it happened. The noise registered in her consciousness just enough to pull her eyes from her reading. She looked quizzically around the yard. She was pretty sure she had heard something, but had absolutely no idea what it might have been. Putting her finger in the book to mark her place, she pushed herself up to the front edge of her chair and listened.

After a few seconds, she heard it again, this time more clearly. It was a soft, mewling sound, the kind a wounded animal might make. She thought it might be a dog. It was definitely coming from behind the trees, and not very far behind them, either. She put her bookmark into *Breathless* and laid the book on her chair behind her, then pushed herself to her feet.

The mewling sounded again, longer and lower this time. Whatever it was, the poor creature seemed to be weak and in great pain. Kristi moved toward the row of spruce, separating the boughs with her hands and getting ready to step to between them.

Three shadowy figures moved easily through the dark woods, heading south and east. There were few paths here, but they weaved their way effortlessly among the leafless trees, making almost no sound. They could have moved faster—much faster—but they had no need for haste.

The leader was a woman, short in stature, with full lips and black hair cut just below her chin. She looked to be in her twenties, but she was older, much older. Her name was Victoria, and she was nearly four hundred years old. She was a vampire. Victoria had been turned by an eccentric Austrian nobleman in the early 1700's, but had the good fortune to encounter Ricard soon after. When the vampire leader decided to journey to the New World, Victoria joined him, sensing her existence would be far safer and more rewarding than life with the Count. She had been with Ricard ever since.

Her two companions were also vampires, following the Council's decree that they leave the caverns only in groups of three or four. Behind Victoria came Wallace, a tall, stocky, vampire of English descent who still maintained the vestiges of his upper class London accent, despite having left the city almost three hundred years before. The final member of the trio was another female, Candice, a slender, aristocratic blonde who like to call herself Countessa, despite having been born to a poor Massachusetts silversmith and his wife nearly two hundred years ago.

The three vampires had no specific destination in mind, wanting only to get far enough from their lair to be safe, in a direction different from those taken by other hunting parties.

They skirted the edges of several southeastern Connecticut towns, seeking a lone human in some isolated place where there would be no witnesses.

As with many of the younger, weaker vampires, Candice's hunger was becoming increasingly difficult to deny. She needed blood, and she needed it soon. Victoria and Wallace were there to make sure she did nothing foolish. The two older vampires were still in near complete control of their urges. Wallace kept a feeder back in the vampire lair, and Victoria had long grown accustomed to satisfying her needs with the blood of animals, taking a human only rarely.

Candice sensed the human first. Her keen hunger sharpened her senses, bringing the scent of the human female to her a moment before her companions noticed it. The human was not far away, behind a row of evergreens. She laid a hand on the shoulders of her companions to bring them to a halt. Her fangs were already dropping into place, but a harsh look from Victoria made her pull them back up.

"Patience, Candice," Victoria cautioned.

"But she's alone," Candice protested. "Can you not sense that?"

Wallace sniffed the air. "Yes, she's alone," he agreed. "But alone does not mean unwatched or unseen by others."

Candice's thirst was spiking from the nearness of the potential prey. She could almost taste the hot blood pouring down her throat.

"I can take her before anyone can stop me."

"But can you take her without anyone seeing you?" Victoria asked. "When we don't know who might be watching?"

"I don't care," Candice said. She inhaled deeply through her nose. "She smells so young and sweet."

"But we care," Victoria said. "You know we must draw as little attention to our kind as possible."

"I want her," Candice said determinedly. "I *need* her."

Victoria studied her younger friend. Candice's need radiated from her in such strength Victoria knew Candice would not be able to deny it much longer.

"Perhaps you shall have her," she said.

Silently, Victoria crept closer to the line of pine trees. She motioned her companions to join her. Through tiny openings in the thick branches, they saw a girl, reading.

"Watch," Victoria whispered to Candice. "And learn."

She squatted low, bringing her face but a few feet from the ground. A low mewling sound issued from her throat, the perfect imitation of a wounded animal.

The vampires sensed movement on the other side of the hedge. Victoria waited a few seconds and repeated the sound, longer and lower this time. They watched the girl rise to her feet and move toward the trees. Her hands appeared first, parting the branches, and then she stepped through the opening.

Candice was on her in a flash, her fangs sinking into the girl's throat.

Kristi Brolen barely felt the cold, strong hands that gripped her shoulders. An intense burning pain erupted in her neck, and then everything turned black.

21. DANGEROUS TIMES

"**O**h, dear," Aunt Janet said, "not another one."

"Another what, Aunt Janet?" Leesa asked, emerging from the kitchen with her mom where they had been doing the dishes. It was the first time since Leesa arrived in Connecticut that her aunt had permitted her to help with the clean up for any meal. Since all Leesa's previous visits had been for just a few days or less, Aunt Janet had brushed off all Leesa's offers to assist by saying she was a guest and guests did not do dishes in her house. This time, Leesa was staying for more than a week, which apparently moved her out of the guest category. She was happy to finally have the chance to pitch in.

"Another young woman has disappeared," Aunt Janet said.

Aunt Janet was sitting on the couch next to her husband, watching the news on television. Max lay on the floor by their feet. Bradley was perched on the front of the big easy chair, staring intently at the TV. Anyone who vanished mysteriously held special interest for him.

"That's the second one in two days," Aunt Janet continued. She eased over to make room for her sister as Judy sat down beside her. "Plus, a young man went missing yesterday, too."

"That's horrible," Judy said.

Leesa slid onto the wooden rocking chair that was her favorite place to sit when she was here. Max immediately took up his post beside the chair, where Leesa could pet his head easily while she rocked.

"Three people just since yesterday?" Leesa said, more to herself than to anyone else. She did not like the sound of that. Yesterday was the first day after the solstice. She wondered if Rave's fear was coming true—that the solstice was magnifying the effects of *Destiratu*. Were the vampires becoming less careful with their hunting, driven by their increased thirst for blood? She hoped there was a simpler explanation.

"I heard about the guy who got lost hiking down by Haddam," Bradley said. "Where did the first woman go missing?"

"Up by Tolland," Aunt Janet said. "Her husband said she walked four blocks to the mini-mart to get some chips and dip yesterday evening, and she never came back. They've been searching for her since last night, but haven't found any sign of her."

Leesa pictured a map of Connecticut in her head. Tolland was fifty or sixty miles north and east; Haddam was much closer, to the south and slightly east.

"What about the woman today?" she asked.

"Over in Ledyard," Uncle Roger said. "She was a junior at UConn, home for the holidays. Her parents said she was sitting in the backyard, reading. Her mom went out to tell her something, and she was gone. The book she'd been reading was still on her chair."

Leesa frowned. Unless the girl had taken off on her own for some reason, her abductor had been very bold. She shuddered to think about vampires being so driven they would snatch someone from her own back yard.

"Where's Ledyard?" Leesa had heard the name, but couldn't place the town.

"Over by New London," Uncle Roger said. "A bit north of it."

Leesa pictured the map in her head again and felt her heart speed up. If you made a triangle out of the incidents, the area where Rave said the vampire lair was hidden would be inside that triangle. She doubted it was a coincidence. She especially did not like that this was happening on the heels of her dream the other night.

"I think it might be vampires," she said quietly.

For a moment, no one spoke. Any other group would have scoffed at such a statement, but not this family. They knew well that vampires existed and they had suffered at the creatures' hands. Judy was wringing her hands now, and Bradley had grown pale.

"What makes you say that" Uncle Roger finally asked.

Leesa thought for a moment. She couldn't tell them what Rave had said without giving away his secret. Still, she had to say something. An idea popped into her head.

"Something Dr. Clerval told us in Vampire Science. He said sometimes the solstice magnifies their thirst, making it hard for them to control themselves. The solstice was just two days ago."

"Oh, my god," Judy said quietly. "What should we do? We have to tell somebody."

"Tell them what, Mom?" Bradley asked skeptically. "That we think vampires are behind these attacks? They'd put us in straitjackets and lock us up."

"But people need to know they have to be extra careful."

"I don't think we need to worry about that too much," Uncle Roger said. "With all the attention these disappearances are getting, people will already start being careful."

"Uncle Roger's right," Leesa said. "It doesn't matter whether people think it's vampires or some psycho serial killer. They'll either be extra careful or they won't."

"They're likely to be *more* careful if they think there's a psycho running around," Bradley said. "That's something they can believe."

"Did the professor say how long this solstice thing would last?" Aunt Janet asked. "With the vampires, I mean?"

Leesa shook her head. "He didn't know. Not much longer, I hope."

For the first time, she felt a bit of anger toward Rave and his people. They were vampire hunters, after all—they should be here, acting as a check upon the creatures, not hiding somewhere up in New Hampshire. Her anger faded as quickly as it had appeared. An all out war between volkaane and vampire was something nobody wanted. Vampires hunting humans was nothing new—they were usually just a bit more circumspect about it. The last thing the vampires wanted was human armies searching for them. They would rein themselves in, she was pretty sure, before they drew too much attention.

At least she hoped they would.

22. A MERRY CHRISTMAS

Christmas had ceased to be special for Leesa a long time ago. She had a few faint memories of joyous mornings and big, beautifully decorated trees from when she was very young, but once her father left all of that ended. Bradley tried to keep the day special for her, but he was just a kid himself, and there wasn't much he could do. He usually managed to find a small, scraggly "Charlie Brown" Christmas tree they could hang a few decorations on and always provided one small present for Leesa, but that was about it. Not the stuff memories were made of, not by a long shot.

This morning was different, though. This was a real family Christmas.

It started late yesterday afternoon, when they all piled into Uncle Roger's Expedition and headed to a nearby Christmas tree farm. Aunt Janet and Uncle Roger had a tradition of not purchasing their tree until the last moment, insuring it would be as fresh and lovely as possible for the actual holiday. They all wandered around the huge farm, enjoying the pine-scented air and looking for the perfect tree. Finally, they selected a beautiful, seven-foot-tall Blue Spruce. Uncle Roger did the bulk of the sawing, but they all took at least one turn with the saw, so that it would truly be the whole family's tree.

After dinner, they had spent more than an hour decorating the tree with brightly colored decorations and tiny white lights.

All the while, Christmas carols played joyfully from the stereo. They finished by wrapping strands of silver garland around the tree, and the result was the most beautiful tree Leesa had ever seen. When she had finally gone to bed, she had fallen asleep with "Frosty the Snowman" playing over and over in her head. Something about the magic in the song was especially appealing to her.

And now, this morning was even better than last evening.

They were all gathered in the living room. Leesa was sitting her in favorite place, the rocking chair. Max was beside her, as always, and she absently scratched his furry head. Her mom, Aunt Janet and Bradley were all on the couch. Uncle Roger, looking jolly in a worn Santa Claus hat, was taking his time pulling presents from beneath the tree and passing them out to the proper recipient one by one. The room was fragrant with the scent of the recently cut tree and more Christmas carols played in the background.

Even the Old Man Winter had cooperated, sprinkling a light dusting of snow over the area last night while they slept. The snowfall totaled barely an inch, but it had still managed to turn everything into a white, winter wonderland. For a girl from San Diego, an inch was more than enough. Leesa was a bit disappointed they wouldn't be able to build a snowman, but it sure looked beautiful outside. She was planning on going out later to make a snow angel or two on the front lawn.

Uncle Roger pranced over to her, chortling "Ho, ho, ho," for what seemed like the hundredth time that morning and carrying a small package wrapped in candy cane wrapping. A bright red ribbon bow covered most of the front of the package. He handed the present to her.

"This one's for you, from your Aunt and me."

Ever the practical one, Leesa carefully pulled the bow from the box and set it aside so it could be used again next year. Sliding her finger under the wrapping paper, she gently peeled it off. Inside was an i-Phone.

"Wow! Thank you, Aunt Janet and Uncle Roger." Leesa got up and gave her uncle a big hug.

The phone was the perfect gift. She had been thinking it was probably time to get a cell again, and now she had one. Even better, this was from a totally different service from her last one, so if that guy who claimed to be her father was still trying to find her, it would be that much harder for him.

Uncle Roger turned to Leesa's mom. "Judy, don't you have something for Leesa that goes along with this?"

Judy crossed to the tree and pulled another small package from beneath it. This one was wrapped in red paper decorated with small Christmas trees. She smiled and handed it to Leesa.

"This is from Bradley and me."

Leesa smiled back. Her mom and brother didn't have much money, so any gift was thoughtful. She unwrapped this present with equal care. Inside was a purple rubber bumper for her new phone. She laughed.

"Since you broke your last one, we figured we should get you some extra protection for this one," Bradley said, grinning.

"Ha! You're right about that," Leesa said as she began working her phone into the bumper.

"You've been without a phone for awhile now," Aunt Janet said. "Your uncle and I figured a college girl needed a phone—especially a girl with a boyfriend."

"Thanks, Aunt Janet, but Rave doesn't use phones, remember?"

Leesa wondered if the rubber bumper would keep Rave's magical energy from frying the phone if he touched it, but she doubted it. She stifled a giggle as a totally absurd thought popped into her head. If the rubber bumper did manage to protect the phone from Rave's heat, maybe she could get a pair of those thick rubber lips people wore for costumes and use them to protect her when she and Rave kissed. She shook her head and chased the foolish thought away.

"Oh, that's right," Aunt Janet said. "I forgot. Still, your uncle and I will feel better knowing we can get in touch with you anytime we want, and that you can reach us if you need to. I'm sure that goes double for your mother."

"It's great, Aunt Janet," Leesa said. "I'd been thinking it was time to get a new one. Now I don't have to."

"Speaking of Rave," Judy said, "where has he been? Are we going to see him for the holidays?"

"No, I don't think so," Leesa said. "His clan has all gone away for a bit, on some kind of pilgrimage."

"All of them?" Uncle Roger asked, puzzled. He had grown up not too far from the Maston settlement. "I don't remember ever hearing about them doing that."

"Is it a religious thing, for Christmas?" Aunt Janet asked.

Leesa shook her head. "No, it's not really religious. It has something to do with the solstice. I don't completely understand it, but it's not something they do every year. There's something special about this year."

"Where did they go?" Judy asked.

"Somewhere up north… in New Hampshire."

Uncle Roger grinned. "Never heard of anyone making a pilgrimage to New Hampshire," he said. "Those people are certainly strange. No offense, Leesa."

Leesa smiled. "None taken."

She noticed Bradley was watching her, a very thoughtful look on his face.

"What is it?" she asked him.

Bradley hesitated, clearly uncomfortable. "Is Rave a vampire," he asked, finally.

Leesa was stunned. Where had that come from?

"What?" she managed to stammer. "Not hardly. Why on earth would you ask that?"

Bradley looked chagrined. "Just something I was thinking,"

he said. "You told us the other night the solstice makes vampires extra hungry or something. And now you say Rave is gone, also because of the solstice."

"So?" Leesa asked, not clear yet where her brother was going with this.

"So I was wondering if maybe Rave's gone away right now so he wouldn't be tempted, to…you know."

Leesa suddenly got it. "To drink my blood, you mean?"

"No… I mean, yes. Don't get me wrong, Rave seems like a really great guy, and I can tell he's crazy about you. So, when you started talking about the solstice again, I thought, maybe…because he's crazy about you…maybe that was why he's not around right now."

"Oh, come now, Bradley," Judy said. "Just because Rave's people left for a pilgrimage doesn't make him a vampire."

"There's more to it than that," Bradley said. Now that he had opened up the subject, he was determined to follow through with it. "There's the whole thing about no phones or cars or anything. And how easily he caught that *grafhym* when we needed its blood for you, Mom."

Leesa shook her head. Not much got past her brother. He was so far from the truth it was laughable, but at the same time, he was closer than he knew. Before she could reply, Uncle Roger joined in.

"Didn't you say he had Special Forces training or something, Leesa?" he asked. "Back when Rave captured the one-fang for you?"

"Not Special Forces, but lots of special training," Leesa replied. "Trust me, Bradley. Rave is *not* a vampire. I assure you."

"If Rave was a vampire, honey," Judy said to Bradley, "why would Leesa have had to offer herself to that monster Stefan in order to free you?"

Bradley had no answer to that. "I guess you're right. That wouldn't make any sense." He turned to Leesa. "I'm sorry, pumpkin. I was just worried about you."

Thank you, Mom, Leesa thought. "That's okay, big brother." She smiled to let him know it truly was okay. "Old habits are hard to break. You looked after me for a lot of years. No reason you should stop now."

"Now that we've got that settled," Judy said cheerfully, "there's still a few more presents under the tree."

Leesa was relieved to have the focus taken off Rave. Still, she wondered how much longer she would be able to keep his true nature a secret—and what would happen when her family finally learned the truth.

23. A WELCOME GUEST

Three days after Christmas, Leesa and Bradley were in the new apartment, assembling inexpensive furniture purchased from the IKEA store in New Haven. They had driven down the day before in Uncle Roger's Expedition and picked out everything they thought they would need for their mom and Bradley to be at least semi-comfortable. Leesa would be going back to school in less than a week, so they had just borrowed an air mattress from Uncle Roger for her to sleep on up in the loft. They didn't really have to figure out how to furnish the loft until school ended for the summer.

They had already put together a bed for their mom and one for Bradley. The instructions were clear and simple and few tools were necessary. Leesa was now assembling a pair of dining chairs to go with the table Bradley was building. Their mom was at the bakery, working. Bradley had set up a CD player, but all of Leesa's music was back at the dorm, so they were listening to a collection of Christmas carols borrowed from Aunt Janet. Leesa did not mind extending the holiday spirit a little longer at all.

A knock on the door surprised them both. They were not expecting visitors—indeed, no one other than Aunt Janet and Uncle Roger even had the new address yet.

Leesa looked over at Bradley and saw he was in the middle

of attaching one of the legs to the table.

"I'll get it," she said.

She laid the chair she was working on down on its side and stood up. She guessed it was probably the apartment manager at the door, or maybe one of the maintenance staff, but when she opened the door she found herself looking at the last person she expected.

"Rave!" she exclaimed joyously.

Without thinking, she leaped into his arms, wrapping her legs around his waist and hugging him tightly. She had missed him fiercely, but hadn't known just how much until this moment.

Rave held her weight easily. "It's nice to see you, too," he said, smiling.

"It's a good thing you are not human, Rave," a voice from behind him said in a joking tone. "Otherwise, this one might have broken your back."

Leesa looked over Rave's shoulder and saw two volkaanes grinning at her. She felt herself blush as she disentangled herself from Rave's arms and lowered her feet back to the ground.

That Rave's companions were volkaanes was obvious. They were both outrageously handsome—though not quite as gorgeous as Rave, of course—with the same dark copper locks and bronze skin. They appeared to be around Rave's age, though with volkaanes you could never be sure. All three were wearing jeans and long-sleeved flannel shirts. Rave's was black and white, the other two red and black.

Rave eased to the side and introduced his friends.

"Leesa, this is Dral and Bain. They are my birth mates and my friends."

Leesa grinned sheepishly, still a bit embarrassed about her recent display, and held out her hand. The two volkaanes each shook it in turn. Both exuded the same warmth from their hands as Rave.

"She is as pretty as you described, Rave," Dral said,

grinning.

Leesa blushed again and began twirling her fingers in her hair. Still, she was thrilled to hear that Rave talked about her to his volkaane friends.

"Nice to meet you both," she said. "I'm not sure what birth mates are, but any friend of Rave is certainly a friend of mine."

"We were all born from the same Festival of Renewal," Dral explained.

"We grew up and trained together," Bain added.

Leesa remembered Rave telling her that volkaane offspring were raised communally and were not considered adults until they were forty. No wonder they were close.

"How did you find me, Rave? We just moved in here yesterday."

"We stopped at your aunt and uncle's. Your aunt gave me the address."

"Oh. Well, come in, everyone," Leesa said, grabbing Rave's arm.

Dral and Bain exchanged glances.

"Thanks," Dral said, "but we will wait outside."

They each moved silently about twenty feet to the side and stood with their backs against the wall. Leesa understood immediately they were acting as sentries. She wondered whether Rave's visit meant she was in danger, or if the volkaanes were just taking normal precautions.

"Is everything okay, Rave?" she asked while they were still outside. If something was wrong, she didn't know if he would be able to tell her in front of Bradley.

Rave kissed her forehead and her knees immediately felt weak. It had been way too long since she had felt even a brief touch of his lips.

"Everything's fine. The Elders insisted that if I wanted to return to Connecticut to see you, I had to bring two companions for safety, just in case. By the way," he added, "I got Max's message."

Leesa blushed yet again. She grabbed his arm and led him inside.

"Bradley, look who's here."

Bradley was stretched out on the floor, screwing in a fastener for one of the table legs.

"Don't get up," Rave said.

"Hi, Rave," Bradley said from where he lay. "Thanks. I've almost got this thing finished."

Leesa still had a tight hold on Rave's arm. "I've missed you sooo much," she said.

"Hey, c'mon Sis, don't get all gooey on me," Bradley said, chuckling.

Leesa gave Rave's arm a squeeze. "Sorry, big brother," she said to Bradley. "I'll try to control myself—at least until I get Rave alone."

Rave grinned. He loved seeing Leesa interact with her family, because volkaanes had no real families of their own. Balin was the closest thing he had to a father, and Dral and Bain the closest thing he had to brothers.

"Done," Bradley said. He got up from the floor and extended his hand to Rave. "Nice to see you again, Rave."

Leesa watched as the two shook hands. Bradley's expression didn't change, so she guessed Rave still had enough control of his inner heat to make his hand normal temperature.

"You, too, Bradley," Rave said. "You look much healthier than the last time I saw you. It's good to see."

"Thanks," Bradley said. "I feel great."

"I hope you'll excuse us," Leesa said to her brother. "Rave and I are going into the kitchen to talk."

"No problem." Bradley nudged an unopened box with his foot. "I've got plenty to keep me busy."

Leesa led Rave by the arm into the kitchen.

"Oops," she said, standing in the middle of the kitchen floor.

"I forgot there's nowhere to sit in here yet."

"Sure there is," Rave said. He picked her up effortlessly and deposited her onto the tiled counter between the sink and the stove, leaving his hands on her hips. "See?"

"Ha! I guess you're right," Leesa said. She draped her forearms over his shoulders and gave his ribs a gentle squeeze with her knees. "This is pretty comfortable. Pretty sexy, too." She cocked her head slightly. "So, what brings you all the way down from New Hampshire?"

"I missed you. Isn't that enough?"

"I've missed you, too. But why do I think missing me might not be quite enough to get you to go to the Council of Elders and to bring two friends down here with you?"

Rave looked at her sheepishly. Leesa loved it when he looked that way, because it did not happen often. He was usually so confident and in control.

"Well, I did miss you," he said. "And I wanted to check on you and make sure everything was all right. But you are right. There is more. I might be gone a bit longer than I originally expected."

That was definitely not something Leesa wanted to hear. "Oh, no. Why?"

"The Council has decided it is safer for everyone that way. For volkaanes, vampires and humans."

"How long will you be gone, then?"

Rave shrugged. "I'm not sure. Unless we hear that vampires are running out of control and our presence is needed, it could be awhile."

Leesa's heart sank. Why did she have to fall in love with a volkaane? She quickly squashed the thought. Rave was by far the best thing ever to happen to her, despite the obstacles. And there were more than a few, for sure.

"Three people disappeared within two days of the solstice," she told him. "Plus one more the other day. There's no way to know if it was vampires, but even if it was, I'm guessing four isn't enough to count as 'out of control' yet, right?"

Rave shook his head. "No. I'm afraid it will take more than that."

"That sucks—no pun intended. So, how long can you stay?"

Rave's handsome features seemed to darken. "Just this afternoon, I'm afraid. We must leave before dark."

Leesa was disappointed, but that still gave them a couple more hours.

"Want to go for a walk?" she asked.

"Sure," Rave said, smiling. "Walking with you is one of my favorite things."

"Oh? And what are some of your other favorites?" Leesa asked flirtatiously.

Rave's grin widened. "Well, let's see. I love carrying you, of course."

Leesa smiled. She couldn't argue with that—she loved it, too. She knew Rave understood that was not what she wanted to hear, though.

"And what else?" she asked.

Rave leaned forward and gave her a quick peck on the mouth. His lips were gone almost before they touched her, but Leesa still felt the familiar thrill shoot through her body.

"And I really love kissing you," Rave said. "I just wish we could do it more."

Leesa sighed. "Me, too. I hope you're not wasting your time up there in New Hampshire. You'd better be practicing that *Rammugul* thing—practicing it a lot."

Rave laughed. "Trust me, I do little else." He lifted her down from the counter. "Let's go get started on that walk."

Out in the living room, Bradley was sitting on the couch, taking a break from assembling furniture. He had managed to complete a small end table while Leesa and Rave were in the kitchen. He stood up when they emerged.

"Rave, can I ask you something?" he said.

Leesa watched her brother carefully. She recognized the curious look he always got when he wanted to know something. She hoped he wasn't going to ask Rave about being a vampire.

"Sure," Rave replied.

"If your people don't drive or ride in cars, how did you get down here from New Hampshire? Is there a horse and buggy parked outside?"

Rave laughed, but Leesa was worried. How *was* Rave going to explain how easily his kind covered long distances?

"No, there is no horse and buggy, I'm afraid," Rave said easily. "Sorry to disappoint you. When we have somewhere important we need to go, if it is not walking distance, we are allowed to ride the bus. We have a different definition of walking distance than most people, though."

Leesa smiled, amazed at how easily the lie came from Rave's lips. She knew just walking onto a bus would probably fry every electrical system on the thing. The Mastons had lived on the edges of society for so long, she guessed they had come up with plausible explanations for most of the questions curious humans might ask.

"Important things like coming to see my sister?" Bradley asked.

Rave smiled. "I can't think of anything more important. Can you?"

Leesa smiled. She *loved* hearing that. She took Rave's hand.

"Nope, I can't," Bradley said.

"We're going for a walk," Leesa told him. "I hope you don't mind me leaving you here with all this stuff for a couple of hours."

Bradley grinned. "Of course not. Rave rode the frigging bus to come see you, after all."

They all laughed. Leesa grabbed her parka and cap and led Rave out the door.

Outside, it was cool but not freezing. The mid-afternoon sun shone down from a mostly clear sky, providing a bit of warmth. Leesa guessed the temperature was in somewhere in the mid to upper thirties. Not bad for New England at the end of December.

The light layer of snow from Christmas Eve had long since melted. Dral and Bain crossed the small lawn and fell silently into step behind Leesa and Rave as soon as they started toward the side walk.

Leesa had no particular destination in mind. She simply led them out to the main road and turned east, toward Middletown. She didn't care where they went—it was enough to be walking with Rave and holding his hand. They talked lightly, easily. She told him about Christmas, about her mom's job at the bakery, about the trip to New Haven for furniture. Rave told her about the caverns in New Hampshire and the temporary shelters his people had erected outside them. She hoped the shelters would be *very* temporary.

For the most part, Dral and Bain walked silently behind them, though now and then one of them would make a comment. Whenever Leesa looked back, she saw the same alert vigilance in their manner that she always sensed from Rave. The volkaanes were not really worried about vampires right now—it was a bright afternoon and they were walking along a fairly busy road, so it was unlikely any of the creatures would be in the area. This was simply the way they were—careful, alert and attentive to the things around them.

They walked for almost two hours, all the way to the downtown Middletown and back. The sun hung just above the horizon when they returned to the apartment complex. The day had grown much colder as the sun ebbed, but with her hand in Rave's hand, Leesa scarcely felt it. It had been a wonderful walk, a wonderful afternoon, but she knew it was now time for another good-bye.

She turned and wrapped her arms around Rave, pressing her

cheek against his chest as she felt his strong arms encircle her, trying to absorb as much of him as she could while he was still here. Finally, she pushed her head away from his chest and looked up at his face. Dral and Bain had moved a few steps back, giving them some privacy.

"Thanks for coming, Rave. It was a wonderful surprise."

"The pleasure was mine," Rave said, smiling. "A two hundred mile jog is nothing—not when you are at the end of it."

"You're such a flatterer," she teased. "Two hundred miles isn't that much for you whether I'm at the end of it or not." She rose up on her toes and gave him a quick peck on the lips. "I like hearing you say it, though."

She stepped back out of his embrace. "Now get out of here. I hate long good-byes."

Rave grinned. "As you wish." He nodded to Dral and Bain, who started down the walk.

Rave kissed the top of her head. "Keep yourself safe, my love," he said, then he turned and followed his companions.

Leesa watched until they disappeared around the corner. It wasn't until she had turned to go inside the apartment that she realized she'd forgotten to tell Rave about her vampire dream. Oh, well, she thought, there was no sense worrying him over a stupid dream anyway. She pulled the door open and went inside.

24. A NEW FRIEND

The first thing Leesa did when she got back to school, after putting her stuff away in her room, was go down to Cali's room. She had only seen her friend once over the break, when Cali had borrowed her mom's car and driven to Meriden two days before Christmas. That had been nearly two weeks ago, and Leesa missed her best friend. Texts were nice, but there was nothing like getting together in person.

Cali's door was wide open. Inside, Leesa could see Cali and Stacie sitting at Cali's desk, their backs to the doorway. She knocked lightly on the door to let them know she was there and entered the room.

The two girls turned at the sound of Leesa's knock, and she immediately saw she had been mistaken. The second girl was not Stacie—this girl's long straight black hair, so similar to the half-Japanese Stacie's—had fooled Leesa. She had never seen this girl before. She was very pretty, with large, almond-shaped dark brown eyes and high cheekbones that gave her an attractive, exotic look, as did her café au lait complexion.

"Hey, Leesa," Cali said happily. She got up and crossed the room to give Leesa a big welcome back hug.

Cali was wearing black jeans and a bright, pinkish-orange lightweight sweatshirt with I LOVE PINK printed across the front in giant block letters. Smaller letters proclaiming PINK RULES ran down the length of one sleeve. Leesa had never seen this sweatshirt on Cali and guessed it was probably a Christmas present. One thing about the Pink people—they were certainly not bashful about letting the world know which clothes belonged to their popular line.

"This is my friend Vanina," Cali said when she let Leesa go.

The new girl rose gracefully to her feet and extended her hand. When she stood up, Leesa saw Vanina was a couple of inches taller than she was, at least five-ten, maybe taller. Her outfit was much less colorful than Cali's, but almost as attention grabbing. Black leggings showed off her long, slender legs, while on top, she wore a loose, long-sleeved dark gray shirt unbuttoned over a crimson cami.

Vanina's hand was soft and smooth. Leesa wondered why she had never heard Cali mention her before. Maybe she was an old friend from high school.

"Hi, Vanina," she said. "That's a pretty name. And so unusual. I've never heard it before."

"It's Corsican," Vanina said. This girl was, in fact, Edwina, but she knew Leesa would recognize that name instantly, so she had introduced herself to Cali using the name of Vanina, her long departed mentor.

"Corsica…isn't that were Napoleon came from?"

Edwina smiled. "Very good. I'm impressed. Not many people know that nowadays." She winced, hoping Leesa wouldn't make anything out of the "nowadays" comment. Edwina was skilled at blending in with the humans, but every now and then something slipped past her lips that could lead an astute observer to wonder where the statement came from.

Leesa thought she saw a strange look flicker momentarily in Vanina's eyes, but it was gone before she could make anything out of it. The girl had just a hint of some kind of accent, too.

"Is that where you're from?" Leesa asked. "Corsica?"

Edwina laughed. "Don't I wish. How cool would that be? But no, I was born in Virginia. I haven't lived there in a long time, though."

"She lives in East Hartford now," Cali said. "We met at the mall over break."

Leesa nodded. That explained why she had never heard Cali mention Vanina before. She was a new friend. "What dorm do you live in?" she asked, assuming Vanina was a Weston student.

"Oh, I don't go to Weston, I go to UConn," Edwina said, using the cover story she had come up with to explain why she wouldn't be around all that much. "We don't start back at school until tomorrow, and I live at home, anyway."

"She drove me back to school this morning," Cali said. "Saved my mom the trip."

Edwina had learned to drive more than a decade ago, taught by a human boyfriend, when she realized the skill would help her blend in. As far as she knew, she was the only vampire in the entire coven who knew how to drive. Of course, most vampires had little use for a car. Cali did not know the car Edwina had said was her mom's was in fact stolen.

"It was no big deal," Edwina said. "Besides, I wanted to see where Cali lived."

"Pretty luxurious, huh?" Cali said sarcastically.

"It's not bad," Edwina said. "At least you have your own room. All the rooms at UConn have at least two people in them." She knew this, because she had often hunted at UConn. "That's one of the reasons I decided to live at home."

"Yeah, I guess having our own rooms is pretty cool," Cali said. "Leesa lives up on the fourth floor."

"Cool. It must be nice to live so close to each other."

Cali draped her arm around Leesa's back. "Yep. Sure is. Leesa's my BFF."

"What year are you in at UConn?" Leesa asked.

"I'm a junior, but I took a year off and traveled after high school."

Leesa nodded. She had guessed Vanina was probably a little older than her and Cali.

"How's Rave?" Cali asked. "Is he back yet?"

"Not yet. I only saw him that one time I told you about."

"That sucks," Cali said sympathetically.

"Who's Rave?" Vanina asked. "Your boyfriend?"

"Yeah," Leesa replied.

"He's smokin' hot, too," Cali said. She licked her fingertip, then held it out and made a sizzling sound to emphasize just how hot she thought Rave was.

Edwina laughed. Now she knew the volkaane's name: Rave. She had already carefully scouted the area where the volkaanes lived—another of the coven's rules she had broken, going so close to their settlement—and discovered they had all departed. Where, she had no idea, but she would not have risked being in an enclosed space like this with Leesa if there was any chance her boyfriend might show up. Even so, she did not want to remain here too long, because she didn't know when the volkaane might decide to return.

"If he's that hot," Edwina said, "I hope I get to see him one of these days. Sounds like you've got a good one, Leesa."

"Yeah, I do," Leesa said, smiling. "Rave's the best."

"Well, I'd better get going," Edwina said. "My mom might be needing her car. It was nice to meet you, Leesa."

"You, too," Leesa said. "I hope we'll see you again."

"Oh, you will, I'm sure of that," Edwina said.

She grabbed a black coat from Cali's bed. How easy, she thought, it would be to kill one or both of them, right here, right now. But what would be the fun of that? As delicious as their blood might be, her thirst for revenge was even stronger than her thirst for blood.

25. DREAM COME TRUE

Leesa awoke in a cold sweat. She had just suffered another one of those powerful, all too realistic dreams. This time, she could only recall the final image, but that haunting vision was more than enough. She had seen a teenage girl standing outside a window peering in. Her hair was long and lank, her eyes wide but lifeless, her mouth hanging slightly open. Everything was dark behind her, but the light coming from inside the window partially illuminated her face. The total effect was one of longing, sorrow and terrible suffering.

It was a horrifying image, one Leesa wished she could wipe from her memory. But no matter how hard she tried, the picture remained clear as a photograph. The girl's face seemed to be seared onto her retinas.

Unable to make the image go away, Leesa changed her focus, struggling instead to recall details from the dream. Who was this girl and where had she come from? What horrors had she suffered to make her look the way she did? And why had she appeared in Leesa's dream in the first place?

No answers came. The first part of the dream remained as elusive as the girl's despondent face was persistent.

Frustrated, Leesa sat up and swung her legs over the edge of the bed. The dorm was silent. A glance at her clock told her it was only 4:35. Out from under the covers, she felt the chill of the room enfold her. Enough light leaked in from the night outside for her to make out the dark outlines of her furniture. She got up and grabbed a terrycloth robe from her closet and slipped her feet into a pair of fleece-lined moccasins.

Warmer now, she crossed to the sink and splashed cold water onto her face, rinsing away a film of dried sweat and hoping that becoming more fully awake would make the image go away. The sweat disappeared quickly; the distressing image of the girl's face remained.

Leesa was in no hurry to go back to bed—she doubted she would be able to fall asleep even if she tried. Instead, she crossed carefully to her desk and sat down. Usually, she did not mind the dark, but tonight the dimness seemed especially oppressive, so she switched on her desk lamp.

This was the third one of these strange dreams to assault her sleep. People said things often came in threes—she hoped it was true, for that would mean this was the last one. She doubted she would be so lucky, though. Where were the dreams coming from, she wondered? She'd never had nightmares before, though if anyone had reason to suffer from them it was her, with her mom's story of the one-fanged vampire and her dad abandoning the family when she was so young. Growing up, she had dreamed, of course, and some of them were scary. Every kid had scary dreams now and then, and she was no different. None of those dreams had been anything like these three—not even close.

She asked herself the same questions she had asked after the first two dreams, and got the same frustrating lack of answers. There was nothing she could point to that might have caused the nightmares, no precipitating event she could recall. They seemed to spring up out of nowhere, for no rhyme or reason, but a part of her knew that could not be true. Nothing so powerful and realistic could spring out of nothingness. There had to be some reason, some cause—she just could not find it.

* * *

Two days later, the haunting image of the girl came rushing back to her.

Things had been going smoothly these first few days back at school. Her classes were good—no more physics, thank god. None of her choices this semester were going to be as much fun as Vampire Science, but her second psychology class looked like it would be as interesting as the first one, and since she had always liked history, she expected American History to be good as well. Sociology promised to be okay, as did part two of the required English literature series, which ran from 1900 to the present. There was even an Anne Rice book on the reading list. Chemistry would be her hardest class, but there was no way it could be as difficult as physics.

Her professors had taken it easy on the students this first week, assigning minimal homework as the kids recovered from their vacation and got back into the swing of school. Leesa had spent the last couple evenings hanging out with Cali, Caitlin and Stacie, having fun and swapping stories from Christmas break. Caitlin sported a blue rubber sleeve on her right elbow, courtesy of a slip on the ice back in New Jersey, so when Guitar Hero came out, she could only watch and cheer—and sing along to the music, of course.

Tonight, though, Leesa was alone. She planned to go down to see her friends a bit later, but right now she was sitting on her bed, doing some reading for history. The television was turned to the news, providing background noise. Ten minutes into the show, a story caught her attention. It was the words "dead daughter" that pulled her from her reading. She closed her book and listened as a reporter in New Orleans interviewed the parents of a seventeen-year-old girl who had died in a car accident a few months ago.

The mother was crying, while the father recounted how they both swore they had seen their daughter standing outside their window the night before, peering sadly in at them. The tale of distraught parents imagining they had seen their dead daughter, as heartbreaking as it was, would not have been newsworthy, especially on a national level, except for one thing. When the police went to the girl's gravesite the next day, they found the plot dug up and the casket open. The girl's body was still inside, but no one had any explanation for why it had been unearthed, or by whom.

The thing that caused Leesa to cringe in horror was not the desecration of the grave, however. It was the picture of her daughter the mom tearfully displayed to the reporter—the daughter looked an awful lot like the girl Leesa had seen in her dream just two nights before!

The television switched to a car commercial, but Leesa's eyes remain fixed on the screen. She was not seeing the commercial, though. She was once again seeing the haunted face of the girl from her dream.

Leesa's fingers danced furiously in her hair. What on earth was going on? This was the second time one of her dreams had seemed to come at least partially to pass, and both had to do with dead people. Were her dreams really seeing into the future? How was that possible? And why did two of them have to do with dead people coming back to life? If she had dreamed of people turning into vampires, that she could understand—she had been bitten by one of the creatures, after all. But corpses rising from their graves and wandering around made no sense.

There was one thing that troubled her even more than the dreams of reanimated corpses, and that was the third dream, the one where a girl was chained to a wall by a vampire—a girl she had come tantalizingly close to recognizing, but just hadn't been able to see clearly enough. What if that dream were to come true? What if, like the other two, it already had? And who was the poor girl? Was there anything Leesa could do to save her? She had plenty of questions, but no answers.

A sudden, terrifying thought struck her. What if she was not just seeing things in her dreams that were coming to pass, but somehow was *causing* these events to occur? She immediately tried to banish the thought from her brain. No way could she be making these things happen. The idea was ridiculous, impossible—wasn't it? But was it any more unbelievable and impossible than seeing into the future, or visualizing events she had no knowledge of? It was all crazy. There was only one thing she was sure of—something incomprehensible was happening with her dreams.

If this kept up, she would soon be afraid to close her eyes at night.

26. AN IMPORTANT CLUE

Unbeknownst to Leesa, the one person who could have answered some of her questions was still almost three thousand miles away, growing more frustrated by the day in San Diego.

Dominic had finally decided he needed help, so he had hired an investigator, paying cash and contacting the man once a day via a different public phone each time. After four days, the man had provided Dominic an address in the North Park section of San Diego.

The place turned out to be a small, run-down apartment complex. Dominic had been stealthily watching apartment five for two days now, but had not seen a single person come out of the apartment. A check of the mailboxes showed a name he did not recognize, but it was possible Leesa's mother had remarried over the years and now had a different name. He had walked casually past the window a few times and was able to see that the place was furnished, so at least he was not wasting his time watching an empty apartment. But whether Leesa, or even her mother, still lived here, he was becoming increasingly doubtful.

If he had anywhere else to look, he would be there, but he did not. Still, he decided he needed to become a bit more proactive, despite his desire for discretion and secrecy. He crossed over to apartment six and knocked on the door. He waited a few moments and then knocked again. There was no response. The apartment's occupants were probably at work.

He walked past apartment five and knocked on the door to number four. He was about to knock a second time when a smiling, gray-haired lady opened the door.

"Yes?" she said.

"Hello," Dominic said in as friendly a voice as he could muster. "My name is Fred." He plucked the name out of the air, continuing his practice of using a different name every time he inquired about Leesa or her family.

"I'm a friend of the Nylands," he said. "I know they used to live next door in apartment five, but I've been gone for awhile. Are they still around?"

The woman shook her head. "I'm sorry, no. They moved out a few months ago."

Dominic cursed silently to himself. He had reached another dead end.

"Did you know them at all?" he asked, hoping to get at least some useful information from this friendly woman.

"Not very," she said. "Especially considering how long we were neighbors. The mother never seemed to come out of the house—I'd see her standing at the window looking outside sometimes. The kids seemed sweet enough, although Leesa was kind of shy."

This was news to Dominic. He remembered Judy Nyland as a friendly, outgoing woman and wondered what had happened to turn her into someone who never left her apartment. He hoped it did not have anything to do with Leesa.

"Do you have any idea where they might have gone?" he asked, hoping against hope for some kind of lead.

"No, I don't. I'm sorry."

Dominic could see on her wrinkled face that she was genuinely sorry. Unfortunately, her being sorry did not do him any good.

"Well, thanks for your help," he said.

As he was preparing to turn away, the woman laid her hand on his forearm.

"Leesa was going to college somewhere in Connecticut, I think. Maybe her mom moved back there to be near her."

Dominic smiled. This was something, at least.

"Do you happen to know which school?"

"I'm sorry, I don't. But Connecticut isn't very big. How many colleges could there be there?"

Dominic had no idea, but he was going to find out as quickly as he could.

"Is there a public library nearby?" he asked.

The woman gave him directions to a local branch only four blocks away. He thanked her for her help and headed for the library, covering the sidewalk with long, quick strides.

The answer to the question "how many colleges could there be in Connecticut?" turned out to be "quite a few." Dominic stared at the list he had pulled up on one of the library's computers. He counted more than thirty—even more if he included all the branches of the state university. The number was disappointing— he had expected fewer. Still, it was something to go on, a starting point at least.

He printed out the list, then folded it carefully and put it in his pocket. It was time to get back on the train. Destination: Connecticut.

27. A NIGHT OUT

Leesa poked through the clothes in her closet, trying to decide what to wear. She was going to some place called The Joint that hosted open microphone nights on Fridays. Andy had been there once with some guys from his fraternity and said it was really fun. Cali knew how stressed she had been lately—Leesa had shared her most recent dream with her—and had insisted Leesa come along, saying a night out having some mindless fun would be good for her. Caitlin was also going, so Leesa wouldn't feel like a "third wheel" on Cali and Andy's date.

Cali had said to dress casual and "funky," and Leesa was not exactly certain what that meant. She was pretty sure none of her stuff was very funky, though. She settled on a purple and black striped sweater and black jeans. She hoped her dark brown Ugg boots might add a bit of funk to her look. Checking herself in the mirror, she thought she looked fine, but fine was probably a long way from funky. Oh, well, she thought, it's the best I can do.

She stuffed her leather gloves and favorite ski cap into the pockets of her parka and headed down the stairs to Cali's room. Maybe she would leave the cap on inside the place—perhaps that would be funky enough.

Cali was studying herself in the mirror when Leesa walked in. She was wearing an outfit Leesa remembered well—how could she forget it?—from one of the first parties they had gone to together. Her button shirt was plaid with a Peter Pan collar and rows of skulls and hearts leading diagonally down the front to a frayed edge. She had paired it with a short black skirt that sat low on her hips and red fishnets ripped in several places. Her black platform shoes made her nearly as tall as Leesa. Leesa wasn't sure she would have been able to stand in those shoes, much less walk in them.

"Is that what you meant by funky?" Leesa asked as she limped into Cali's room.

Cali grinned. "Yeah… I'd call it hip and funky."

Cali stepped away from the mirror and gave Leesa's outfit a quick once-over. Her frown told Leesa all she needed to know about Cali's opinion of her outfit.

"Don't you have anything with skulls on it?" Cali asked. "Or polka-dots?" Her face lit up like she had just had a great idea. "Polka-dots are funky. Big ones, anyhow."

"Ha! Sorry. No polka-dots. And definitely no skulls." Leesa smiled sweetly. "I guess you'll just have to deal with the embarrassment of being seen with me."

Cali bent in front of her dresser and rummaged through one of the drawers. She pulled out an orange bandana adorned with big purple polka-dots and folded it into a two-inch wide band.

"Tie this around your head," she said, offering the bandana to Leesa. "It'll give your outfit some edge, at least."

Leesa took the bandana and studied it briefly. The purple circles almost matched the stripes in her sweater. What the heck, she thought, and tied it around her head.

Andy arrived a moment later. His outfit showed why he and Cali made such a good pair.

He was wearing a tight black T-shirt over a gray long-sleeve shirt. The T-shirt had a big gray screaming skull on the front. His black jeans were pretty normal, but they were held up by a wide black leather belt with a giant silver buckle shaped like a winged demon. He was sporting a cloth fedora hat, the kind Justin Timberlake and Jason Mraz often wore. The pale pink and dark brown plaid pattern was eye catching, but the hat was sedate compared to his shoes—bright pink and white checkered canvas sneakers.

"Wow. Cali wasn't kidding when she said dress funky," Leesa said, smiling.

Andy grinned and doffed his hat. "You like?"

Leesa laughed. "I'm not sure," she said. "But I bet Cali does, and that's what counts."

"You look great, Andy," Cali said.

"And you look hot, babe," Andy replied.

The two of them exchanged a hug and a quick kiss.

"Caitlin should be ready by now," Cali said. "We can pick her up on the way out."

They headed down the hallway and found Caitlin waiting in her doorway. She was wearing a plain white shirt and short black skirt over black leggings. A pair of wide, dark blue and black elastic suspenders stretched over her shoulders. Looking at her three companions, Leesa almost felt like *she* was the one who was dressed weirdly. She could not believe everyone at The Joint was going to look like her friends. At least, she sure hoped they wouldn't, or she was going to stand out like a sore thumb.

The Joint was a small restaurant and bar located just off campus. It wasn't too far a walk, but the night was cold, so they piled into Andy's car for the short drive. He parked in a lot behind the building and they circled around to the front, where they paid a three dollar cover charge and went in. Cali led the way, with Leesa following close behind her.

Leesa was surprised by how small the place was, but the owners had crowded enough tables inside to hold nearly a hundred people. The room was already three-quarters full. The chattering conversations were a bit louder than she would have expected, and she guessed that at least some of the kids already had a few drinks in them.

Leesa recognized the hostess from her English class last semester, and the two of them exchanged quick hellos before the girl guided them to a small round table on the far side of the room. They were closer to the back of the room than the front, but still not all that far from the makeshift stage, which was nothing more than a raised square platform covered with black felt. An old acoustic guitar leaned against the wall at the rear of the stage and there was a beat up piano just to the right.

Leesa studied the people seated near them. Most were college kids, but there were a few older folks sprinkled in the crowd. She spotted a couple of fedoras, some pink and green streaked hair, and a one guy in a bright green, blue and yellow plaid sports jacket he had to be wearing as a joke. She figured he must be a comedian—if not, she felt really sorry for the girl sitting next to him, who seemed pretty normal. She saw a fair number of other people dressed relatively conservatively, for which she was very grateful.

A tall waiter with short blond hair threaded his way to their table. He was wearing a loose white button shirt with the sleeves rolled up and black pants. The dark edges of an intricate tattoo peeked out from beneath the sleeve on his right forearm, but not far enough for Leesa to identify the design.

"What can I get you guys?" he asked.

Andy asked for a beer and the girls all ordered diet sodas. Leesa was surprised but pleased that Cali did not try to use her fake ID to order a drink.

"Have you been here before?" Caitlin asked Andy when the waiter was gone.

"Once. Last semester with some friends. It was pretty fun."

"Cool," Caitlin said. She looked at Leesa and Cali. "Any of you Guitar Hero stars thinking about getting up on stage tonight?"

Leesa laughed. "Not a chance. Not in a million years."

"I might," Andy said. "You never know. It could be fun."

"What?" Leesa exclaimed, totally surprised. "You're kidding, right?"

Andy grinned. "Why not?"

"What would you do?" Leesa asked. "Sing? Tell jokes?"

"Nothing so boring. Maybe I'll recite some poetry."

Leesa hoped he was kidding. She had never been here, but she was pretty sure this crowd would not react too kindly to a poetry recital.

Movement at the front of the room drew their attention. A tall, dark-haired guy wearing the same white shirt and black pants outfit as their waiter stepped up onto the stage and grabbed the microphone. He tapped the mic with his fingers and waited for the crowd to quiet.

"Welcome, everyone, to open mic night at The Joint," he said. Some whoops and whistles arose from the crowd. "We're going to start with our traditional opening act," he continued when the noise subsided. "Give it up for one of your favorites, Tony Phillips!"

The whoops and whistles grew louder and were joined by applause. Leesa guessed this Phillips guy had a lot of fans here tonight, or maybe it was just a boisterous crowd ready to let loose and have some fun. The cheers continued as a chunky guy with long brown hair stepped up onto the stage. He carried his own guitar, much newer and nicer than the one leaning against the wall. The overhead lights dimmed and he began to play a customized version of Toby Keith's "I Love This Bar."

"We got winners, we got losers," he sang in a deep baritone voice, "pot smokers and boozers. We got freshman, we got juniors, and we've got *lots* of slacker seniors."

People laughed and clapped, and when he got to the chorus and sang "I love The Joint," the place erupted. Leesa and her friends laughed and clapped along with everyone else.

When Phillips finished, the MC jumped back onstage and

grabbed the microphone. "Tony Phillips, folks!" he said as the applause finally faded. "Thanks for getting us started, Tony. And as always, The Joint appreciates the plug."

Phillips waved to the crowd and stepped down off the stage.

"Before we open the mic completely, we've got one more regular eager to entertain you," the MC continued. "You know him and you love him. Let's hear it for the always popular Stefan Handlemenn!"

A slender blond guy dressed in an old black leather bomber jacket and a military cap with a shiny plastic bill stepped onto the stage. The audience began chanting something that sounded to Leesa like "ga...ga" over and over.

The guy set up a music player on a small table, fiddled with the controls briefly, and then stood with his back to the crowd. A driving electronic dance beat began to blast from the player. The rhythm was familiar, but Leesa couldn't place it. She watched Handlemenn bend forward and do something with his cap. When he spun around, the crowd erupted. Under the cap, he was now wearing a platinum colored, page-boy style wig.

He launched into a surprisingly good impression of Lady Gaga's "Paparazzi." The audience loved it, joining in with a rambunctious "papa-paparazzi" whenever he reached the chorus. By the time he finished, a bunch of kids were on their feet, dancing.

The MC returned to the stage. "Thank you, Lady Gaga...uh, I mean Stefan. Wasn't that something, folks?" The crowd roared once again. "Now, let's see who's brave enough to follow that performance."

Apparently, the guy in the wild plaid sports jacket was the only one. His appearance was met with a few groans—Leesa didn't know if it was for his outfit or because they had seen him before. He pulled the microphone from the stand and walked casually to the very front of the stage. He did not seem the least bit nervous.

"Is everyone having a good time tonight?" he asked. There wasn't much of a response, but he pushed on. "Did you hear about the guy on the track team who won a gold medal? He was so proud he had it bronzed." He waited for a reaction, but except for a few groans, the audience remained silent. He seemed to like the groans, though. Leesa guessed any reaction was better than no reaction at all.

He told a few more lame jokes, then stepped from the stage to a mixture of polite applause and not so polite boos.

Before the MC even reached the microphone, Andy was on his feet.

"That's an act I can definitely follow. Wish me luck."

Leesa looked at Cali. She did not seem bothered in the least that Andy was heading for the stage. Leesa hoped he wasn't really going to recite poetry.

To her surprise, Andy did not get up onto the stage at all. Instead, he sat down at the piano. She had to admit, he looked pretty cute sitting at the piano with that fedora on his head. She worried this was not a piano music kind of crowd, though. Cali did not seem to share her concern—she was smiling broadly.

Andy started slowly, barely touching the keys. The tune was somber and hauntingly familiar. The low hum of conversation in the room began to quiet, as people strained to hear the music. Andy began to play louder, more forcefully, and Leesa finally recognized the song. It was "Hurt"—the original Trent Reznor version more than the Johnny Cash. The music grew more powerful and the room grew quieter. His playing wasn't perfect, but it was pretty darn good.

Suddenly, the melody changed. Andy's fingers started pounding the keyboard and his head was bobbing up and down. Without missing a beat, he had shifted from "Hurt" to "Whole Lot of Shakin'" by Jerry Lee Lewis. When his fingers slid across the keys in a loud glissando, the crowd roared.

"Go get 'em, Jerry Lee," someone yelled. "Yee-haw!"

Andy banged the keys for another few moments, then lifted his right foot from beneath the piano and began bouncing his heel on the keyboard, playing the high notes with his foot. The crowd went wild, and Leesa now knew why he was wearing those wild sneakers.

Finally, he lowered his foot back to the floor and finished with a flourish, sliding his fingers along the entire length of the keyboard three times in row. The crowd cheered and whistled as he stood up and took a deep bow, then weaved his way back through the tables.

"That's my guy," Cali said, laughing. She stood up and gave Andy a big hug.

"That was amazing," Leesa said when he sat down.

"Twelve years of lessons," Andy explained. "Mostly church music and show tunes, but when I learned my assignments well, I was allowed to have some fun."

"Well, you looked like you were having fun tonight, for sure," Leesa said. "Especially when you did that thing with your foot."

He grinned. "Too much?"

"No way," Cali said. "It was perfect. Just right for this place." She grabbed his hat and placed it atop her head. "I want to make sure everyone knows I'm with the superstar."

They listened to lots more acts, some pretty good, some not so good. Only one got a reaction anywhere near as loud as the one Andy received, a pair of girls in sexy leather jump suits who brought the house down with a sultry rendition of Katy Perry's "I Kissed a Girl."

By the time they got back to the dorm, it was nearly midnight. Leesa said good-night to her friends and headed up to her room, pleasantly exhausted. She was glad Cali had talked her into going out tonight—she had not thought about dreams or zombies for hours. She hoped her sleep would be as untroubled as the evening had been. As tired as she felt, she was pretty sure it would be.

Pulling off her coat as she entered her room, she stumbled over her straw wastebasket, knocking it over. Half its contents spilled out onto the floor, including a not quite empty can of soda whose syrupy brown contents were now beading up on her throw rug. Leesa cursed silently. She must have pulled the basket from its normal place beside her desk for some reason before going out and forgot to put it back. Angrily, she aimed a fake kick at the overturned basket and was astonished to see it go flying across the room and crash into her dresser, spilling the rest of its contents.

"What the…?" she said half-aloud as she stared dumbfounded at the basket, thinking she must be even more tired than she thought. Because she was absolutely certain her foot had never touched the thing.

28. COUNTING SHEEP

Leesa sat down numbly on the edge of her bed, her eyes moving back and forth from the soda stain on her rug—where the wastebasket had started—to the basket itself, now lying on its side across the room against the dresser. How had it gotten from one spot to the other? Sure, she had kicked at it after she stumbled over it, but she hadn't actually connected with it. Or had she? The evidence was right there in front of her, lying against the dresser. She must have kicked it. What other explanation could there be? Wastebaskets did not fly across the room on their own. Unless....

She thought back to the Red Bull can. Maybe the darn thing had actually slid a few inches across her desk. Maybe the can and the basket hadn't moved on their own—maybe *she* had somehow caused them to move. She remembered a special she had seen on TV, about a guy who claimed he could move objects with his mind. Maybe she was doing the same thing. But that was crazy, right—moving stuff with her mind? Either that was crazy, or she was. More likely, she was just imagining things.

She shook her head, unable to believe it was just her imagination. Sure, she might have imagined the can moving—it was only a couple of inches, after all—but no way had she imagined the basket flying across the room. Could she have kicked it without realizing it? Maybe. She guessed perhaps she was tired enough for that.

The Red Bull thing had occurred during finals, when she had been exhausted. Maybe she wasn't crazy—maybe her mind just played tricks on her whenever she was overly tired. Between her dreams and her tossing and turning, she certainly had not gotten anywhere near enough sleep lately. She wished more than ever that Rave was here. Not that she expected him to have an answer about any of this, but she was pretty sure if she could just lie down cradled in his arms, she could get a much needed good night's sleep.

But Rave was not here, and she had no idea when he would be back.

She wondered if Dr. Clerval might know anything about vampires being able to move things with their minds. She had never heard of them doing it, but that did not mean it wasn't true. And if they could, maybe Stefan's aborted bite had been enough to transfer a bit of that power to her. She definitely needed to ask the professor about this. First chance she got on Monday, she was going to head to his office.

There were no answers she could get tonight, though. Still, there was one thing she could do now, something she should have done already if she hadn't been so stunned by all this. She got up from the bed and wet a washcloth in the sink. Dropping to her knees, she began cleaning up the soda spill.

Ten minutes later, Leesa had cleaned up the spill as much as she could. A faint brown stain was still visible on the rug, but that would need some real carpet cleaner or shampoo to get rid of. She had also put the spilled trash back into the wastebasket and returned the basket to its normal place beside her desk, where there would be no chance a fake kick would send it flying again. Her eyes were growing heavy, so she washed her face, brushed her teeth and climbed into bed.

Once again, sleep did not come easy. Her body was tired, but her mind refused to turn off. Just because her eyes were closed and she was tucked comfortably under the covers did not mean the questions racing through her brain were going to stop. She tried focusing on other, more pleasant things, recalling memories of favorite times with Rave, but the relief was only temporary. Warm and fun, for sure, but temporary. As soon as she began to drift off, images of the wastebasket flying across the room or dead bodies coming to life reappeared.

Finally, after what seemed like hours of tossing and turning, she fell asleep.

Sleep did not offer the succor she had hoped for. A familiar dream rose up from her unconscious, returning her to the cave, where she once again faced the dark figure with glowing eyes. Behind the vampire was the same poor girl, chained to the cavern wall. No, not to the wall—the girl was now tied to a small tree. What a tree was doing here deep inside the bowels of the mountain, Leesa had no idea. As before, she was certain she knew the captive, but something kept the image blurred. The girl was tantalizingly familiar, yet frustratingly unrecognizable.

Leesa's eyes snapped open, only to be met by more darkness. At least this was real darkness, not some magical dream dimness that revealed some things and kept others hidden. Why couldn't she see the girl more clearly, she wondered? Her other two dreams had been so clear—much clearer than she wanted—but not this one. Why had she been able to see every detail of the rotting corpses coming back to life, but the one figure she desperately wanted to see remained just out of her grasp? Was her brain protecting her from something? Or was this another kind of dream, not related to the other two? All three dreams felt the same, different in some profound, powerful way from her usual dreams, yet they differed in this one very crucial element.

Another thought struck her—one that brought both comfort and despair. Each of her zombie dreams had occurred just once, and then had seemingly come to pass, at least as far as she could tell from the television news and the YouTube video. This one she'd had twice now, more than two weeks apart. Perhaps the repeat signaled that this dream had not yet come true, that no girl was being held captive in a dark cavern somewhere. Maybe there was still something Leesa could do to prevent it from happening. But how was she supposed to stop it, when she had no idea who the girl was?

The only thing Leesa knew for sure was that she needed to get some sleep. Unable to turn her mind away from her problems, she decided to concentrate on them instead, to count them, sort of like counting sheep. One, Rave was several hundred miles away...Two, even if Rave was around, she would not be able to kiss him, because something had weakened his control over his inner fire...Three, magical energies were inflaming the blood thirst of the vampires...Four, some guy was looking for her and claiming to be her father...Five, objects in her close proximity were moving without apparent reason...Six, there was a chance that in some unknown way, *she* was making them move...Seven, she'd had two dreams of dead bodies reanimating, and both had apparently come true...Eight, she had twice dreamed of a girl in trouble, but despite a strong feeling of familiarity, she could not recognize who the girl was....

Somehow, in a perverse and unexpected way, listing her problems sent her drifting off into much needed sleep.

29. EDWINA'S HUNT

Edwina glided through the darkness, getting ready to leave the vampire lair yet again. She was nearly to the cavern entrance when Stefan appeared out of nowhere and grabbed her lightly by the elbow.

"Going out again?" he asked.

"Yes, I am," she said, her tone neutral, hoping he was not going to give her trouble.

"This is the fourth time," Stefan said.

"But who's counting?" Edwina replied lightly. "Don't worry, I'll be careful." She looked down at his hand, still gripping her elbow.

Stefan released her arm. "Is it so difficult to find a feeder?"

"I keep my feeders for a long time, as you well know." It didn't hurt to remind Stefan just why she needed to go out. "I have to find the right one."

She could feel Stefan's eyes probing hers, seeking some sign of deceit or guile. Edwina was not new to this game, though, and kept her gaze flat, revealing nothing.

"Try to find one quickly," Stefan said finally. "Remember, it is only by my permission that you are allowed out by yourself."

Edwina recognized the implied threat—his permission could be revoked at any time. Still, Stefan owed her, and she was fairly certain he would not be changing his mind just yet. She would not hasten her plans—not yet, anyway. She was enjoying herself on the outside too much.

"Believe me, Stefan, no one wants to find a feeder more than I do." She did not want to raise his suspicions by seeming overly compliant, so she decided a little dig was in order. He would be expecting it. "I've grown used to feeding whenever I wanted," she added.

Stefan nodded, apparently satisfied with her tiny rebellion. "Well, let's both hope you find one soon, then."

"Yes, let's," Edwina replied. She certainly was not going to tell him she had already found her victim. She just wasn't ready to take her yet—she was having too much fun.

The night was dark. Thick clouds blanketed the moon and stars, and there were few lights along this part of the Connecticut River's eastern shore. As Edwina glided swiftly north along the river, she hoped the clouds remained in place tomorrow. Her plans would go much more smoothly without the sun.

No human eye could see her in this blackness, but despite her speed, her senses were alert for any sign of danger. There were other beings that roamed the night, creatures whose eyes could pierce the darkness as easily as her own. The volkaanes may have abandoned their settlement, but some might still be around. Not that she would mind testing herself against a lone hunter—she had heard how sweet and hot their blood was—but with *Destiratu* growing ever stronger, she knew it was unlikely any volkaanes would be hunting alone. By nature, the volkaanes were a cautious race, and *Destiratu* would be making them even more so.

In less than an hour, she was across the river from the city of Hartford. She crossed the river by swinging on the support girders beneath a highway bridge and made her way downtown. It was just past one o'clock, and the area was alive with people celebrating the beginning of the weekend. Dance music and laughter spilled from the open doors of the most popular clubs. She strolled past a string of bars, ignoring an invitation from a group of drunken humans to join them for drink—she was pretty sure they were not offering the kind of drink she preferred. Across the street, the yawning mouth of an underground parking garage beneath a towering office building beckoned her. She toyed with the idea of flashing through the lines of traffic to the other side, but instead waited for the light to change and crossed dutifully at the crosswalk. She turned into the entranceway and walked past the black and yellow automatic arm blocking the drive. Her plans for later today required a car, and this was the perfect place to obtain one.

She took the stairs down to the second level, which was less crowded with cars than the first but still held an acceptable number of vehicles. The place was dimly lit, with plenty of dark shadows to conceal her. She melted into the darkness beside a concrete pillar and waited. This time, she could not just steal a car by hotwiring it, the way a motorcycle-riding bad boy "boyfriend" had taught her years ago. She wanted the keys as well. An expectant smile curved her lips—she did not think getting the keys would be a problem.

She waited only a few minutes before the elevator dinged, sounding unnaturally loud in the stillness. The doors slid open and a lone guy stepped out. While she was prepared to deal with two or even three humans, one by himself was perfect—just what she had been hoping for.

The man's leather shoes echoed unevenly on the cement floor as he crossed the garage. His lumbering gait provided clear evidence that he had downed at least a few drinks this evening. Edwina's smile widened. The guy should not be driving. She would merely be doing her civic duty tonight.

Her plan was a simple one—kill him with a blow to the back of the head and relieve him of his keys and phone—but as he drew nearer, her bloodlust grew. It was *Destiratu*, she knew, magnifying her hunger. She could have fought it, but decided why should she? They were alone, and she was thirsty. Besides, slaking her thirst now would make the coming day easier. As long as she disposed of the body properly, no one would ever know.

She waited as the guy fumbled with his keys, finally managing to press the button to deactivate his car alarm. The horn of a silver Camry a few spots down beeped as the taillights blinked twice. Edwina flashed silently across the garage floor and grabbed him from behind.

There would be no playing with her meal this time. She gave his neck a sharp twist, paralyzing him but keeping his heart pumping blood. His keys fell from his hand, but she caught them easily in one hand before they hit the ground. Her fangs dropped from her jaw and she bit deep into his neck, tearing open his jugular vein. She dragged him back into the shadows and began drinking deeply of his sweet, hot blood. She thought she had never tasted anything more delicious.

When she had drained him of the last drop, she ripped off a piece of his shirt and wiped his blood from her lips. She ruffled through his pockets and pulled out his cell phone and his wallet, removing close to a hundred dollars in cash before shoving the wallet back into his pants. They were still alone, so she lifted him effortlessly over her shoulder and carried him to his car.

She popped the trunk open and dumped the body unceremoniously inside. After slamming the lid closed, she gave the lock a sharp blow with the heel of her hand, jamming it shut and insuring no one would be able to get inside and discover her cargo.

Whistling softly, she got behind the wheel and drove out of the garage, favoring the attendant with a sweet smile and paying the fee with the dead guy's cash.

30. A DROP OF BLOOD

Pink's hit anthem "Perfect" rang out from Leesa's cell phone, pulling her from her sleep. The song told her it was Cali on the other end. Leesa thought the line about people not liking the singer's jeans and not getting her hair was the perfect ringtone for Cali, and Cali had laughed delightedly when Leesa told her about her choice.

She wiped the sleep from her eyes and checked the clock, surprised to see it was already twenty minutes past nine. She almost never slept this late, even on the weekend. Her tossing and turning and dreaming must really have exhausted her, she thought. At least she had finally managed to fall asleep, and to stay asleep until after nine. She wondered how long she would have slept if the phone had not awakened her.

She pushed herself up from the bed and grabbed her cell.

"Hey," she said.

"You sound tired," Cali said. "Did I wake you?"

"Yeah, you did, but it's okay." Leesa's feet were growing cold, so she slipped her feet into her moccasins. "What's up?"

"Some fun is up, that's what," Cali said. "So get your lazy butt out of bed. I'm coming up to tell you about it."

"Do I get a choice?" Leesa asked, fighting a yawn.

"Nope," Cali said, laughing. "See you in a few."

The phone went silent. Leesa barely had time to put on a pair of jeans, T-shirt and a sweatshirt before Cali knocked twice on the door and let herself in.

Leesa was happy to see Cali was also dressed casually, in gray sweatpants and a baggy purple and gray sweatshirt. Leesa knew Cali would never be caught dead in that outfit outside of the dorm, so at least she wasn't planning on going anywhere immediately.

"What's got you so fired up this morning?" Leesa asked, sitting down atop her bed.

Cali pulled the chair out from under Leesa's desk and sat down. She had a big smile on her face. "We're gonna blow this joint today," she said. "Gonna take us a road trip. How's that sound?"

Leesa was surprised. No one in the dorm owned a car, and the only person she even knew with one was Andy. Nothing about a road trip had been mentioned the night before when they were all together at The Joint.

"And just how are we going to do that?" she asked. "Did you steal a car this morning?"

"Ha, ha, pretty funny," Cali said. "Vanina called and said she has her dad's car for the day. She's coming to get us at ten-thirty."

Leesa was glad to hear she would have time to shower and eat. From Cali's enthusiastic tone, she had been afraid Cali would want to get going much sooner. Still, she was pretty tired and not sure just how ready she was for whatever adventure Cali and Vanina had in mind.

"I don't know," she said. "I'm kind of tired. I didn't sleep very well last night."

"How come? Too wound up from our big night at The Joint?"

"Ha! I wish. That was pretty fun." Leesa pulled her feet up onto the bed and wrapped her arms around her shins. "Remember that dream I told you about, with the girl and the vampire? I had it again last night. And it was just as disturbing. I had trouble getting back to sleep afterward."

"And you still couldn't recognize the girl?" Cali asked.

Leesa shook her head. "Nope. That's the worst thing about it. I feel like I should know her, but the dream always ends before I can see her clearly enough." She got up off her bed and limped over to the window. "I wouldn't be quite so bothered about it if it wasn't for those other two dreams. They've got me worried this one might come true, too. I hate feeling so helpless."

Cali joined Leesa by the window.

"I don't blame you. I'd be freaked if I had a dream like those zombie ones and they came true." She put her hand on Leesa's shoulder. "But those two happened pretty quickly, right? Within a day or two of when you had the dream?"

"Yeah. They did."

"Well, maybe that's a good sign. You first had this one a couple of weeks ago. Maybe this dream isn't like those other two."

"Maybe," Leesa said, hoping what Cali said was true. "But it sure feels real when I have it."

"I think this is another good reason for us to get out of here and have some fun," Cali said. "Sounds to me like you sure could use it."

Leesa thought Cali was probably right. It certainly wouldn't hurt to take her mind off all the stuff bothering her. She just wondered if that were possible.

"Where are we going?"

"Up to the big mall in Farmington. We'll hang out, try on some hot outfits, get something to eat. It'll be great."

Leesa had never been to the Farmington mall, but she had heard it was one of the most upscale malls in Connecticut. It might be cool to check it out, even though she doubted she'd be buying anything, not with her bank account as puny as it was. She was pretty sure Cali would have a lot more fun trying on outfits than she would, but it would be a kick to see what kind of stuff Cali picked out to model. You could always count on Cali to pull some fashion surprises.

"Okay, I'm in," Leesa said.

Leesa and Cali stood just inside the front door of the dorm, waiting for Vanina to show up. It wasn't all that cold out, especially for January, but it was chilly enough that Cali preferred to wait inside. Leesa had her parka draped over her arm—she would have been fine outside with it on—but Cali was dressed for the enclosed mall, not for the outdoors. She was wearing her new fluorescent Pink brand sweatshirt, a short, pleated black skirt, knee high black boots and black fishnet stockings that peeked out only about two inches above the top of her boots. Somewhere, she had found nail polish that matched the bright color of her sweatshirt almost exactly, and she had replaced the blue streaks in her hair with pink. Leesa didn't know how Cali did it, but inexplicably, the look worked on her.

Leesa was dressed much more conservatively, in an acrylic sweater with wide, alternating stripes of light and dark blue and plain jeans. Since she expected to do a lot of walking at the mall, she had opted for a pair of Sketcher walking shoes rather than her Uggs. Cali had not wanted to bother with a jacket, but Leesa planned to leave her parka in the car when they got to the mall.

A silver Camry a couple of years old pulled to the curb in front of the dorm and beeped once. Leesa slipped into her parka while Cali pushed the door open and strode quickly toward the car. Leesa followed behind and climbed into the back seat while Cali slid into the front. It was cool inside the car, so Leesa kept her parka on.

Edwina turned and smiled at them both. She was wearing tight black jeans, with a black sweatshirt unbuttoned over a blood red collarless shirt. The shirt extended about three inches below the sweatshirt, creating a red band between the black jeans and black sweatshirt.

"Hi, guys," she said. "You ready to have some fun?"

"Yeah, if we don't freeze to death first," Cali said, making a show of hugging her arms in front of her against the chill. "Doesn't this thing have heat?"

"I told you to bring your coat," Leesa said, grinning. "It's winter, in case you've forgotten."

"Yeah, yeah, I know," Cali said. "But I wasn't planning on being outside. You might as well have the windows down, Vanina."

Edwina laughed. She actually had been driving with the windows down, but had put them up before reaching the dorm.

"Sorry," she said. "I kind of like the cold, but I guess we could spare some heat." The cold did not affect her, of course, but she had another reason for not turning the heat on until necessary—the body still crammed into the trunk. She didn't think much heat would seep into the trunk, but figured the colder it stayed back there, the longer it would take for the corpse to begin to decay. She reached for a knob on the dash and warm air began blowing into the car. "Better?"

"Much," Cali said, holding her hands in front of one of the vents. "Now let's get this show on the road."

They followed Highway 9 north, through a series of towns Leesa had never been to before, but did not look all that different from Meriden. The drive was pleasant enough, and in about forty minutes they were pulling into a wide parking lot. At Cali's urging, Vanina circled the lot until she found an open spot not too far from the mall's shiny glass and steel main entrance. Giant blue letters along the top of the curved entranceway proclaimed WEST FARMS.

They got out of the car and walked quickly toward the entrance. A thick layer of clouds blanketed the sky, keeping the morning cool, but they did not have very far to go. Leesa was impressed with the design of the place. A pair of restaurants flanked the entrance building. Each had a different look, but both bore clean, sharp lines and pleasing colors.

Inside, the mall was just as nice.

"This place is pretty cool," Leesa said, looking around at all the glass storefronts filled with colorful, eye-catching displays.

"Nothing but the best for us, huh?" Edwina said, smiling.

"Have you been here before, Vanina?"

"A couple of times, yeah. But it's been awhile."

"Let's go to Nordstrom first," Cali said. "We can check out the expensive stuff."

They spent nearly an hour in Nordstrom. Leesa guessed that Cali probably tried on three outfits for every one Leesa or Vanina tried. Some of the combinations Cali put together were never meant to be paired and went beyond even Cali's outrageous fashion sense. Leesa loved watching her prance out of the dressing room with one wild outfit after another. Even the two sales girls got into the fun, laughing and applauding at some of Cali's wilder creations.

Leesa thought Vanina did not seem to be having quite as much fun as the rest of them. Whenever Leesa looked at her, Vanina was smiling, but there was something not quite joyful about her smile, like she was forcing herself to enjoy it all. Leesa wondered if maybe Vanina also had things weighing on her mind and was trying to use the outing to forget them. She didn't feel she knew Vanina well enough to ask her about it, so she just let it slide.

From Nordstrom, they moved to the bebe store. The contrast between Nordstrom and bebe was dramatic. The former was huge, with large, well-appointed dressing rooms that seemed almost as big as Leesa's dorm room. Bebe was smaller and less ornate—except for all the trademark rhinestones, which seemed to sparkle from every corner of the store.

"Hey, check this one out," Cali said.

She pulled a royal blue T-shirt off the rack. It had a giant pair of slightly parted pink lips stenciled on the front, with a much smaller set of white lips superimposed over the corner of the pink ones. The pink lips were decorated with dozens of tiny rhinestones.

"It's so you," Leesa said, grinning.

"Ha, ha. It is, isn't it?" Cali held the shirt up in front of her chest, displaying how it would look on her. "You can never go wrong with pictures of sexy lips," she said. "It gives guys all sorts of nasty ideas. And I love that it's blue—most of their stuff is black. But a girl's got to wear a little color now and then."

"A little?" Leesa said, laughing and tugging playfully at the sleeve of Cali's fluorescent sweatshirt.

"I wish I could pull off some of the colors you do, Cali," Edwina said. "I'd hate to see what a sweatshirt like yours would do to my skin tone."

"When you've got it, flaunt it," Cali said, grinning. She reached inside the shirt, looking for the price tag. "Ouch!" she exclaimed. "Damn."

"What happened," Leesa asked, moving closer.

"I stuck myself on something."

Cali held her hand out in front of her. She pressed her thumb against the top of her index finger, and Leesa saw a tiny drop of blood well up from the pinprick.

Edwina's head snapped around at the sweet scent of fresh blood. Before she could stop it, a low groan escaped her throat. She quickly turned her back to Cali, thankful she had feasted just last night. If she hadn't, she did not know if she would have been able to control herself. Killing a girl—or two girls—in a public place like this would definitely not be a good idea, no matter how much fun it might be.

At the sound of Vanina's moan, Leesa turned her head and caught a quick glimpse of a strange expression on her friend's face. She almost thought it looked like excitement, but Vanina spun around before Leesa could be sure.

"I'm sorry," Edwina said, thinking quickly and keeping her back to the other two girls. "I hate the sight of blood. It makes me sick."

"I never would have taken you for such a wuss," Cali said teasingly. She sucked at the blood on her fingertip, then pressed her thumb tightly against the spot. When she pulled her thumb away a few moments later, the bleeding had stopped.

"You can turn around now, Vanina," she said. "No more blood."

Vanina turned around slowly. Leesa watched her face, but her expression had reverted to normal. With Vanina's dark skin tone, it was impossible to tell if the incident had caused her to turn pale at all, the way some people did when seeing something that upset them.

"I'm sorry," Edwina apologized again. "I've never been any good with blood, ever since I was a kid. I don't know why."

"Don't worry about it," Cali said. "We all have our little things." She held her hand out. "See, no more blood."

Even though the blood was gone, Edwina could still smell its traces. She fought to keep her expression flat. "Thank goodness for that. I'd hate to have the nurse come for me when you were the one who was wounded."

Cali laughed. "Yeah, I'm glad you didn't faint or anything. Leesa knows how much I hate having any attention taken away from me."

Leesa laughed, too. "I'll vouch for that. I'm surprised you didn't prick yourself again, just to add a little extra drama."

"Darn, why didn't I think of that?" Cali said, grinning. She hung the shirt back on the rack. "I can't be buying a shirt that made me bleed. What do you say we go get something to eat?"

"I don't think I could eat anything right now," Edwina said, putting her hand on her stomach. She was glad to have an excuse not to eat—not eating was one of the biggest problems she had to deal with when she was around humans. "But you two should get something."

Leesa was still wondering about Vanina's reaction to the sight of Cali's blood. Had she really seen disgust on Vanina's face, or had it been something else—like anticipation, maybe? She shook her head, feeling silly. Maybe she just had vampires and zombies on her mind. Yeah, that must be it; she was imagining things. She pictured Stefan's pallid face. Vanina certainly did not look anything like him, nor did she resemble the only other vampire Leesa had ever seen close up, the young vampire Rave had killed right in front of her on Halloween. That vampire's skin had been equally pale. And she had never heard of a vampire with a car—except in *Twilight*, of course, and that was just a book.

No, she had simply misread Vanina's expression, that was all. She pushed any thoughts of vampires from her mind.

"I could use some food," she said.

And I could use something to drink, Edwina thought, feeling her blood thirst rise as she eyed the two sweet young necks in front of her. She forced the hunger down. Waiting was hard, but it would be worth it. Soon, she promised herself. Soon.

But not yet.

31. ULTIMATUM

Edwina had been back inside the vampire caverns for just a short while when Stefan approached her.

"I trust you enjoyed your outing," he said, moving close in front of her. There was a hint of controlled anger in his voice.

Edwina took a half step backwards, startled by his comment and his tone. What was he saying? How much did he know? She decided that if he knew she had been with Leesa, his anger would have been far more furious. It had to be something else.

"What do you mean?" she asked, buying time.

"Don't act the innocent with me. You have taken human blood. I see it in your eyes, and I can smell it."

"So what?" Edwina straightened her posture and pushed her shoulders back. She had to show him she would not be cowed. "I was careful, and I disposed of the body where it will never be found. No one will ever connect his disappearance to our kind. He is just another missing human."

"You said you were seeking a feeder," Stefan said, continuing to press her. "Your permission to go out alone was for that purpose—not so you could hunt."

"I was not hunting," Edwina lied. "But the opportunity was so perfect, I just could not resist."

"Exactly," Stefan said. The satisfaction in his voice was

clear. "That is why the rules were put in place, because *Destiratu* can make it impossible to resist the urge."

"That is not what I meant," Edwina replied calmly. "I was never out of control, not even for a moment. The chance was just too good to pass up. Trust me."

"That is the problem, I'm afraid. I do not trust you. Not at all. I should rescind your permission to venture out by yourself right now."

Edwina laid her hand gently on Stefan's forearm. "No, please don't," she said, trying to sound as compliant as possible. "I need a feeder. I've grown used to having one." It never hurt to remind him of that.

Stefan studied her closely. He didn't trust her, but he did owe her. He cursed the *grafhym* blood that had somehow found its way into Leesa's veins and kept him from being able to turn her. He had put himself into Edwina's debt for no gain.

"Very well," he said finally. "You may go out one more time. But you had best come back with a feeder, or you will go hungry. My patience has its limits."

Edwina breathed an inward sigh of relief. She didn't know if Stefan would hold firm to his ultimatum, but there was a chance he might. She would need to plan her next trip out very carefully.

32. ANSWERS AND QUESTIONS

Leesa trudged up a musty, dimly lit stairwell, heading for Dr. Clerval's third floor office. This was one of the oldest buildings on campus and had no elevator. She was pretty sure someone with the professor's tenure could have had a bigger and newer office somewhere else on campus if he wanted, but Dr. Clerval seemed comfortable here.

It was barely nine o'clock, but Leesa hoped the professor would be in his office. She had classes today from ten o'clock until one, so she was hoping to catch him before her first class. Pushing through a heavy fire door, she stepped into the third floor hallway. The corridor was silent and empty, and her footsteps echoed lightly off brown plaster walls badly in need of a fresh coat of paint.

She limped down the hallway until she reached an old wooden door about halfway down the hall. In contrast to the shiny nameplates affixed to the other doors she had passed, Professor Clerval's brass nameplate was tarnished dark with age, testimony to his long tenure here. Leesa knocked softly on the door.

"Just a minute," came the professor's voice from inside.

"It's Leesa Nyland," Leesa said, letting him know there was no reason to put any of his secret stuff away. He had already shown her his most precious treasures, including one that only one other person had ever seen, his genuine vampire skull.

A moment later, she heard the lock click and the door swung open, revealing a smiling Dr. Clerval. As always, he was dressed in a dark, rumpled suit and black converse high top sneakers. Candlelight flickered behind him. Leesa was pretty sure she knew what the candles meant.

"What a pleasant surprise," Dr. Clerval said. "How's my favorite student?"

Leesa knew the professor's comment was sincere. They had experienced a lot together last semester, culminating with Dr. Clerval getting to meet a real vampire when she had chosen him to drive her to meet Stefan to fulfill her bargain. Until then, the professor had been absolutely convinced vampires existed, but had never actually seen one. The meeting with Stefan was enough to insure Leesa's place as his favorite, but they had shared other experiences as well, including curing Leesa's mom with the blood of a *grafhym*.

"I'm fine," she said. "At least, I hope I am."

"Where are my manners?" the professor said, stepping aside. "Come in, come in."

Leesa limped into the dimly lit office, and Dr. Clerval closed the door behind her, clicking the lock back into place. As usual, the air inside his office was thick with the fruity scent of pipe tobacco, and Leesa saw his pipe smoldering in the old brass ashtray on the corner of his desk. A thin ribbon of smoke twisted up from the bowl in the candlelight, dissipating in the dimness above.

Even though she had been here several times, Leesa was still surprised by how small the office was, smaller even than her dorm room. Tall bookcases crammed with books—most of them dealing with vampires—lined every wall, making the room feel even smaller. A glass-fronted bookcase housed the professor's oldest, most valuable manuscripts. Black curtains were drawn across an arched window similar to the one in Leesa's room, and only the tiniest a bit of daylight leaked in around the edges. Beneath the window was a beautiful antique roll top desk, cluttered with papers. Sitting in the center of the desk was the reason for the closed curtains and candlelight—his vampire skull.

When Dr. Clerval had first shown her the skull, Leesa had been amazed and fascinated, especially by the twin fangs. That was back when she didn't know vampires truly existed, before she had watched Rave destroy one, and before she had been bitten by Stefan. The ancient skull had been the first real evidence she had ever seen for the existence of vampires. It turned out vampire bone was even more sensitive to light than vampire skin, so the professor only examined it by candlelight.

Leesa still thought the skull was very cool, but it had lost its power to amaze her.

"Sit down, sit down," the professor invited.

Leesa sat down carefully on an old wooden chair with a dark burgundy cushioned seat. Dr. Clerval lowered himself gingerly onto his desk chair.

"Let me put this thing away," he said, indicating the skull. "And then you can tell me what's troubling you."

Professor Clerval carefully wrapped the skull in the black velvet cloth he always stored it in, clipping the top of the cloth closed with a brass clip. He carried it across the room to his old-fashioned metal safe and placed it gently inside, then pushed the heavy door closed and spun the combination lock. When he sat back down, he switched on the red and gold glass Tiffany table lamp on his desk and blew out the candles. He grabbed his pipe from the ashtray and took a deep puff.

"So, what brings you here this morning?" he asked after he exhaled a cloud of smoke.

Leesa was not sure where to start. Zombies? Strange dreams that seemed to possibly be coming true? Objects moving for no apparent reason? Each time one of those things happened, it seemed critically important, but when she looked at them from a distance and got ready to talk about them, they all seemed almost silly. Still, she was certain they were not silly, and was pretty sure Dr. Clerval would not think so, either.

"I'm not even sure where to begin," she said.

"You've been through a lot these last few months, Leesa. If something is troubling you, I'm sure it must be important. So start wherever you want."

She decided to start with the dreams.

"I've been having some really strange dreams the last month or so."

"Strange, how?"

"Well, for starters, they're totally realistic," Leesa explained. "Much more real than my usual dreams, for sure. But that's not what bothers me so much. What's really strange is two of them apparently came true."

She saw a tiny hint of surprise in Dr. Clerval's eyes, but that was the extent of his reaction to her claim. She could only imagine how skeptically any of her science professors would have reacted to such a claim.

"What do you mean by 'came true?'" he asked.

She described the dreams, and then told him about the news stories and the YouTube video.

"I remember hearing about that thing in Higganum," Dr. Clerval said. "I didn't pay too much attention to it—I just figured it was a prank of some sort, probably teenagers with too much time on their hands. Your dream certainly casts a different light on it, though."

"I might have chalked it up to coincidence," Leesa said, "except for that tri-cornered hat. And then I had the dream about the dead girl at the window."

Dr. Clerval took another long pull from his pipe and blew the smoke out through pursed lips. "Precognition," he said.

"Huh? What's that?"

"The ability to see future events. For some people it happens in dreams, others have visions. Have you experienced anything like this before?"

Leesa shook her head. "No, never. Not even close."

"So, if you *are* experiencing precognition," Dr. Clerval said, "one question would be, why now?"

"I've been wondering that same thing. I was hoping you could help. Do you think it could have anything to do with being bitten by Stefan? Do vampires have any of this precognition stuff?"

"I've never seen it mentioned in any texts or histories," the professor replied. "But just because it's not a vampire power doesn't mean it's not related to Stefan's bite. Perhaps the bite triggered something already inside you—unlocking it, if you will."

"Well, if that's the case," Leesa said glumly, "it might not be the only thing it triggered.

Dr. Clerval's eyes widened with interest. "What do you mean?"

"I'll tell you in a minute," Leesa replied. "But can we stick to the dreams just a bit longer? I can understand why the one dream has to do with a vampire, given everything that happened last semester. But zombies? I have no idea where that's coming from. Why am I suddenly dreaming about dead people returning to life? And is it truly happening? Or is someone just digging up bodies as a prank? Even if it's just a prank, why am I dreaming about it?" She smiled. "That's a lot of questions, I know. Do you know anything about zombies?"

Dr. Clerval took a last puff from his pipe and placed it carefully back into the ashtray. "Reanimated corpses have been a theme of old folk tales for centuries," he said, lapsing into his teaching voice. "They are especially connected to the voodoo practiced in places like the Caribbean and Africa. It's usually a witch doctor or sorcerer who brings the person back to life with a ritual spell. In the last hundred years, zombies have become increasingly common in literature, and a bit later, in film. In these modern stories, it's usually some kind of plague or radiation that turns hordes of corpses into flesh-eating monsters."

Leesa nodded. She had been right to come to Dr. Clerval. He knew at least a little bit about lots of supernatural stuff.

"I know there've been lots of books and movies in the last few years," she said. "Is there any chance some of it could be based on something real? Like the vampire stories are?"

The professor closed his eyes for a moment and stroked his chin with the fingers of one hand. It looked to Leesa like he was remembering something.

"When I was a much younger man," he said finally, "and far more energetic than I am now, I took a long trip to Eastern Europe in search of vampire lore. During my journey, I heard repeated stories of someone—or something—called the Necromancer. It's a common term, used in many tales and legends about a person who can control the dead, but the stories I heard seemed to refer to a particular being. People spoke of grandparents or great grandparents who had lived through a scourge of walking dead. Since my main interest was vampires, I didn't pay too much attention to these tales, but I still remember having the feeling there might be some germ of truth to them."

"So you think zombies could be real, then?"

"I believe they might have existed at some time in the past, in very local situations," Dr. Clerval replied. "But I haven't come across anything in the last fifty years or so that carried the same quality of truth as those stories. Nowadays, every mention of the living dead is just popular fiction. It's as if zombies disappeared, similar to the way werewolves also seem to have vanished."

Leesa remembered Rave saying something about werewolves being wiped out several hundred years ago. Could the same thing have happened to zombies? But if so, why were they suddenly reappearing now, in her dreams, at least?

"Do you think there's a chance what I'm seeing could

actually be happening, then?" she asked.

Dr. Clerval shrugged. "In my line of work, I seldom rule anything out. You've made a pretty good case for it, with the YouTube video and the old colonial hat. Of course, none of this tells us *why* you're suddenly having these dreams."

"I know. But at least hearing you say the dreams could be real makes me feel better, like maybe I'm not imagining all this." With first Rave and now Professor Clerval mentioning that old stories of flesh-eating corpses could have been based on real occurrences, Leesa was definitely not going to rule the possibility out. Unfortunately, that meant her dream of the girl and the vampire might also be real.

"Is there any chance you could ask Stefan about zombies?" Dr. Clerval asked. "Perhaps the undead know something of their purported cousins."

"I haven't seen him," Leesa said. "Not since, you know...."

"Well, I guess that's really for the best," Dr. Clerval said, though he sounded a bit disappointed. Leesa was pretty sure he was hoping to get another chance to meet Stefan.

"You said there was something else you wanted to talk about?" the professor asked.

Leesa had almost forgotten about the Red Bull can and the wastebasket. In for a penny, in for a pound, she thought.

"Yeah, there is. I hope all this isn't making you think I'm going crazy, Professor."

Dr. Clerval smiled. "After all the things I've seen you deal with, Leesa, I'd be a fool not to take anything you say seriously."

Leesa described the two incidents, admitting she could not be absolutely certain either of them had actually happened the way they seemed, but that she believed they did, especially the wastebasket.

"Fascinating," Dr. Clerval said when she was finished. "Telekinesis. The ability to move objects with one's mind. Once again, that's not a vampire power, so I think we can rule out it being caused by Stefan's bite. You appear to be an extraordinarily gifted girl, Leesa."

Gifted? More like cursed, Leesa thought.

"Maybe if I had an ounce of control over either thing I might agree with you," she said. "The way things are right now, I don't feel very gifted."

Dr. Clerval thought for a moment, then opened his desk drawer and took out a pencil. He laid the pencil atop the desk.

"Let's see whether you do have any control," he said. "Try to make this pencil move."

Leesa stared at the pencil. She did not have a clue how to begin. "How?" she asked.

"I don't know," the professor admitted. "Try concentrating on it, to the exclusion of anything else. Will it to move."

Leesa focused her full attention on the pencil, trying to command it to move. Nothing happened. She felt foolish.

"I'm sorry," she said.

"Nonsense. There's nothing at all to be sorry for. I would have been quite surprised if you'd actually done it, but it was worth a try." Dr. Clerval returned the pencil to the drawer. "You said both times this happened you were tired, and that you were angry the night you kicked at the wastebasket. Perhaps fatigue knocks out some of your logical defenses, allowing you to do something that would otherwise seem impossible and foolish. Maybe emotion plays a role as well. Perhaps this will happen again sometime soon and we'll have more to go on."

Leesa glanced at the professor's clock. "I've got to be getting to class," she said, getting up from her chair. "Thank you for all your help."

"I'm here whenever you need me. And please, let me know if any of this happens again."

As Leesa left the professor's office and headed down the hallway, she wasn't sure whether she wanted it to happen again or not.

33. ATTACK!

Sixteen-year-old Nicky Kappes and fifteen-year-old Teri Smith would have preferred to be almost anywhere on this frigid Friday night instead of where they were right now—huddled in down sleeping bags inside a canvas tent in the Berkshire Mountains of western Massachusetts. The campground was officially closed for the winter, but that hadn't stopped their fathers. For the past three years, the divorced dads had brought their kids here for a weekend of what they called "uninterrupted bonding time." That meant no cell phones, no computers, no nothing—not even other people, except for their pesky little brothers, who hardly counted. Their fathers had their cell phones for emergencies, and Nicky's dad always brought his rifle. Why, the girls didn't know, since nothing was in season to hunt, and the Berkshires were not exactly known for harboring dangerous predators. The few bears that still roamed the mountains were all hibernating comfortably in their dens.

It could have been worse, Nicky and Teri knew—they could have been forced to share a tent with their eight-year-old brothers instead of with each other. But thankfully, the boys were in tents with their dads.

The six of them had spent the last couple hours sitting around a blazing campfire, taking turns telling scary stories. Most of the stories were pretty lame, but Teri's father raised some goose bumps with a tale of a crazed psychopath who preyed on campers, dragging them from their tents back to a cave where he slowly ate them alive. By the time he was done, the youngsters found themselves peeking over their shoulders into the darkness.

"When do you think we'll be old enough so we won't have to come out here anymore," Teri asked Nicky. "I hate not being able to text, or talk, or even email my friends."

Both girls had their flashlight turned on beside them, illuminating the inside of their tent while they talked.

"Me, too," Nicky said, reaching one arm out of her sleeping bag and into her backpack. "That's why I snuck this into my pack this year." She pulled out her cell phone.

Teri gasped. "I can't believe you brought that. Your dad will kill you if he finds out."

"I know, right? But no way am I going all weekend without at least texting Adam." Nicky's fingers began pecking at her phone. "Not when we've only been going out two weeks. I don't want him to forget about me."

"I can't believe you're dating a senior. That's way cool."

"I know. And he's sooo cute, too."

"Shhhh…what was that?" Teri asked anxiously. She pushed her shoulders up out of the sleeping bag and propped herself up on one elbow. The frigid night air immediately seeped in through her sweatshirt.

"What was what?" Nicky asked, shoving her phone back into her pack.

They listened in worried silence. Something was moving around outside, like footsteps on the dead leaves, but not quite footsteps—an animal of some kind, maybe? A dark shadow crossed in front of the moonlight that painted the front of their tent, growing larger as it moved nearer. The shadow seemed human in shape, but it was making an eerie, moaning kind of sound, like an animal in distress.

Nicky aimed her flashlight at the zippered front flaps. "Dad, is that you?" she asked quietly, thinking one of their fathers was out there trying to frighten them. The shadow was much too big to be one of the boys. "Mr. Smith?"

Whoever was out there began pawing at the entrance to the tent. Nicky grabbed her pack and scrabbled for her phone.

"Dad? Mr. Kappes?" Teri said urgently "Stop it, please. This isn't funny. You're scaring us. I mean it. Stop!"

The zipper began to slowly rise, moving up unevenly in fits and starts, as if whoever was outside could not quite get a proper grip on it. Terrified, both girls shined their flashlights at the entrance. When the zipper was half way up, a face poked into the opening. The girls screamed.

The face was more horrible than anything either of them had ever seen. One eye socket was empty, surrounded by an ugly red and yellow fibrous scab. The thing's grayish skin seemed to be rotting away, exposing pieces of bone and skull. Its lips were gone as well, revealing hideous yellow teeth. Dark yellow saliva so thick it looked more like mucus dripped from the upper teeth. The awful moaning sound grew louder as the creature continued pulling at the entrance flaps.

Suddenly, the thing disappeared, jerked away from the entrance by Mr. Smith.

"Get out here, girls, now!" he shouted.

Nicky and Teri scrambled from their sleeping bags. Nicky yanked the zipper on the front flap all the way up and the two girls tumbled out into the darkness. A gunshot echoed through the night, first one, then another and another.

More of the hideous creatures lurched across the campsite, each one as frightening and ugly as the one who had tried to get into the girls' tent. Kappes was shooting at them. His bullets thudded into the creatures with a wet, sickening sound, but the gunfire seemed only to slow them, not stop them. The two boys were huddled behind him, and Smith was wrestling with the creature he had pulled away from the tent.

Nicky had seen enough horror movies to know what was happening. It was impossible, but the campsite was being attacked by zombies! Never in a million years would she have believed it.

"You have to shoot them in the head, Dad," she shouted, recalling the movies she had seen. People always shot the creatures in the head. "In the head—it's the only way to stop them."

Kappes shoved the two young boys back toward the girls.

"Take care of your brothers," he ordered. "Get them to the car!"

He raised his aim and shot the nearest zombie in the face. The creature crumbled to the ground. The girls and their brothers remained frozen behind him.

"I said get to the car!" he screamed again. "And if anything comes near you other than one of us, drive out of here. That's an order."

Nicky and Teri grabbed their brothers and scrambled toward the SUV, parked at the edge of a dirt parking lot nearly a hundred yards away. Luckily, there were no zombies in this direction. Gunfire continued to split the night. The boys were screaming. Nicky climbed behind the wheel and tossed her cell to Teri.

"Call 911," she said as she started the engine and turned on the headlights.

The gunfire suddenly stopped. Nicky hoped her dad hadn't run out of bullets, or worse. Two dark figures lumbered toward the car, still too far away to recognize. She prayed it was her father and Mr. Smith.

More than a hundred miles to the south and east, Leesa's eyes shot open.

34. BAD NIGHT

Leesa's heart pounded in her chest and the long-sleeved T-shirt she slept in clung to her skin with sweat. She felt like she had closed her eyes and fallen asleep only minutes ago. The sounds of music and voices from somewhere down the hall told her it couldn't be very late, and a glance at her clock confirmed her thought—the blue numerals read 11:24. She had gone to bed a little before eleven, pretty early for a Friday night, but she had been feeling tired a lot lately, courtesy of all the tossing and turning she seemed to do almost every night now. If she didn't figure out some remedy for her restless sleep soon, she wasn't sure how she was going to make it through the semester without her grades suffering.

Going to bed early tonight had not been any big deal—she hadn't been doing much of anything anyhow. Cali was out with Andy, and Stacie and Caitlin were on dates as well. With Rave still up in New Hampshire, Leesa had been left to fend for herself, so she'd just hung around her room, doing a little studying and watching parts of a sappy romantic comedy movie on television.

She pulled herself out from under the covers and swung her legs over the side of the bed. Wide awake despite the tiredness she felt in her body, she knew she would not be going back to sleep anytime soon—not after this dream.

The cold air immediately attacked her damp shirt and bare legs, and she felt goose bumps begin to pimple her arms and legs. Moving carefully across her dark room, she switched on the desk lamp and retrieved a new, dry shirt from her dresser. She shivered as she pulled the wet shirt off and replaced it with the new one. The cloth was cool against her skin, but a big improvement over the sweat-soaked garment. She grabbed her terrycloth robe from the closet and slipped into her moccasins, then wrapped her arms tightly across her chest and waited for her body to warm itself up.

The warming seemed to take longer than it should have, and Leesa knew why. It wasn't just the cold and the sweat that chilled her—it was the nightmare that had yanked her from her sleep.

Tonight's dream had been the most realistic and most disturbing yet. It was the raw violence of this new vision that was so upsetting. None of her other dreams had contained any violence at all. Even the vampire nightmare, as dangerous and threatening as it felt, had not displayed any actual violence. This one was different. The zombies tonight had not just stumbled around a graveyard or peered plaintively into a window. No, these creatures had attacked the campers, forcing the men to defend themselves and their children. Leesa had heard the bullets penetrating the monsters' rotting bodies with a wet, almost sucking sound. She had seen their heads explode when the shooter adjusted his aim at his daughter's instructions.

And such realism! That was what made the whole thing so much more frightening. When the zombie stuck its gruesome face into the girls' tent, Leesa had almost felt like the thing was trying to get at her. She could still hear the creature's low, gasping moans, and swore she'd been able to smell its foul, decaying stench as well. She shuddered at the memory.

The worst thing about the dream was the way it ended. Leesa could still picture the two black forms lumbering through the darkness toward the car, but she could not make them out in the darkness. Were they the fathers, escaping from the zombies? Or were they two of the creatures, seeking more flesh to feast on after finishing off the men? Leesa hoped and prayed it was the fathers, about to rejoin their children and drive away from that cursed place.

A sudden realization struck her. Not knowing how the dream ended was *not* the worst thing. No, the worst thing by far was that she didn't know whether this horrible vision was also going to come to pass—or if it already had!

35. GOOD MORNING

Leesa paced in small circles around her room, unsure what to do with herself now that she was awake. Her friends probably weren't even home from their dates yet. If they were, their boyfriends would still be with them and wouldn't be too thrilled if she suddenly showed up at their door. Some of the girls on her floor were still up—she could hear music and voices down the hall—but she didn't really feel like hanging out with anyone but her close friends.

She thought about using the time to do some studying, but the way she felt right now she knew she wouldn't retain anything she read. There was always the TV, if she could find something that wasn't scary, stupid or boring—not always the easiest thing this late on a Friday night.

On a whim, she sat down at her desk and switched on her laptop. When it booted up, she went right to the Google search page. She stared at the screen for a few moments, trying to decide exactly how to word her search. This was no ordinary inquiry. She knew her efforts would most likely be futile—it was probably much too soon—but as long as she was up anyhow, she wanted to see if she could find any mention of a story that might match her dream in any way.

She typed in several dozen searches, using different

combinations of words like "zombies," "attack," "camping," "girls" and any other words she could think of. Lots of choices popped up—zombies were an incredibly popular topic—but as she expected, none of them were even remotely close to what she was seeking. For future use, she made a mental note of the search combinations that seemed to produce the most promising results and then turned the computer off.

Now what to do? The dorm had grown quieter during her internet search, though she could still hear faint strains of music from down the hall. Just for something to do, she limped to over to her back window and peered out. She saw two people walking at the far end of the courtyard, but other than that, the quad was empty.

For what seemed like the ten thousandth time since she had met him, she wished Rave was here with her, or that she at least had some way to talk to him. *Oh, Rave, why are you so far away? I need you here with me.* Feeling his strong arms around her would be the best, of course, but just hearing his voice would be pretty good, too. Unfortunately, neither was a possibility. She thought about calling her aunt tomorrow and asking her to bring Max out for a visit, so she could at least send some loving thoughts to Rave. It wouldn't be anywhere near as good as a phone call or text, but it would be better than nothing. She decided if she still felt this way in the morning, she would call her aunt.

She moved away from the window and sat back down on her bed. She was exhausted, but she wasn't sleepy. She never would have imagined someone could be so tired without being sleepy, but she knew it was true. Grabbing the remote from her desk, she switched on the television and lay down on her side. She flipped through a bunch of channels before settling on a Train concert on MTV—not her favorite band, but passable. Watching a music show wouldn't require any real concentration from her tired brain.

Finally, her eyes grew heavy and she drifted off to sleep. Just before she fell asleep, she managed to flick off the TV.

For a change, her sleep was peaceful and untroubled. She dreamed she was with Rave, the two of them lying close together on a soft blanket in a meadow filled with red and gold flowers, his wonderful warmth soaking into every inch of her body. The sky was a bright blue canopy above them, the sun a shining yellow jewel, and the air was filled with the sweet fragrance of the colorful blossoms. She had never felt happier or more relaxed. She wished she could remain there forever.

When she finally felt herself coming awake, she didn't want to open her eyes, did not want to let the illusion vanish. She snuggled her cheek against her electric blanket, pretending it was Rave's warm chest, and let out a contented sigh.

As she came more fully awake, she realized something was not right. The bed beneath her blanket was firm and uneven, not soft and smooth like it should have been. She opened her eyes and found herself looking not at her blanket, but at a brown waffle-knit shirt. Twisting her head upward, she saw Rave smiling down at her. She was cradled in his arms, her head against his chest.

Was this another dream? If so, it was one she definitely did not want to end. She was tempted to close her eyes again to prevent this wonderful vision from slipping away. Instead, she reached up and caressed his smooth, warm cheek.

"Rave?"

His smile widened. "Good morning, sweetheart."

She wrapped her arms around him and hugged him tightly. This was no dream—it was a dream come true! No wonder she had slept so peacefully.

"I can't believe you're here," she said when she finally let go of him. "I'm so happy to see you." She settled her neck into the crook of his arm, so she could look at him and savor his gorgeous features.

"Me, too," Rave said. He gently stroked the side of her head with his fingertips. Every stroke sent waves of pleasure shimmering through her.

"How long have you been here?" she managed to ask.

"A couple of hours. I don't know why, but I had an almost irresistible urge to see you last night. So I grabbed Dral and Bain and headed south. When we got here, I could hear through the door that you were sleeping. It was unlocked, so I let myself in. You were on top of the covers, so I just lay down beside you."

"I think I fell asleep watching TV. I can't believe I didn't wake up when you got here. I must have really been out."

Rave grinned. "We volkaanes can be quite stealthy when we want to."

Leesa returned his grin. "I had the most wonderful dream about us. And now I know why."

She picked her head up and looked over Rave's chest. They were alone in the room.

"Where are your friends?"

"Outside in the hall," Rave said.

"Why didn't you let them in?"

"We can't all be in the same enclosed space," Rave explained. "It's too risky."

"You think we might be in danger here?" she asked, surprised.

"No, not really. But it's best to be careful, especially now."

A yell from outside the door interrupted them.

"Holy crap!" exclaimed a female voice.

Leesa smiled. "Cali," she said to Rave. "And I'm pretty sure I know what's got her so excited."

She got up from the bed and crossed to the door. Behind her, Rave stood up as well.

Leesa pulled the door open and saw Cali standing a few feet back from the doorway, her eyes shifting back and forth between Dral and Bain. She was wearing a camouflage pullover shirt and dark jeans with faded thighs. Leesa was pretty sure part of the "holy crap" came from Cali wishing she was more stylishly dressed for her surprise encounter with the two handsome Mastons. She had a big grin on her face anyhow.

"Hi, Cali," Leesa said. "You want to come in?"

"I'm not sure. The scenery out here is pretty freakin' nice." Cali looked over Leesa's shoulder and saw Rave. She raised her hand in a brief wave. "Since your guy is here," she continued, "I guess that leaves these two hotties for me."

"Ha! Don't you wish." Leesa introduced Cali to Dral and Bain, then stepped aside and let her enter the room.

"Here I was feeling sorry for you last night," Cali said when she was inside, "stuck here by yourself while the rest of us were on dates. I didn't know you were hosting a hunk convention."

Leesa laughed. "Me, neither. Rave came by after I was asleep." She moved beside Rave and put her arm around his back. "It sure was a great way to wake up, though."

"From the way you're dressed, I'm guessing you didn't wake up very long ago, either. I hope you two behaved yourselves." Cali grinned. "Actually, I hope you didn't."

Leesa felt herself blushing. "Rave was a gentleman," she said. "As always."

"Well, I guess no one's perfect," Cali said, laughing.

"Oh, I don't know," Leesa said. "He's pretty perfect for me." Perfect, she thought, except for the tiny problem that kissing him could kill her, and she didn't know if they were ever going to solve that problem.

"Well," Cali said, "I just came by to see what you were up to today, since we all abandoned you last night. But I can see you're in good hands." She turned to Rave. "So, are you Mastons all done with that pilgrimage thing?"

Leesa realized she hadn't had a chance to ask Rave that same question. She felt herself holding her breath while she waited for his response.

"No, not yet," Rave said.

Leesa tried to hold back her disappointment.

"But I couldn't go another hour without seeing Leesa," Rave continued, squeezing Leesa lightly around the waist. He gave an exaggerated shrug. "It was a long walk, but here I am."

Cali laughed and Leesa felt herself grow warm inside.

"Okay, I take it back," Cali said. "Maybe he is perfect."

36. WONDERFUL DAY

Leesa and her perfect guy lay side by side again, this time on a dark gray cotton blanket they had spread out in the middle of Brennan Field, a wide, grassy meadow a short distance from the Weston campus. They lay on their backs, Leesa's head cushioned by Rave's arm, looking up at a bright blue sky striped with wispy cirrus clouds. Dral and Bain sat comfortably on the ground on either side of them, twenty feet from the blanket. No one expected any trouble from vampires on such a bright sunny day, but the two volkaanes maintained their vigilance nonetheless.

Leesa had seldom felt so happy and relaxed. She wanted to try to mimic last night's dream as closely as possible, to extend the wonderful feelings it had brought her, and Rave had readily agreed. Of course, there were no meadows filled with flowers within a thousand miles this time of year, so the thin green and brown grass of Brennan Field had to do. That was okay with her, though. An outing like this would normally have been impossible in the middle of winter. The ground beneath the blanket was frozen solid and the temperature of the air lingered somewhere in the mid-twenties, with a bit of wind adding to the chill. No girl in her right mind would want to lie out on the ground like this on a cold January day—unless the boyfriend she was snuggled up against happened to be a volkaane, of course.

Rave's inner fire provided all the heat she needed, somehow even keeping the blanket underneath her warm. She felt as if it were July, not January. Now if only she could roll over and kiss Rave deeply, she would be in paradise. Still, she would happily settle for this, for now.

"This is wonderful, Rave," she said, turning onto her side so she could look at him. "I'm so happy to see you. You couldn't have picked a better time to come."

"I had such a strong feeling last night that you needed me. Almost like you sent a message through Max, but I knew you hadn't. I have never felt anything quite like it."

Leesa smiled. "Maybe that's what love does. It syncs two people's hearts and minds, linking them."

"Perhaps," Rave mused. "I've never been in love before, so this is new to me. Whatever it was, it was pretty strong last night."

"I've read stories of parents and their children, or identical twins, who said they've known what the other was thinking or feeling despite being miles apart. Maybe this is something like that."

Rave eased his arm out from beneath Leesa's head and propped himself up on his elbow so he could look at her more easily. "Do you remember that first night we walked together?"

Leesa smiled as the memory flooded into her. This time, the warmth flowing through her body had nothing to do with Rave's inner fire.

"How could I forget it? I was walking home from the library. You'd been stalking me and finally decided to say hello."

Rave grinned, remembering how Leesa had teasingly accused him of stalking her. "Not stalking," he reminded her. "Just keeping an eye on you."

"That was a wonderful night. I'll never forget it."

"This may sound a bit strange, but do you remember if you wanted me to hold your hand that night?"

Leesa let her mind drift back to that unusually warm October evening. New England had been enjoying an Indian summer, and she was wearing only a light sweatshirt and shorts. She remembered noticing how silently Rave walked, even over fallen leaves, while she seemed to crunch every dead leaf in sight. She had been afraid he would think she was a clumsy oaf, with her limp and all that noise. And yes, she remembered wishing desperately for him to take her hand.

"Yeah, I did," she said. "Very much."

Rave's brow furrowed in thought. "Hmmmmm...what would you think if I told you that part way through our walk, I suddenly had an almost irresistible urge to hold your hand? The only thing that stopped me was I could not allow you to feel my heat. Not back then, before you knew what I was."

Leesa swung herself up into a sitting position and crossed her legs loosely in front of her. Rave did likewise.

"Are you saying what I think you're saying?" she asked.

"Yeah, I am. I think what happened last night has happened before. It's like sometimes I can hear your thoughts...or feel them, anyway."

"How is that possible?" Leesa asked. If what Rave was saying was true, then she possessed magic—or something close to it. She thought about her strange dreams, and the wastebasket and Red Bull can. Who—or what—was she? And what good were any of these powers if she had no control over them?

"I'm not sure," Rave said. "But maybe this connection explains why I was so drawn to you, right from the start. I have always known it was more than just your beautiful face."

Leesa blushed. She remembered Rave teasing her about being drawn to the vampire blood in her veins, courtesy of the *grafhym* bite her mom had suffered. She had thought there might be some truth to that, but this was something more, much more. What if Rave wasn't really in love with her, but was just pulled to her by some kind of magic she couldn't understand much less control?

Rave must have guessed what she was thinking by the look on her face, because he reached forward and took both her hands in his.

"It doesn't matter what pulled me toward you in the first place," he said. "I'm not in love with you because of any of that. I'm in love with you because of who you are, because of the way *we* are when we're together. Can you understand that?"

Leesa nodded. She could understand it very well, because something similar was going on inside her. She did not love Rave because he was a volkaane, and not because his very touch filled her with magical warmth. She loved him for his gentleness, his thoughtfulness, his sense of humor. His magic was just a bonus. And a danger, too, she reminded herself.

"Yeah, I do get it. It's the same for me. But where does my magic, if that's what it is, come from? My *grafhym* blood? Stefan's bite?"

"Not Stefan's bite," Rave said. "That happened way too late. And not from the *grafhym*, either. The one-fangs have fewer powers than other vampires, not more."

"Then where?"

Neither of them had a ready answer, so they sat in silence for a few moments.

"I wonder...?" Rave said finally.

"What?"

"The guy who claimed to be your father. What if somehow he really is your father? Maybe you got something from him."

Leesa thought about it. She still could not believe the guy could actually be her father, but she didn't have any better answer to offer. She suddenly wished she hadn't dropped her phone that day. For the first time, part of her began to hope he would find her again. She had so many questions, questions maybe he could answer.

"There's some stuff I haven't had the chance to tell you yet," she said.

"More nightmares?" Rave guessed.

"Yeah. And something else, too."

Rave looked surprised. "Start with the dreams."

"I've had two more. In one, there's a vampire with a girl chained behind her. I've had it twice so far, which really bothers me. The girl seems familiar—I think I should know her—but she's never clear enough to recognize. It's very frustrating and disturbing."

"I'm surprised you don't dream about vampires more often," Rave said sympathetically, "with everything that's happened to you. What about the other dream?"

"It's another zombie nightmare, but this one is different from the first two. This dream was much more frightening and seemed so much more real. I swear, I could almost smell one of the zombies. In this one, they actually attack a couple of families camping in the woods. The fathers try to fight them off to save their kids, but I don't know if they survive or not. The dream ended before I could see."

Rave shifted around so he was sitting next to Leesa. He put his arm around her back.

"That does sound scary. I hope you're not going to tell me you saw this one on the news, too."

"No… not yet, anyhow. I just had it last night. I was so upset when I woke up I couldn't get back to sleep. That's when I really started wishing you were here." She rested her head on his shoulder. "Maybe that's what you felt."

"Perhaps," Rave said. "I wonder why it hasn't happened more often, though." He grinned, wanting to lighten the mood. "Maybe most of the time you don't miss me enough."

"Ha! You know that's not true," Leesa said, smiling back at him. "I miss you all the time—like crazy!"

Rave gave her a gentle squeeze. "I know. Me, too."

"Dr. Clerval says this stuff might have to do with strong

emotions combined with fatigue. He thinks somehow being tired breaks down some of my logical defenses and lets out whatever might be inside me."

"That makes sense. Most humans have trouble truly believing in anything magical or supernatural. Look at you. You spent eighteen years being skeptical of your own mother's story. Maybe all your encounters with the supernatural in the last few months have started weakening your psychological defenses. Then when you're tired and feeling strong emotions, whatever is inside you manages to break through."

"Maybe," Leesa agreed. "But that still doesn't tell us what the heck is inside me, if anything."

"No, it doesn't." Rave pursed his lips, thinking. "You said before there was something else, besides the dreams?"

"Yeah, there is." Once again, as Leesa got ready to talk about the incidents Professor Clerval had called telekinesis, she began to feel foolish and unsure. It seemed so impossible, that she was moving objects with only her mind, but was it really any more unlikely than any of the other things she had seen and experienced?

"You're hesitating," Rave said. "Do I detect those 'logical defenses' coming into play again?"

Leesa flashed a sheepish grin. "Yeah, you do," she admitted. She paused for a moment. "I think I may have moved a couple of things with my thoughts," she said finally.

Rave's eyes widened. "Really? Tell me about it."

Leesa told him what had happened with the Red Bull can and the wastebasket.

"I can't really be sure of either," she said when she was done. "I don't know if that stupid can actually moved, or whether or not my foot might have hit the basket. But I'm pretty sure it didn't."

Rave's gaze seemed to drift off into the distance.

"Waziri," he said after a moment, only half aloud.

"What?" Leesa asked, not sure if she had heard the word correctly.

"Waziri," Rave said, more clearly this time. "A clan of wizards. Some of them had the power to move things without touching them. Others were said to get glimpses of the future in their dreams, or to see things happening far away. My people had dealings with them far in the past. There's been no word of them for more than a hundred years, though."

"I've never heard of them. Are you sure they were real?"

Rave smiled. "You had never heard of volkaanes, either. But we exist, and so did they. Like most of those who don't prey on humans, they chose to remain out of sight, the waziri even more so than most. That's why you have few, if any, stories about them, unlike creatures such as vampires, werewolves and zombies."

"Are you saying that I somehow have some of these waziri powers?"

"I don't know. I don't see how you could, but your stories brought the waziri to mind. And I have always known there is more to you than meets the eye."

This was all too much for Leesa. Nervous energy filled her. She needed to move, so she stood up. The cold air immediately assailed her, until Rave stood up close in front of her and his heat enfolded her once more.

"Let's walk for a bit," Leesa said.

Rave took her hand and they began walking across the field, not really heading anywhere, just walking. Dral and Bain fell into step behind them.

Moving helped calm Leesa a little. "I don't understand any of this," she said after a few moments. "How would I get wizard powers, if that's even what they are? It doesn't make any sense."

"I have no idea," Rave said. "It was just a thought. Who knows if there's anything to it."

"Were the waziri good wizards or bad wizards?"

"They were good, for the most part, at least until the end."

"What happened to them?"

"I'm not certain. I was very young then. Some kind of strife within their ranks, I think. Like a miniature civil war. It is said they wiped each other out. Balin would know more."

Leesa was more confused than ever. If the waziri had wiped themselves out, how on earth could she have gotten any of their powers a hundred years later? A sudden thought struck her. She stopped walking and turned to face Rave.

"I always thought wizards were men," she said, "and that women with magic were witches, or sorceresses. Were there any female waziri?"

She could see her question caught Rave off guard. It was obviously something he had not thought about.

"Not that I know of," he said after a few seconds. "They were all men, I think."

"Well, there goes your theory, then. Unless you think that somehow I'm the first female waziri."

"It does seem a bit far-fetched," Rave admitted. "But stranger things have happened."

"Ha! Name one."

Rave smiled. "I fell in love with a human."

Leesa rose up on her toes and kissed his cheek. "Well, there is that."

Rave wrapped his arms around her back and she nuzzled her cheek against his chest. Whenever he held her like this, all her worries seemed to melt away.

Finally, she stepped out of his embrace.

"I guess we're back where we started," she said, a half smile on her face. "We don't really know a darn thing."

"I'll talk to Balin. Perhaps there were female versions of the waziri I am not aware of. Or maybe hearing about the things happening to you will trigger some other idea in him."

"And maybe the guy who claimed to be my father will find

me again. This time, I'll make sure to ask him some questions, to see what he might know."

Leesa took Rave's hand and they began walking back across the field.

"I'm supposed to go back tonight," Rave said when they reached their blanket. "But I don't like leaving you, especially with all that's going on."

"Don't worry. None of this stuff seems really dangerous—not yet, anyhow." Leesa picked up the blanket and began folding it. "If the dreams start getting scarier and begin coming true, I'll tell Max. Besides, you need to go back to New Hampshire so you can talk to Balin about the waziri."

"I know. But that doesn't mean I have to like the idea."

"That's good," Leesa said, smiling. "I don't ever want you to like the idea of leaving me."

37. SEARCHING

Only thirty miles to the south, the man Leesa was hoping would find her again exited a grimy bus at the edge of the Yale University campus. Neither Leesa nor he knew how close to each other they actually were, but until Dominic found her, the distance did not really matter.

With no clues to guide him about what college Leesa might be attending, Dominic had been systematically working his way up the Connecticut coast. Yale was the sixth school he had visited in the last five days. Searches of campuses in Stamford, Fairfield and Bridgeport had all come up empty. The New Haven area contained six different colleges he would have to check, so he expected to be here five or six days, at least. Then he would have to decide whether to head north toward Hartford and its collection of colleges, or to continue east along the coast. He thought he would probably go north, since there were more schools in that direction, but he didn't have to make that decision until he was finished here in New Haven.

The afternoon was cold, and a chill wind blew off nearby Long Island Sound, making the day feel even colder. The first thing Dominic had done when he disembarked from his cross country Amtrak trip in New York City was to purchase a worn black jacket and a pair of black leather gloves at a used clothing store. He wouldn't need them unless it got much colder than even this, but he wanted a jacket and gloves to help him blend in.

As soon as he stepped off the bus, he donned the jacket and gloves. He would search Yale the same way he had checked the other schools—by systematically walking up and down every street or walkway on campus, and climbing the stairways of any building taller than three stories. Despite his past failures in locating Leesa, he was pretty sure he would be able to sense her if he got close enough, and vertical distance counted just as much as ground distance.

Fortunately, all the campuses he had searched so far had been urban schools, with their necessarily more compact grounds. Still, his painstaking searches were time consuming, but he had no other choice—not unless he chose to unleash a magical search. Such a search would draw his enemies to him as surely as if he had lit a beacon fire atop a mountain. No, that had to remain a last resort, to be used only if his present tactics failed and he saw no other options.

There were holes in his methodology, he knew. If Leesa was off campus for any reason while he was seeking her, he would miss her. She could even be on campus, but moving in a direction that would keep her too far from him, despite the thoroughness of his search. Still, this was the best strategy he could come up with, without resorting to magic. He wished college administration offices were not so protective of the names of their students, but several attempts to find out if Leesa was at a college had been met with stiff resistance.

He turned his back to the wind and opened the map of the city he had obtained at a tourist kiosk in the New Haven train depot, protecting the paper from the wind with his body. He folded the map into a smaller square that showed only the Yale area and was able to handle it much more easily. The campus was about seven short blocks wide and slightly more than a dozen much longer blocks long. That was the good news. The bad news was that parts of the campus were built in quadrangles with lots of walkways and plazas, and there were many dorms and other buildings taller than three stories. The stair climbing would not really tire him, but it would take valuable time.

There was nothing he could do about it, though, so he tucked the map into his coat pocket and set off down the first block.

38. WAZIRI

Sunday morning, Leesa slept late. Her sleep had been peaceful and relaxed, the result she guessed, of leftover feelings of contentment from Rave's visit. He had departed late last night, but the chance to spend an entire day with him had been wonderful.

She got out of bed and slipped into a comfortable pair of sweats. Turning on her stereo, she fixed herself a breakfast of bran flakes and raisins and a big mug of hot chocolate. Part way into her meal, Semisonic's "Closing Time" started up on the stereo. She stopped chewing and listened to her favorite line about new beginnings. She had experienced so many new beginnings in the last few months and most of them had been great. There was Rave, of course, but also Cali, and college, and Aunt Janet, Uncle Roger and Max. Some of the beginnings were not so good, like her troublesome dreams, but maybe even they would turn out to be positive eventually. There had been a number of "ends," too. Good ones like the end of her mom's affliction and the end of Bradley's captivity. And most importantly, she had managed to avoid the most horrible end of all—the end of her humanity after she had agreed to become Stefan's consort. She wondered whether this waziri thing she and Rave had discussed would turn out to be a beginning or an end....

Her breakfast finished, she washed the bowl and mug in the sink and then stretched out contentedly on her bed. She wondered if Dr. Clerval would be in his office today, and whether he knew anything about those waziri wizards. She was pretty sure he would have at least heard of them, and he might have some useful knowledge. A glance at the clock told her it was after ten. Might as well give his office a call, she thought.

Not surprisingly for a Sunday morning, she reached his voice mail. She left him a message telling him she had something important to talk to him about and to please call her back, especially if he was going to be in his office later today.

She ended the call and sat back down on the bed, not sure what to do with her morning. Homework was always an option, but Sunday was supposed to be a day of rest, so she wanted to keep that as a last resort. Maybe Cali would have some fun ideas.

Before she could even call Cali, her phone began playing "Rolling in the Deep." She had made the Adele hit her generic ringtone, so she had no idea who was calling. Not Cali, though, and not her mom or Bradley, or Caitlin or Stacie. They all had their own special ringtones. And it's certainly not Rave, she thought, grinning.

She picked up her cell and saw it was Professor Clerval, returning her call already. He said he would be in his office in an hour or so, and would be happy to see her anytime after. Leesa thanked him and said she would be there.

Yesterday's sunny sky had transformed overnight into a gray, leaden one. The air was still cold, without even the meager benefit the winter sun had provided yesterday. Leesa didn't have Rave to keep her warm, either. So she bundled up in her parka, gloves and ski hat, and even wrapped a dark blue woolen scarf around her neck before stepping out into the cold.

Even so, the frigid air stung her cheeks and her breath steamed out in front of her. Luckily, Dr. Clerval's office was little more than a ten minute walk, so she tugged her scarf up over her chin and mouth and headed across campus.

She wondered if a storm might be on the way. The winter had been unusually dry—the meager dusting they had enjoyed on Christmas Eve had been the only snow so far. The benign winter surprised Leesa, especially after an early winter ice storm paralyzed the state way back in November. She had expected that massive storm to be a harbinger of lots more ice and snow to come, but she had been disappointed. Some real snow would be fun—she hadn't played in the snow since she was seven years old and living in New Jersey.

She saw very few fellow students as she walked, not surprising for such an uninviting Sunday morning. Winter might be fun when there was snow to play in, but cold and windy provided little joy to most. A small pond on the other side of campus had been frozen for awhile, and Leesa guessed there would be some kids ice-skating there, but the section where she was walking was mostly deserted.

Inside the professor's building, the air was warm and toasty. Leesa quickly unwrapped her scarf and took off her gloves and hat as she headed up the stairwell. By the time she reached the third floor, she had pulled off her parka as well.

Dr. Clerval's door was open, so she knocked lightly and walked in. As usual, the air smelled of fruity pipe tobacco—cherry, she thought. The professor was sitting at his roll top desk, a book open on the desk in front of him, his wooden pipe hanging from his lips. He twisted around at Leesa's knock and smiled.

"Hello, Leesa," he said, placing the pipe into the brass ashtray on the corner of his desk. "It's always good to see you."

"Hi, Professor. Thanks for letting me come by, especially on a Sunday."

"Nonsense," Dr. Clerval said, smiling again. "I'm always happy to see you. You bring me the most interesting questions."

"Ha! That's for sure, huh?" Leesa said, returning his smile.

She took her usual place on his old cushioned wooden chair. "I hope that stops one of these days soon, though."

Dr. Clerval chuckled. "I don't blame you," he said. "So, what do you have for me this time? Another dream? More objects moving about? Or are we perhaps back to vampires again?"

Leesa wasn't sure how to reply. "I did have another dream—more zombies and much scarier this time. But that's not why I'm here. At least not directly."

Professor Clerval leaned back on his chair and clasped his hands on his lap. His posture was one of relaxed ease, but his eyes sparkled with keen interest.

"Go on," he said.

"Have you ever heard of some wizards called the waziri?"

Dr. Clerval raised his eyebrows. "I have, yes. But I'm surprised you have." He smiled. "You never cease to amaze me, Leesa."

"Yeah, me, too," Leesa said wryly.

"May I ask where you heard of the waziri? They were always very secretive. Very few people know that name, especially nowadays."

Leesa hesitated. She should have known he would ask her that, but she hadn't thought it through. He knew so much about her and her family, but he didn't know Rave was a volkaane. That secret was not hers to share.

"I'm sorry, Professor, but I can't tell you that. It would mean betraying a very important trust."

Dr. Clerval studied her from under his thick white eyebrows. With all she had already shared with him, he was clearly a bit surprised by her response. Leesa hoped she hadn't offended him.

"I'll respect that," Dr. Clerval said after a moment. "What do you wish to know about the waziri?"

Leesa leaned forward. "Anything you can tell me. They were wizards of some kind, right?"

"Wizards, sorcerers, magicians… call them what you will.

213

But yes, they were said to possess magical powers."

"What kind of powers?"

Leesa watched the professor's face as some of the pieces clicked into place.

"I see where this is going," he said. "Precognition and telekinesis. Those were said to be among their powers." He stared hard at Leesa. "The very same powers you and I just happened to be discussing just last week."

"Yeah," Leesa admitted. "That's how this came up."

"Tales of the waziri are most common from Eastern Europe. They were a small, very reclusive clan. It's said they used their powers for good, against the forces of darkness, outside the view of humanity for the most part. The tales seem to have died out more than a hundred years ago."

Leesa listened closely. So far, all this fit with what Rave had told her. The part about the waziri acting as a check against the forces of darkness was new, though, and very welcome.

"My friend said they disappeared after some kind of civil war," she said. "Do you know anything about that?"

"That's one of the stories—that some of them began to turn to the dark side." Dr. Clerval smiled. "I don't mean to sound like something from Star Wars. I'd like to meet this friend of yours some day. He or she seems to know a lot about a subject most people have never even heard of."

"Maybe you will," Leesa said. She looked forward to a day when everyone close to her knew about Rave's true nature. She didn't know if that day would ever come, however.

"Are you thinking the things that have been happening to you—the dreams and moving objects—might have something to do with the waziri?" Dr. Clerval asked.

Leesa stood up. She felt like pacing, but there was very little space to walk in the professor's cramped office.

"I don't know," she said. "It was something that came up, so I thought I might as well try to learn what I could about them."

"Well, apart from the question of how you suddenly acquired magical powers from a group that seems to have died out over a hundred years ago, there's another problem. Every tale I've ever read or heard about them said the waziri were all men. I've never seen any mention of female waziri."

Leesa nodded. "That's what my friend said, too."

She sat back down. "There's one other thing. I don't know if it's related to any of this or not."

She told Dr. Clerval about the call from the man claiming to be her father.

"I haven't heard from him since I broke my phone," she said at the end of her story. "At first, I was glad. I was hoping he'd never find me again. But now I'm wishing he would. Maybe he has some answers for me."

"It sounds like a long shot, but you never know."

"Yeah, I know it's not much. But if nothing else, if he calls again, maybe I'll be able to solve one mystery, at least."

"I'm sorry I'm not able to be more help. I'll do some research on the waziri and see if I can find anything more. I'm afraid there's not a lot of information out there about them, though. Like I said, they were pretty reclusive."

"Thank you, Professor. Every little bit helps, I guess."

Dr. Clerval picked up a pencil and placed it in the center of his desktop.

"As long as you're here, do you want to try one more time to move it?"

Leesa shrugged. "Sure. Why not?"

She closed her eyes and tried to picture the pencil rolling slowly across the desk. When she opened her eyes, the pencil was right where it started. Not that she had expected anything different—but a tiny part of her had hoped there might be.

"Never hurts to try," Dr. Clerval said, smiling.

"I guess not," Leesa replied, wondering if she would ever be able to do anything more than try.

39. BAD NEWS

Leesa sat on her bed, her back propped comfortably on a pillow against the wall, watching the news. Since her latest dream, she checked the news every evening, either the six o'clock broadcast or the late night one, looking for any story that might in some way match the nightmare. Sometimes she watched both broadcasts. The zombie attack on the two camping families had seemed even more realistic than her first two dreams. Since those two had apparently shown real events, she was afraid this one might, too.

Two, then three, and now four days passed without any story. She hoped the absence of any news meant her nightmare was just that—a nightmare—and not some kind of special dream like the others. There was another possibility, though one she prayed was not the case. The lack of any story might just mean the kids and their fathers had not survived the horrible attack. With no witnesses, there would be no one to recount the tale.

Still, even if everyone had been killed, six missing people should have been newsworthy. Of course, there was nothing in her dream to tell her how long the families had planned to camp—it was possible no one had even missed them yet. There was also nothing to indicate where it had taken place. If the attack occurred in a far away state, six missing people would probably not make the local news here in Connecticut, and might not make any national broadcasts, either.

She was lost in her thoughts and only half paying attention when the words "missing families" suddenly registered in her ears. She grabbed the remote and quickly turned up the volume.

The reporter, a pretty woman with black hair who looked very cold, stood a few yards away from a dark red SUV. The car was parked at the edge of a dirt parking lot adjacent to some barren woods. Yellow police tape had been strung around the car, keeping the reporter and a small knot of onlookers away. A longer barrier of tape snaked through the trees, marking off a large section of woods. Leesa tried to recall the color of the SUV from her dream, but she had been much more focused on the two dark forms stumbling toward the vehicle than on the actual car itself.

The woman was in the middle of her story. Leesa leaned closer to the television.

"Police report that there were signs of a struggle in both the car and at the campsite, but are not revealing what those signs are, other than to say no blood has been found in either place."

Leesa's heart lightened at the no blood comment, but what she heard next did little to keep her mood up.

"Lead Detective Tannis Conner has confirmed that no bodies have been found," the reporter continued, "but that only heightens the mystery. Where did two capable adult men and their four children vanish to, leaving their car, tents and equipment behind? They were expected home Sunday night and have now been missing for four days."

The woman tucked a stray lock of raven hair behind her ear.

"This is Teresa McMillan, reporting from the Berkshires."

The picture switched to two female anchors, who made sympathetic comments on the story and then segued to a commercial.

Leesa stared numbly at television for several minutes before finally switching it off. She got up and began pacing around the room.

Her worst fears had come true. Not only had her dream apparently come to pass, but the shadowy figures heading for the SUV could not have been the two fathers—which meant they were zombies instead. For some reason, the kids hadn't escaped either, despite the father's admonishment to drive away at the first sign of danger. Leesa imagined the two girls hoping against hope it was their dads approaching out of the darkness, and when they finally realized what was coming toward them instead, they had been too paralyzed with fear to drive away. She wondered what happened to the four kids, but quickly chased that thought from her head. She was better off not knowing.

Once again, she cursed this stupid power that continued to torment her with images she did not understand and had no power to stop. She sat back down on the bed and drew her feet up in front of her, hugging her knees to her chest. What good was it to see such horrid events but not be able to do anything about them? The old refrain "ignorance is bliss" had never sounded so wise to her. If those waziri wizards had been burdened with powers anything like this, she thought, they had probably wiped themselves out simply to put an end to their frustration.

She did not know how much more of this she could take.

40. EDWINA'S REVENGE

Barely a week after receiving her warning from Stefan, Edwina slipped out of the vampire caverns into the gray morning light. Thick clouds blanketed the sky from horizon to horizon, bringing a smile to her lips. The sun's absence would make things that much easier and more comfortable for her today. Only the barest hint of a breeze brushed her cheeks, lending hope the clouds would remain in place the entire day.

Heading north, she glided silently through the woods along the river's edge, in no real hurry. Her pace betrayed no indication of her eagerness, lest one of her fellows happen to see her leave. Nor would her speed draw attention from any sharp-eyed humans who might be watching from across the river. With the leafless trees providing little cover, a dark blur racing through them at vampire speed would raise eyebrows—and questions. Questions the coven would not be too happy about.

When she felt she was far enough from the vampire lair, she pulled a cell phone from the pocket of her black hoodie. The phone belonged to the guy she had killed in Hartford a week ago—he certainly had no more use for it. Keeping the cell for herself broke another of the coven's rules, but she didn't care. Most of her brethren would not know how to work a phone even if it was allowed, but she used one now and then during her interactions with the humans. Today, she definitely needed one for her plan. She had turned it off and removed the battery, leaving no chance the phone could suddenly go off and reveal her transgression, or that its location could be traced.

Sitting down on the smooth trunk of a fallen tree, she pushed the battery back inside the cell, making several attempts before it slid in properly. She switched the phone on and tapped in a number, waiting anxiously while it rang. If she got no answer she would have to disassemble the cell and hurry back to the caverns, hoping her brief stay outside would not be noticed by Stefan, or if it was, would not count as the one last outing he had allowed her. If her target answered, she would proceed with her plan.

The ringing stopped, replaced by a familiar female voice. Edwina smiled and licked her lips. It was time to put her plan into motion.

Just before noon on Saturday morning, Leesa lay on her bed reading "Catch-22" for her lit class. She was having a little trouble following the book's unusual narrative style, but she was enjoying its absurd, satirical humor. She had just reached the part where the actual "Catch-22" rule is first explained when Pink's "Perfect" suddenly sounded from her cell, startling her. Slipping her bookmark into the book, she wondered what Cali wanted. They already had plans to get together later that afternoon. She hoped Cali wasn't cancelling.

She pushed herself up from the bed and grabbed the phone from her desk.

"Hey, what's up?" she asked.

"Hi, Leesa," said a female voice on the other end that was not Cali. The girl sounded familiar, but Leesa could not identify her voice.

She looked down at her cell, checking the caller screen. Only Cali's phone should have played "Perfect." The screen confirmed the call was from Cali—or from her phone, at least.

"Who is this?" Leesa asked.

"It's Vanina, Leesa."

Now that Vanina had identified herself, Leesa recognized her voice. Vanina had always called Cali in the past, so Leesa had never heard her voice through the phone. She wondered why Vanina would be calling her now—and from Cali's phone.

"What's going on, Vanina? Where's Cali?"

"She's right here," Edwina said. "But she can't come to phone right now."

"I don't understand. Why not?"

"She's in a spot of trouble," Edwina said. "There's no time to explain. We need to you to come here as quickly as you can."

Leesa paced in a small circle around her room. Vanina's call made no sense. *Spot of trouble*? Who talked like that? She had heard the phrase in an old movie or two, but never in real life. And what kind of trouble could they be in? If something dangerous was happening, Vanina had the cell—why didn't she just dial 911? If it was something else, why wasn't she telling Leesa what it was? And what did they expect her to do, anyhow? Was there something she should bring? Someone she should tell?

"I don't get it," she said after a moment. "What do you want me do to?"

"Just get out here to Brennan Field as fast as you can. We're at the far end, by the edge of the woods. Please hurry."

Brennan Field was the grassy field where Leesa and Rave had lain on the blanket a week ago. It wasn't very far. She could make it there in less than fifteen minutes if she hurried. There was no one she could call who could get there any faster.

"I'm on my way," she said. "Call me back if there's anything else you need to tell me."

She hung up and shoved the cell into her pocket. Still puzzled by it all, she grabbed her parka and knit cap and rushed out the door.

Rather than wait for the elevator, she raced down the stairs as quickly as her limp would allow. Outside, the day was cloudy, but not overly cold. She pushed her cap into her pocket and hurried down the sidewalk. While she prided herself on being able to walk as fast and far as almost anyone, her leg prevented her from running at anything faster than an awkward half-walk, half-jog pace. She knew she probably looked ridiculous clomping across campus, but she didn't care. She had to get to Cali and Vanina and find out what was going on.

Brennan Field was empty, except for two figures standing at the far end. When the weather was warmer the field was a popular spot for throwing Frisbees or kicking soccer balls, but it got little use in the dead of winter—unless you happened to have your own portable volkaane heater with you, Leesa thought. She could not imagine what had brought Cali and Vanina out here today.

Cali was leaning against a slender tree, her hands behind her back. Leesa was surprised to see a scarf wrapped over Cali's mouth and chin—it wasn't that cold out. Vanina stood a couple of feet closer, watching Leesa approach. They did not seem to be in any immediate trouble, so Leesa slowed to a walk. As she drew near her friends, Cali began shaking her head vigorously back and forth. Leesa had no idea what that was about. She noticed a black hoodie lying on the ground behind Vanina, who was wearing only a charcoal gray long sleeve shirt and dark blue jeans.

"What's going on?" Leesa asked, trying to catch her breath and talk at the same time. She wondered why Cali was still leaning against the tree.

"Oh, just a little surprise for you," Edwina said, smiling.

Something about Vanina looked different today. Nothing Leesa could put her finger on, but somehow the girl looked less friendly. The word "sinister" popped into her head.

"What do you mean?" Leesa asked. She looked over at Cali, who still had not moved from the tree. "What kind of surprise?"

Edwina crossed to Cali and pulled the scarf from around her

chin. Cali immediately spat a wadded up rag from her mouth.

"I'm so sorry, Leesa," she said. "I didn't know."

"Didn't know what?" Leesa asked as cold fingers of fear began to prick at her.

"Didn't know this," Edwina said. Two curved fangs slowly descended from her mouth.

Leesa's jaw dropped. Her stomach felt hollow. She could not believe this was happening. Suddenly Vanina's strange behavior at the mall when Cali pricked her finger made sense. Vanina had not been disgusted by the blood—far from it. She had turned away to hide her desire for it.

"You're a vampire," Leesa managed to say finally.

"Aren't you the bright one," Edwina said, smirking. Her fangs retracted back into her jaw.

Leesa did not understand why Vanina had gone through this elaborate ruse, befriending them, going to mall, hanging out with them. *Oh, Rave, how I need you now*, she thought. She remembered Rave saying he could sometimes feel her thoughts, but that would do her little good now. Even if he did feel them, he was two hundred miles away.

"What do you want with us?" she asked.

"With you? Not much...not much at all. Just that you suffer, that's all. From Cali I will take more—much more."

Leesa glanced at Cali, who was straining to pull herself away from the tree, but with no success. Leesa could see now why Cali hadn't moved. Her hands were tied to the slender trunk of the tree with thick cords of rope.

"Haven't you figured it out yet?" Edwina asked. "Who I am?"

Leesa turned back to Vanina and stared hard at her face. She looked evil now, yet still beautiful, in some macabre, exotic way. *Exotic*—the word echoed familiarly in Leesa's head. She had heard that word before. People had described Bradley's girlfriend Edwina as exotic. Edwina... Vanina. The two names were too close. It was starting to make sense. Horrible sense.

"You're Edwina," Leesa said bitterly. "You took Bradley."

"Yes, I did. And then he was taken from me—taken from me because of you, Leesa. I miss your brother. His blood was sweet." Edwina grinned, but there was nothing pleasant about her smile now. "Did you know my kind can tell whether someone is a good person or a bad one by the sweetness of their blood? Bradley was one of the good ones—one of the very good ones."

Leesa stepped closer to Edwina. "Then why not take your anger out on me?" she asked. "Why punish Cali? She doesn't have anything to do with this."

Edwina's eyes darkened. "Because I'm forbidden to hurt you. But that doesn't mean I can't make you suffer. And making you suffer will make Stefan suffer."

The pieces began to fit together in Leesa's head. Stefan had taken Bradley from Edwina—his part of his bargain with Leesa. He was probably the one who had forbidden Edwina to harm her, so Edwina was going to take Leesa's best friend instead—and make Leesa watch while she did it. The third dream finally made sense. She knew why the girl in the cavern seemed so familiar and why the rock wall had been replaced by a tree. The girl was Cali, and the dream had foretold this moment. The full horror of Edwina's plan hit Leesa like a punch to the stomach. Edwina was going to make Cali her feeder.

Edwina grinned again. "I can see by the look on your face that you finally understand. Cali will replace your brother. But not here in Connecticut, where your volkaane boyfriend knows how to find our caverns, and where Stefan has the power to release her. No, I'll keep her far from here, in a place where none of you will ever find her."

Edwina's fangs descended slowly from her jaw again, glistening with saliva this time. She moved closer to Cali. "Say good-bye to your friend, Leesa. But do not worry, I'll take very good care of her, I promise."

"No!" Leesa shouted, stretching her hand out in front of her chest. "Get away from her!"

Suddenly, Edwina flew backward, soaring through the air with her arms outstretched until she crashed into a tree twenty feet away with a loud thud. Her face bore a stunned, bewildered look.

Leesa looked from Cali to Edwina in disbelief, unsure what had just happened. One second Edwina was leaning toward Cali's throat and the next she was smashing into a tree. An image of the wastebasket flying across her room rose in Leesa's head. Had she somehow done the same thing to Edwina—make her fly across the field with the power of her mind? It did not seem possible, but she could think of no other explanation.

She rushed over to Cali and began pulling at the ropes that bound her. Before Leesa could even partially untie the knots, an icy hand grasped her wrist.

"I don't know how you did that," Edwina said, her voice cold with anger. "But I am not done with Cali."

She yanked Leesa away as if she weighed next to nothing. Leesa struggled to free herself, but Edwina's grip was unbreakable. She dragged Leesa a few feet from the tree then suddenly kicked out at her good leg. Leesa fell sprawling to the ground.

"Let's see if you can do that again," Edwina said. She bent into a protective crouch, bracing against a possible second onslaught.

Leesa pushed herself up into a sitting position. Despite the pain in her leg, she focused all her thoughts on Edwina, trying to picture her flying back across the field again. But as hard as Leesa tried, nothing happened. She had no control over whatever power was inside her.

"I thought not," Edwina said, her voice dripping with disdain. "Now watch closely, Leesa, while I begin draining your friend of her sweet, hot blood."

Once again, Edwina's fangs dropped down from her upper jaw. Leesa watched helplessly as Edwina opened her mouth and bent toward Cali's neck.

Dominic studied his list of Connecticut colleges as the bus carried him north from Hamden, where he had spent a day searching Quinnipiac College for any sensation of Leesa, toward Hartford. He needed to decide soon whether to go directly to the Hartford area with its half dozen colleges, or to make side trips to two schools a few miles west of the freeway in New Britain and to another in Middletown, ten miles to the east.

If he was going to head to Middletown, he had to decide by the time the bus reached Meriden, just one exit ahead. There was no real reason to decide one way or the other—he would have to choose on instinct.

Suddenly, a brief blast of magic rocked his senses. He whipped his head around to the east—toward Middletown. Could it have been Leesa? The magic seemed far too powerful. How could she have produced such magic without training? Yet the magic felt familiar, though slightly twisted somehow. If it was not Leesa—and he didn't see how it could be—then it could only have been his enemies. He wondered if it might be some kind of trap. That didn't make sense, though. His foes would have no way of knowing he was searching for Leesa or for magic. They should not have any idea where he was, either. There was no reason for them to expect such a trick to accomplish anything—unless he had slipped up somewhere and given himself away.

The bus was nearing the Meriden exit. He had to decide quickly. In the end, the decision was an easy one. This was the first real inkling he'd had that he might be close to finding Leesa. He would be careful, but he had to chance it, trap or no trap.

Grabbing his jacket, he got up from his seat and headed for the front of the bus. He could be in Middletown in less than an hour.

41. VAMPIRE KISS

Leesa watched in horror as Edwina's fangs inched inexorably toward Cali's neck. She knew Edwina was moving so slowly to torment her but was helpless to do anything about it.

Suddenly, out of nowhere, a dark blur flashed across the grass and smashed into Edwina, knocking her away from Cali. Leesa watched in startled amazement as the two figures tumbled across the ground, growling and yelping like two wild animals going at each other. She hoped the pain-filled moans were all coming from Edwina. The battle turned out to be no contest. In less than a minute a black clad figure stood up over Edwina's motionless form, blood dripping from his mouth.

"Stefan!" Leesa cried. Her eyes flew back and forth from Stefan to Edwina. A grisly wound gaped from the right side of Edwina's neck. No blood flowed from the wound though, which made the ragged gash look even more ghastly. Leesa wondered about the blood on Stefan's lips.

Stefan wiped his mouth with his sleeve. "Hello, Leesa," he said. Amazingly, he didn't seem to be breathing hard.

Leesa scrambled to her feet and threw her arms around him. Even through her parka, she could feel the chill from his body. She didn't care. Stefan had saved Cali from a horrible fate. She didn't know how and she didn't know why, but Stefan had sided against one of his own kind for her.

"Thank you, Stefan," she said. "Thank you."

Stefan returned Leesa's hug for a brief moment, then eased back out of her embrace.

"What happened just before I got here?" he asked. "Something sent Edwina sprawling, but I saw nothing. What was it?"

"I don't know," Leesa said. She wasn't lying—she really did not know—but she wasn't telling the complete truth, either. She saw no need to reveal to Stefan that she might have done it with a power she did not understand and could not control.

Stefan's black eyes, so like bottomless pools now, bored into hers, as if he was looking for something deep inside her soul. Leesa didn't know if he found what he was looking for, but after a moment, his eyes became black mirrors once again, completely unreadable.

"Edwina disobeyed my direct order," he said, answering Leesa's unasked question of why he had done what he did. "Such behavior must be punished."

Leesa looked down at Edwina's prostrate form. "Is she dead?"

Stefan's lips curved into a wry smile. "My kind are all dead," he said. "And yet we are not, of course. But no, she is not dead, not in the way you mean. But she will never bother you—or any other human—again. I promise you that."

"Hey," Cali called from behind them. "What does a girl have to do to get a little help around here?" Her voice was remarkably lighthearted for someone who had just gone through what she had endured.

Leesa laughed, the tension finally draining out of her. Stefan moved to Cali's side and ripped apart the ropes holding her as if they were strands of thread. Cali pulled the loose pieces from her arms and began rubbing her wrists, which were red and chafed from her efforts to free herself.

"Thank you, Stefan," she said. "We haven't been properly

introduced. I'm Cali." She held out her hand.

Stefan looked at Leesa, a bemused smile on his lips. Leesa shook her head in amused resignation and shrugged. Cali was just being Cali.

Stefan took Cali's extended hand and kissed it lightly.

"Wow," Cali said. "Kissed by a vampire!"

"Ha! Down, girl," Leesa said. "You know you can never tell anyone about this."

Cali sighed. "Yeah, don't worry, I won't. But *I* know it happened, and that's what counts."

Leesa turned back to Stefan. "How did you know what was happening?" she asked. "And manage to get here just in time?"

"Edwina acted very suspiciously the last time she returned from the outside," Stefan replied. "She has been angry with me for taking your brother, and I guessed that she would be blaming you as well. I gave her specific orders to stay away from you, but I did not trust her. So when she left our caverns this time, I followed her trail."

Leesa had never been quite sure how she felt about Stefan. He had asked a terrible price to rescue her brother, but when he had been unable to complete her transformation, he still kept his part of the bargain. She was a little bit afraid of him, but she admired him for his honor—honor as he saw it, anyhow. And she could not deny the sensual pull she felt toward him on some deep, primitive level.

Now he had saved Cali, so Leesa owed him double. Still, she wouldn't mind if she never saw him again, but she was awfully glad he had been here today.

"I'm sure glad you followed her," she said. "Thank you again."

"I only did what was necessary," Stefan said. "Besides, I have not completely given up."

Not completely given up? Leesa wasn't sure what he meant by that, but the words struck a distinctly uncomfortable chord in her head.

Once again, Stefan's eyes bored into hers. Leesa felt the pull, but this time she forced her eyes away from his. After a moment, the feeling vanished. She thought Stefan looked as if he wanted to say more, but instead he bent and lifted Edwina's limp body effortlessly over his shoulder.

"Be safe, Leesa," he said.

Stefan turned and loped off into the trees without another word. Leesa watched him disappear into the shadows.

"Wow," Cali said. "How cool was that?"

Leesa stared at her friend in amazement and disbelief.

"Cool? I was scared out of my mind."

"Well, me too," Cali said. "But then Stefan ripped into that bitch Edwina and everything was fine." She looked down at the back of her hand. "And I got my hand kissed by a vampire," she added, grinning. "Have I told you lately that you are the coolest best friend ever?"

Leesa shook her head, but couldn't help smiling. "What am I going to do with you?" she said.

42. TOO LATE

One hour after Leesa and Cali left Brennan Field, Dominic strode quickly across the empty meadow. After so many painstaking and frustrating months, he hoped he might at last be drawing near to finding Leesa. The magic was long gone, he knew—it had been at least an hour since its vibrations had jarred his senses on the bus—but it had been so powerful he could still sense where it had occurred, across the field near the edge of the woods. The picturesque Weston college campus spread out behind him, but before he began his search for Leesa there, he wanted to examine the place where the magic had originated to see what he might learn.

He slowed his pace as he neared the trees, his senses guiding him unerringly to a spot a few feet from the boundary of the field. This was the place. He stood perfectly still and slowed his breathing until his chest barely moved, focusing his concentration on the tiny vestiges of magic that remained. That he could still sense the vibrations at all was more evidence of how strong the magic had been. What kind of magic had been performed here, he could not tell. The remnants of the weaves were familiar, yet they were not. In some tiny details, they were different from anything in his long experience. In one way, he knew this was a good thing. Had the magic been identical to his, it would have drawn the attention of the same enemies who for so long had been seeking him. He wondered if perhaps they might have sensed it anyway. They had no reason to be anywhere near here—he hoped the distance combined with the differences in the weaves would be enough to hide the magic from his foes.

When he was certain he could learn no more from the remnants of the magic, he let his focus widen—and was surprised to detect traces of vampire. What had happened here, he wondered? A dozen questions flashed through his brain. Had Leesa somehow become involved with vampires? If so, had she survived the encounter? There was no way to know. He did not even know if the magic had anything to do with her or was something else entirely.

He walked slowly, in an ever-widening circle, seeking answers. He found a spot where the brown grass was crushed and twisted, telling him there had been a struggle here. Kneeling down, he examined the grass and the ground more carefully. He sensed a slightly stronger vampire presence in this spot—more than one of the creatures had been here, he decided. The whole thing was becoming more mystifying by the minute. Had a pair of vampires ganged up on someone or something? He had no way to tell.

He continued on with his search. Happily, he detected no sensation of death. Whatever had happened here, no one had died. He breathed a sigh of relief—if Leesa had been involved in this, she was still alive, at least. He prayed she had not been taken by the vampires; that would be just as bad.

Unfortunately, he still could not detect any direct sense of Leesa. He did not know for sure if she had been here, and if she had, he had no way to follow her trail.

He turned and headed back to begin his search of the Weston campus. If Leesa was indeed here, that was where he would most likely find her.

43. SECRETS REVEALED

Rave showed up at Leesa's door a few hours later.

Leesa and Cali were inside, still talking about their amazing afternoon adventure. Leesa was sitting on the bed, but Cali remained amped up by the excitement and spent most of her time walking about the room and gesturing with her hands. She did most of the talking, of course, describing over and over again what had happened before Leesa arrived, as well as reliving everything that occurred after. Her favorite part was when Edwina went flying through the air like she had been grabbed by an invisible hand, but Stefan kissing her hand was a close second. She also peppered Leesa with crazy questions about Stefan and vampires in general, most of which Leesa answered with "how the hell would I know that?"

"What do you think will happen to Edwina?" Cali asked.

Before Leesa could reply once more that she didn't know, Rave strode in through the open door, his handsome face etched with concern.

"Rave!" Leesa shouted. She leapt up off the bed and flew into his arms.

"Are you all right?" Rave asked, hugging her tightly.

Leesa lifted her head from his chest and looked up into his gorgeous eyes.

"I'm fine. And now that you're here, I'm way better than

fine."

"We had a pretty exciting time a few hours ago," Cali said, her tone hinting at mysterious secrets. "But everything's cool now. I'm not sure how much I'm allowed to tell you, though."

Leesa stepped back from Rave's embrace but kept her hands linked around his arm. She would tell Rave everything, of course, but wasn't sure how much to say with Cali there.

Rave spoke instead. "What happened, Leesa? I felt your need and came as quickly as I could." He laid one hand atop Leesa's hands where they circled his forearm. "I was afraid I was going be too late."

Cali looked back and forth from Leesa to Rave, her confusion evident.

"How did you know we were in trouble?" she asked.

Rave thought for a moment, deciding what to say.

"Can we trust her to keep a secret?" he asked Leesa.

"Yeah, I think so."

"I *know* so," Cali said adamantly. "When I put something in the lockbox, it stays there." She mimed putting a key into a lock and turning it, then theatrically dropping the key down her shirt between her breasts. "So c'mon, what gives?"

"Go ahead," Rave said to Leesa. "She's your best friend. Tell her everything."

Leesa looked at Rave for a moment to make certain he meant what he had just said. He nodded for her to go ahead.

"You can't tell anyone," Leesa said to Cali. "I mean it. Even my mom and Bradley don't know what I'm about to tell you."

Cali made a crossing motion with her finger in front of her heart. "I promise."

"Rave's kinda different," Leesa said.

Cali looked incredulous. "That's it? That's your big secret? Please, tell me something I don't already know. He's a Maston— of course he's freakin' different. They're all pretty strange." She looked at Rave and smiled sweetly. "No offense, Rave."

Rave smiled back. "None taken."

"No," Leesa said. "Much more different than you can imagine. I think maybe you should sit down."

Cali looked more confused than ever, but she plopped herself down on the edge of the bed.

"Rave's a volkaane," Leesa said.

"A volk *what*?"

"Volkanne," Leesa said. "Show her, Rave."

Rave held out his right hand, palm up. "Touch it," he said to Cali.

Cali looked at Leesa and then back to Rave. She reached out and placed her hand in his palm.

"Wow! It's so warm!"

"Wait," Rave told her. He sent more heat into his hand.

Cali's eyes widened. Finally, she lifted her hand away and brought it close to her face, staring at it in disbelief of what she had just felt.

"What does that mean?" she asked after a moment. "How hot can you make it?"

Rave looked at Leesa.

"Go ahead," she said.

Rave let his heat grow, until the familiar tiny blue flames flickered from his fingertips.

"Holy crap!" Cali exclaimed, remembering tales about the Mastons and strange blue fires. "That blue fire stuff is real!"

Rave smiled and let the flames disappear. "Yes, it is," he said. "One of the only stories people tell about us that is actually true."

"What do you do with it?" Cali asked. "It looks pretty and it's way cool and all, but I'm guessing it's not just for show?"

"He kills vampires with it," Leesa said matter-of-factly.

Cali's eyes looked like they were going to pop out of her head. She swung her head back and forth between Leesa and Rave like it was on a swivel.

"You're kidding, right?" she asked Leesa. She turned to Rave. "She is kidding, right?"

"My people are vampire hunters," Rave said. "We use our fire to slay them."

Cali sat silently for a long moment and then broke out into a wide grin.

"Leesa, you definitely are the coolest friend *ever*. First Stefan, and now this. Wow!"

"Stefan?" Rave asked, looking at Leesa. His eyes narrowed. "What's this about Stefan?"

Leesa sensed Rave's barely restrained anger. She took his hand.

"Stefan saved us today. At least, he saved Cali."

"And he kissed my hand, too." Cali held her hand out, displaying it. "Right here." She looked at Leesa. "I'm allowed to tell Rave, right?"

Leesa smiled. "Yes, you can tell him anything." She turned to Rave and began describing the afternoon's events.

"When Edwina first showed us she was a vampire, I desperately wished you were here," she said. "That must be when you sensed my need for you. Edwina took her time with us, threatening and tormenting me. When she finally got ready to bite Cali, I somehow knocked Edwina back...with my thoughts, I think."

Rave seemed to take her statement in stride. "Like the wastebasket," he said.

"Yeah, like the wastebasket."

"Wait a minute," Cali said. "That was *you* who did that to Edwina?"

"Yeah, I think so." Leesa briefly explained about the Red Bull can and the wastebasket.

"Wow," Cali said, her voice filled with amazement. "This just keeps getting cooler and cooler." She grinned. "You're a superhero, too."

"Ha! I wish. I don't have any control over it. I wasn't even sure if those other things really happened, or if I just imagined them." Leesa turned to Rave. "When Edwina went after Cali the second time, I couldn't do anything to stop her, no matter how hard I tried. Then Stefan showed up out of nowhere. He took care of Edwina."

"It was amazing," Cali said. "I never saw anyone move so fast. He ripped half her throat out before I could even blink."

"You haven't seen Rave move yet," Leesa said proudly. "He's faster."

"Why did Stefan turn against one of his own?" Rave asked. Ever since his first encounter with Stefan, which Leesa had bravely interrupted and stopped, Rave had thought he and Stefan were destined to test one another's power again one day. His anger over Stefan's attempt to turn Leesa into a vampire had solidified the feeling. Now, he didn't know. Perhaps fate had something else in store for them. He didn't like the idea of being indebted to a vampire, but if Stefan had stopped Edwina, then Rave owed him a great deal.

"I don't really know why he did it," Leesa admitted. "I know he felt something special for me when he wanted to make me his consort, but I thought that ended when he found out he couldn't turn me. He said he had warned Edwina to stay away from me, and when she didn't, she had to be punished for disobeying him. I don't know if it was more about me or about her disobedience."

"I have no idea what you two are talking about now," Cali said, "but I'm glad Stefan showed up when he did."

"Me, too," Leesa said. She turned to Rave. "How long can you stay this time?" she asked.

Rave smiled. "How about forever?"

Leesa's heart jumped. Had she just heard what she thought she'd heard? She looked up into Rave's smiling eyes. "Forever" had a very nice ring to it.

"Really?" she managed to say finally. "You don't have to go

back to New Hampshire?"

"I told Balin I would not be coming back, that I needed to stay closer to you." Rave's smile widened into a big grin. "I don't know how one girl can keep getting into so much trouble, but somehow you manage to do it. Balin said he would take care of any problem there might be with the Council. My people will all be returning in a few days, anyhow. *Destiratu* remains a problem, but the effects of the solstice seem to be ended."

This was the best news Leesa had heard in a long time. She wrapped her arm around Rave and snuggled against him. Before she could say anything, she felt his body suddenly stiffen. He shoved her behind him and spun toward the door. His fingers began to glow blue, but he kept his hands hidden behind his back.

Leesa peeked out from behind him and saw a man standing in the doorway.

44. A MYSTERIOUS GUEST

The man in the doorway did not appear threatening, but the blue flames flickering from Rave's fingertips told Leesa he thought differently. The stranger was tall and slender, dressed in a worn black jacket and plain khaki pants. He looked to Leesa like he was in his late forties or early fifties, but it was difficult to tell for sure. His tan face was only lightly lined, but his dark hair was speckled with more than a little gray and his neatly trimmed goatee showed even more of the salty color than his hair. His pale blue eyes were so light in color they looked almost gray as well.

The man held his hands up in front of his chest in a gesture of peace.

"Douse your fire, volkaane," he said, making no move to enter. "I am no threat to any of you, I promise."

Leesa was dumbfounded. Rave's hands were still hidden behind his back—how had the guy known Rave was a volkaane? And how many people even knew about volkaanes in the first place? The flames slowly disappeared from Rave's fingertips, but his fingers still glowed blue.

"What is it, Rave? What's going on?"

"I'm not sure. There is more to him than meets the eye. Like me, he is something more than human."

Leesa knew volkaanes could sense the presence of

vampires—did that mean the man standing in her doorway was a vampire? No, he couldn't be. Rave would be reacting much more protectively if he was, she knew that for certain. Apparently, Rave's special senses were not just limited to vampires. That meant this guy was something else—something Rave was not familiar with. The thought was very troubling.

"My name is Dominic," the man said. His eyes went from Leesa to Cali before fixing on Leesa. "And you would be Leesa?"

Leesa nodded. "How do you know who I am?" she asked.

"The answer to that is more complicated than you can know, and will take some time to explain," Dominic said. "May I come in?"

Leesa looked to Rave. The blue was gone from his fingers now, but she could tell he was still alert and ready to react. Standing this close to him, she could feel that his heat was still raised above its normal level, too. Yes, he was definitely ready.

"First, tell me who—and what—you are," Rave said to Dominic.

Dominic leaned against the doorframe and smiled. He looked to Leesa like a man who was finally allowing himself a bit of rest at the end of a long task.

"I am truly glad to find Leesa has a volkaane to look after her," he said. "I never expected such good fortune. I will tell you everything you wish to know, but what I have to say is for Leesa's and your ears only."

Cali got up from the bed. "I can take a hint," she said. She gave Leesa a quick hug and then grinned. "Besides, if I hear any more secrets today, my poor little head will burst." She moved toward the door, then paused. "Just make sure to let me know everything is okay when this is finished, okay?"

"For sure," Leesa said.

Dominic stepped back from the doorway to let Cali by. Leesa was pleased to see him move back, rather than forward into the room. He was clearly waiting for permission to come in.

Somehow, she found that comforting—until she remembered that many stories claimed vampires could not enter a room unless they were invited in. The thought chilled her. Was something similar going on here?

When Cali was gone, Dominic moved back to the doorway. "You asked who I was," he said to Rave. "The answer to that is quite complicated, and will take some time to explain. Let me begin by telling you that I am the man who called Leesa a month or so ago."

Leesa's mouth fell open. She didn't know what she had expected, but it wasn't this. Out of nowhere, the man who claimed to be her father was standing in her doorway. Some of her questions, it seemed, were finally about to be answered. She felt both relieved and anxious.

"You said you were my father. How is that possible?"

"That was probably a poor choice of words," Dominic said, "although it many ways it is true. I think it would be better if you sat down, and if you invited me in."

Leesa hesitated. "Could you come in even if we didn't invite you?" she asked finally.

The corners of Dominic's mouth twitched into a tiny grin, as if he knew exactly what Leesa was thinking.

"Yes, I could," he replied. "And believe me, should I choose to enter, neither of you could not stop me. But I will not do so without your permission. I am a friend—you will see that before long."

Leesa looked to Rave, who nodded.

"Come in, then," she said.

Dominic moved into the room and quietly shut the door behind him. Rave kept himself partially between Leesa and Dominic, still unsure where this was going. He could sense power in the man, but it seemed veiled, at least to his volkaane senses.

"Please, sit," Dominic said to Leesa.

Leesa took two steps backward and sat down on the edge of

her bed. Rave moved alongside her, but remained standing, still protective. She took his hand and squeezed it gently.

"You're limping," Dominic said to Leesa, his voice filled with concern. "Are you hurt?"

Leesa was surprised Dominic had noticed her limp in the two short steps she had taken to get to the bed.

"No, I'm fine. It's something I was born with. It's no big deal."

Dominic was silent for a moment. Leesa could not know it, but he was wondering if her limp was the result of his actions eighteen years ago.

He reached for the desk chair. "May I?"

"Sure. Go ahead," Leesa said.

Dominic lifted the chair and deposited it in the middle of the room. He turned it to face Leesa, took off his coat, and sat down.

"Before I begin, I must ask you a question. Were you responsible for the magic I sensed earlier today?"

The question took Leesa by complete surprise. How had he known about that?

"I think so," she said after a moment. "But I'm not really sure."

Dominic smiled. She saw warmth in his pale eyes.

"I am not surprised by that," he said. "I imagine you have experienced more than a few things in these last months that you have not been able to fully understand."

Again, his words surprised Leesa. Did he know about her dreams, and about her apparent ability to move things with her thoughts? How was that possible?

"Yeah, a couple," she admitted. She was not ready to reveal anything specific yet.

"May I ask what you moved this afternoon?" Dominic asked. "You used quite a bit of power. Much more than I thought you would be able to control at this point."

So much for keeping her ability to move things secret, Leesa thought. She decided she might as well tell him.

"I don't really have any control over it," she said. "It just sort of comes out sometimes. Today, I needed it. I wasn't even trying to do it. When I tried to do it again, I couldn't."

"I'm not surprised. As I said, it was much more powerful than anything I would have expected from you. So tell me, what did you move—to require so much power?"

"A vampire," Leesa said.

Dominic's right eyebrow shot up in surprise.

"She was going to bite my best friend," Leesa explained. "Somehow, I managed to knock her away—once, at least."

"A vampire, you say?" Dominic shook his head in amazement. "I will want to hear more about that, and about any other things you may have experienced as well. But I expect you will feel more comfortable after you have learned a bit more about me."

Rave had been watching and listening with keen interest. "As would I," he said.

"It's a long story," Dominic said. "I will try to cover the highlights now, and fill in any questions later. Does that sound okay to both of you?"

"Yeah, it sounds great," Leesa said. She could feel her heart beginning to beat faster. She was finally about to get some answers!

45. DOMINIC'S STORY

"To start with," Dominic said, "I am a wizard. My people were known as waziri. Perhaps Rave has heard the name. My people had dealings with volkaanes many years ago."

"Yes, I have heard of your kind," Rave said.

Leesa sensed a slight lessening in Rave's guard when Dominic said he was a waziri.

"Rave mentioned the name to me," she said, "when I told him about some of the things that were happening to."

"We are a clan of wizards," Dominic said. "Or, at least we were."

"Were?" Rave asked.

The sadness that descended over Dominic's eyes was unmistakable.

"I am the only one left, the only one I know of, at least," he said after a moment. "The rest are dead—or changed into something no longer recognizable as waziri."

Leesa did not like the sound of that at all.

"What happened?" Rave asked.

"That's another long story, whose details can wait until another time, I think. In brief, some of my brethren were seduced toward the dark arts and were banished for practicing forbidden magic. One night, they returned and attacked. Though they were fewer in number than us, the battle was never really in doubt. They possessed the same powers we did, and more. The surprise attack and their dark arts were the difference. At the end, there were but two of us left, against more than a half-dozen of the renegades. I survived only because Denethon, the most powerful wizard among us, sacrificed himself so that I might escape and keep the hopes of our clan alive, meager as they might be. I wanted to stay and fight, but Denethon insisted I go. I have no doubt he vanquished one or two more of our enemies before he fell, but fall he did. I felt his life force leave him. Fortunately, by then I was beyond the grasp of our foes."

"When did this all happen?" Rave asked.

"More than a hundred years ago. I have been in hiding ever since, biding my time, hoping one day to right this wrong, or at least to thwart some of their plans."

"What are their plans?" Leesa asked nervously.

"Those who were banished joined with an old enemy," Dominic replied. "He goes by many names, most of them unpronounceable in your tongue. He is sometimes called the Necromancer."

Leesa gasped, remembering Dr. Clerval mentioning that name when they were discussing her zombie dreams.

"You have heard the name before, I see. From Rave, perhaps?"

"No, from one of my professors," Leesa explained. "He's an expert about vampires, but he knows lots of other stuff, too."

"What did he tell you about the Necromancer?"

"I don't remember, exactly. Something about dead people, though. He didn't know anything real specific."

"The Necromancer seeks dominion over death," Dominic said. "For centuries, he has sought to raise an army of the dead and to use them to bring the world under his rule. My people long opposed him, until the traitors crossed to his side."

"If the Necromancer has been at this for so long, why

haven't we ever heard anything about it?" Leesa asked.

"You have," Dominic said. "Human cultures are filled with tales of the walking dead. But you couch them in stories meant to scare children, not as histories."

Images from her dreams rose up in Leesa's head. "Are you saying this has actually happened? That the dead have risen from their graves?"

"Not recently, no. But yes, it has occurred, more than once over the ages. Each time, the Necromancer seems to gain a little more control over them. A hundred years ago, when he began successfully raising the dead in isolated areas of Eastern Europe, the waziri stopped him. We pooled our magic and created a seal between the world of the living and the world of the dead. He has undoubtedly been seeking to break the seal ever since."

Leesa recalled Dr. Clerval telling her about stories from Eastern Europe of gangs of walking dead attacking villagers. Dominic was confirming those tales were true. She wondered if her dreams were a sign the Necromancer was beginning to penetrate the waziri seal.

"Do you think that's where he still is?" she asked. "In Eastern Europe, I mean?"

"I sincerely hope so," Dominic said, for that would mean Leesa was still as safe as she could be. "I could locate him if I wished, but doing so would be like lighting a beacon to show him where I am. Indeed, almost any use of my powers would reveal me, and I am not yet ready to face him and his renegade minions."

Leesa decided it was time to tell Dominic about her dreams.

"I've had several dreams about bodies rising from the grave," she said.

Dominic's face grew tight at Leesa's revelation. "Tell me about the dreams," he said.

Leesa described her three zombie dreams and then told Dominic how she had later seen something similar to each one on the news. Halfway through her story, Dominic got up from his chair and began pacing around the room.

"This is ill news," he said when Leesa finished. "If what you say is true, it means the Necromancer is beginning to learn how to break our seals. I had hoped we would have more time—much more time."

Leesa stifled a yawn. It was still early—why was she so tired? It certainly wasn't because Dominic's story was boring her. She was eager to hear everything he could tell her. So why was she having so much difficulty shaking her fatigue?

"You are tired," Dominic said. "Forgive me. I should have expected this, and explained it to you sooner."

"What do you mean? Explained what?"

"The amount of power you employed earlier would have drained even a trained wizard a bit. It has no doubt drained you far more. You need to get some rest. We can continue this tomorrow."

"Not yet," Leesa said. "There's still one thing I have to know, if I'm going to get any useful sleep. Why did you say you were my father? What did you mean by that?"

Dominic sat back down and blew out a deep breath. "That's another very complicated story. For now, I'll try to make it as simple as possible."

He took a moment to gather his thoughts. Leesa watched him anxiously, wondering where this would lead.

"You need to understand a little background on the waziri," Dominic began. "Each of us may pass along our magic but once in our lives. We usually choose a child, someone in whom we sense the proper qualities, and impart out powers to him. From that moment on, we mentor him, training him for the moment he turns eighteen, when his magic becomes active."

"You keep saying 'he' and 'him,'" Rave said. "What does this have to do with Leesa? Were not the waziri always men?"

Leesa was suddenly struck by how similar Rave and

Dominic spoke. Not in the way they sounded—Dominic had a bit of an accent, similar in some ways to Stefan's—but in their cadence and the way they put words together. Rave and Dominic both spoke in a slightly stilted manner, a bit formal almost, using few contractions. She wondered if it had to do with growing up so long ago. Perhaps people spoke more formally back then.

"Yes, the waziri have always been men," Dominic replied to Rave's question. "But that was part of my plan."

"What plan?" Leesa asked.

"My plan to stop the Necromancer and his renegade waziri underlings."

Leesa tried to make sense of what Dominic was saying, but her tired brain was making it difficult. Was he telling her that *she* was part of some grand scheme to stop the evil wizards? She sure hoped not. She'd had enough of this magic stuff and supernatural creatures to last a lifetime—enough of all of them except Rave, of course.

Dominic had been watching Leesa's face closely. "I think you are beginning to understand," he said. "I chose to impart my magic to you."

Leesa's head felt like it was spinning. Dominic had imparted magic to her? Rave sat down beside her and put his arm around her back. His touch was comforting, as always.

"How...when?" she managed to ask.

"Before you were born," Dominic said. "Before you mother even knew she was pregnant with you."

Leesa shook her head. "I don't understand."

"I was afraid that if I tried to pass my magic along in the traditional way, my foes would detect it," Dominic explained. "That would have been dangerous for the child, as well as for me. And remember, I only had one chance to do this. So I decided to take a chance, to pursue a different route by choosing an unborn child—a female child. By doing something that had never been done, I hoped for her to elude detection. So far, that part of my plan seems to have worked." He studied Leesa's face for a long moment. "Are you with me so far?"

"Sort of. I think it will take me awhile to understand completely." Leesa yawned again. She really was exhausted.

Rave kissed her hair. "I told you there was more to you than either of us knew."

"There is much you still need to hear," Dominic said, "but I think I have given you enough to digest for now. Besides, you need some rest."

Leesa smiled. "I can't argue with that. Rave, will you stay with me tonight?"

"Of course," Rave replied. "Nothing could make me leave you right now."

Leesa leaned her head against his shoulder. She had a lot to think about, but with Rave beside her, she hoped she would sleep peacefully.

"I will be nearby, keeping watch." Dominic said. He stood up and moved to the door. "I will see you tomorrow."

With Dominic gone, Leesa gave in to her exhaustion.

"I really am tired," she said. "I want to talk with you about all this, but I hope you don't mind waiting until tomorrow."

Rave kissed her hair. "Not at all. Go to sleep, my love."

Leesa stretched out atop the bed, and Rave lay down beside her. She nestled her head into the crook of his arm. Within moments, she was fast asleep.

46. CHOICES

When Leesa opened her eyes the next morning, Rave was still beside her, smiling. She could not think of any better sight to be greeted by.

"Good morning, beautiful," he said.

Leesa smiled. "Good morning to you, too."

Thin strips of pale daylight outlined her curtains, telling her it was at least eight o'clock. She stretched her arms out over her head, feeling deliciously refreshed. She always slept well with Rave beside her.

"You slept very peacefully," Rave said. "It was good to see."

Leesa ran her fingers through her hair, moving some tangled strands away from her face.

"Don't tell me you were staring at me the whole night," she said, hoping she hadn't done anything gross, like drooling in her sleep.

"No, of course not." Rave kissed her forehead and grinned. "Just most of it."

"Ugghh!" Leesa hid her eyes behind her forearm.

"Don't worry, you're beautiful when you sleep."

Leesa smiled. "Thank you. You look pretty good yourself, considering you spent most of the night watching me."

"I told you, volkaanes don't need much sleep. Did you have

any dreams?"

Leesa thought for a moment. Pieces of a dream began to come to her.

"I did, yeah," she said, remembering. "I dreamed of wizards battling an army of monsters. The wizards were shooting lightning bolts and fireballs from their staffs and wands. The fireballs were blue, of course."

"Naturally," Rave said, grinning again. "We'll make a volkaane out of you yet."

Leesa returned his grin. "Ha! Don't I wish." She thought back to last night's dream. "The dream didn't feel real, though, and it definitely wasn't scary like the other ones. It was more like watching a movie. A couple of the wizards even resembled Gandalf and Harry Potter."

Rave laughed. "We'll have to ask Dominic about getting you a wand, then," he joked.

"Ha! I think not." Leesa pushed herself up to a sitting position. "Has he been around at all yet?"

"I sensed his presence briefly a couple of times during the night. Never for long, though. I get the feeling he does not remain still very much."

"I hope he comes back soon. I've got so many questions."

"I'm sure he will. He seemed so relieved to find you, I doubt he'll waste much time now."

"You're right." She gave Rave a peck on the cheek and got up from the bed. "I'd better get cleaned up and grab something to eat while I've got the chance."

Dominic returned shortly before ten o'clock, giving Leesa time to shower and wolf down a breakfast of vanilla yogurt and a banana. It was not much of a meal, but she wasn't sure her stomach could handle much more, as keyed up as she was about getting more answers from Dominic.

He was wearing the same black jacket and khaki pants as

yesterday, though they didn't appear to be slept in. As a matter of fact, they looked to Leesa as if they had come freshly out of the closet this morning. She wondered if maybe there was magic involved.

"Are you ready to hear more about the magic?" Dominic asked her.

"Definitely. I need to understand what's been happening to me."

Dominic flashed a small smile. "Good. I believe I can give you a pretty good start in the next hour or two." He paused for a moment, before adding, "And then you will have a decision to make."

Leesa wondered what kind of decision he meant, but quickly pushed it from her thoughts. She figured she would learn soon enough.

"Rave doesn't think you like to stay still very long," she said. "Is that true?"

Dominic's smile was wider this time.

He has a friendly smile, Leesa thought, but then remembered Edwina also had a friendly smile. Still, she detected nothing threatening from the wizard.

"Rave is right," Dominic said. "It's an old habit, built from so many years trying to remain hidden."

"Let's go for a walk," Leesa suggested, thinking a walk would make Dominic feel more comfortable and might also make it easier for her to deal with whatever he was going to tell her.

Dominic's eyes strayed involuntarily to Leesa's leg, but he quickly pulled them away. He wondered once again whether his actions had played any role in Leesa's affliction.

Leesa recognized the look. "I told you, my leg doesn't hurt at all." She held her foot out and grinned. "I can't run very fast and I suck at dancing, but I can walk with just about anybody."

"A walk sounds great," Dominic said.

Leesa grabbed her parka and her knit cap. "Let's go."

Outside, the morning was cold and blustery, with a chill wind blowing out of the northeast. Thick, dark clouds covered the eastern half of the sky like a shroud. Leesa wondered if they were finally about to get their first real snow. She had been looking forward to some snow all winter, but wasn't sure now would be the best time for it, with all that was happening.

Though the wind stung her cheeks a bit, the cold did not bother her, not with her arm linked inside Rave's. Dominic also did not seem overly affected by the cold, at least not that she could see. He didn't seem as oblivious to the temperature as Rave was, but he didn't look uncomfortable, either.

"You do walk well, Leesa," Dominic said as they strode at a brisk pace down the sidewalk toward the main gate.

"Told ya," Leesa said, smiling.

"Yes, that you did," Dominic acknowledged. "I'm very glad to see it. I was concerned your leg might somehow be the result of what I did, passing my magic to you before you were born."

"You'll have to get in line if you want to take credit for my leg."

Dominic looked perplexed. "What do you mean?"

Leesa told him about her mom being bitten by the *grafhym* while she was pregnant.

"I've kinda been chalking up most of the stuff that's happened to me to my *grafhym* blood."

Dominic considered that for a few moments.

"That might explain something that has been troubling me," he said, stroking his goatee. "Yes, that might definitely explain it."

"Explain what?" Leesa asked.

"Why I had so much trouble finding you. The magical bond between us should have enabled me to sense your location from a hundred miles away. When I left eighteen years ago to insure your safety, I was counting on being able to find you easily when the time came. Instead, I need to be within a few hundred feet to feel your presence. I think the *grafhym* blood may have altered your vibrations slightly, hiding them from me until I get close."

They crossed through the college's stone gateway and turned west on Washington Street toward downtown. The wind blew almost directly in their faces now, rushing unchecked up the wide road from the river. Leesa's cheeks stung with the cold. She reached a gloved hand up to cover her face from the wind, but before she could do it, Rave's hand was there, gently caressing her cheeks and infusing them with his magical warmth. He has to be the most thoughtful boyfriend ever, she thought. The warm glow she felt blossoming in her chest had nothing to do with his inner fire.

She kissed Rave's fingers and smiled, then turned back to Dominic.

"How long have you been looking for me?"

"Almost a year now, since a few months before you turned eighteen. I wanted time to prepare you for the appearance of your powers. I'm very sorry I was not here. Believe me, you do not want to hear what I have gone through this last year trying to find you."

"If I hadn't dropped my stupid phone, you would have found me sooner," Leesa said, recalling Dominic's phone call, way back on Thanksgiving weekend.

"And you are here now," Rave added. "That's what matters."

"Let me start by telling you a bit about my magic—your magic, Leesa. Waziri possess two kinds of magic—active and passive. Passive magic is what allows me to sense your presence and what keeps me warm in the cold. Your dreams are also passive magic. Passive magic is safe—our enemies cannot detect it and use it to find us."

"So when I learn to control this, I won't feel the cold anymore?" Leesa asked.

"You won't be like Rave," Dominic replied, "but with time, you'll notice the chill far less."

Leesa looked at Rave and grinned. "I guess I'll still have to keep you around," she teased, squeezing his arm affectionately.

Rave smiled back. "I'm very glad to hear that. I was beginning to worry."

Leesa returned her attention to Dominic. "You haven't mentioned my moving things with my thoughts," she said. "I take it that's active magic?"

Dominic nodded. "Yes. Which is why I was able to sense it from the highway."

Rave suddenly stopped walking, so Leesa and Dominic halted as well. Leesa could tell Rave had ratcheted his ever present alertness up a notch.

"If you could sense it," Rave asked Dominic, "could your enemies not also detect it?"

Dominic pursed his lips in thought. "Perhaps, if they were close enough. But I see no reason they should be anywhere near here. Even if they were, I think the alteration in Leesa's vibrations would make it difficult for them to detect her. Her bond with me is direct, like a father to his daughter. Their connection to her is diluted, just waziri to waziri. I also believe Leesa is shielded somewhat by being female. The *grafhym* blood probably lends another layer of protection."

"So you are certain she is safe?" Rave persisted.

"As certain as I can be," Dominic replied. "Remember, my reason for choosing an unborn female was to create something beyond my enemies' ken. With the *grafhym* influence added in, I feel even more confident."

Leesa thought how ironic it was that a story she had never believed, about a one-fanged vampire biting her mom, would be working to protect her once again. Thinking about the *grafhym* blood prompted a second thought.

"What would happen if a vampire tried to turn me?" she asked Dominic.

Dominic was clearly surprised by her question. "I doubt it

could do it," he said after a moment. "Your waziri nature would probably prevent it. Why do ask? This is the second time you have mentioned vampires."

"It's a long story," Leesa said, thinking this might be another reason Stefan had been unable to turn her. She wondered if he had sensed this magical part of her nature. "I'll tell you about it later. Right now, I want to hear more about waziri magic." She linked her arm back inside Rave's. "Let's keep walking."

The three of them headed back down the road. Leesa was glad to see Dominic was paying no more attention to her limp.

"You were about to tell me about active magic," Leesa said.

"Yes," Dominic replied. "Whereas passive magic remains within you—staying warm, sensing magic being used, your dreams—active magic affects external things. There are two forms of active magic. Spells, which must be learned, and innate powers, which are already inside you and must merely be unleashed and controlled. Blasting a vampire away from your friend was a power. Making someone fall asleep or making them forget something would require a spell."

Leesa remained silent while she tried to digest everything Dominic said. Active and passive, spells and powers, learn or unleash, internal or external—it was all pretty confusing, especially for someone who until yesterday had no inkling she actually had any magic inside her. On top of all that, there were renegade wizards and some guy called the Necromancer who would want to kill her if they ever learned she existed. Suddenly, dealing with plain old vampires did not seem quite so bad.

"This is all pretty complicated," she said finally.

"More complicated than you know," Dominic replied. "It is why I wanted to find you before you came of age, to help prepare you for it. Still, I would not have expected you to have experienced so much, so soon. I think *Destiratu* probably has had a hand in that."

"Rave told me about how *Destiratu* affects vampires and

volkaanes. Do you mean it affects wizards as well?"

"*Destiratu* affects all things magical, most often by magnifying them. My renegade brethren attacked during the previous *Destiratu*. I'm certain its pull played a role." Dominic shook his head regretfully. "I never planned for you to come of age during a time of *Destiratu*, Leesa. I never even considered it, I'm sorry to say. That was a mistake on my part, I'm afraid."

"You could not have known," Rave said. "None of us knows when *Destiratu* will arise, not until it begins."

"No, I guess not," Dominic agreed. "Still, it complicates things."

"Things with Leesa are always complicated," Rave said, smiling. He leaned over and gave her a quick kiss on the forehead. "But I wouldn't have it any other way."

"Ha! Don't talk to me about complicated, Mister," Leesa said, grinning. "I'm not the one with a kiss that could fry his girlfriend to ashes." A new thought popped into her head, a very pleasant thought. "Dominic, could my magic make me immune to Rave's fire? Could you teach me to safely kiss him as much as I wanted?"

Dominic smiled. "I'm sorry, no. Nothing can withstand the full force of a volkaane's heat—not even me." He recognized the disappointment that darkened Leesa's face. "But you should already have a bit of innate tolerance to it, and I can train you to be even more resistant."

Leesa remembered Balin's surprise she was not more harmed when Rave lost control. She guessed her magic must have protected her at least a little. She turned to Rave and squeezed his arm.

"You hear that? You'd better get yourself ready for some major making out."

"A guy can only dream," Rave replied, grinning.

Leesa turned back to Dominic. "All of a sudden this magic stuff isn't sounding so bad," she said. "Not bad at all."

"Yes, I can see that," Dominic replied, smiling. "But do not be so hasty. Learning to control even a tiny bit of your power will take much effort." He reached out and gently grabbed Leesa's arm, pulling her to a halt. His voice turned very serious. "And you must understand, the more you learn, the greater the danger from our enemies."

Leesa swallowed hard. With visions of kissing Rave swirling in her head, she had kind of forgotten about the danger part for a moment.

"Is that what you meant when you said I had a decision to make?" she asked. "That I could decide not to have you teach me and just keep dealing with this magic stuff when it pops up as best I can?" She didn't really like the idea, but thought now that she knew where it was coming from, she might be able to handle things with less stress and worry. At least she would know she wasn't going crazy—that was something all by itself.

"That is one choice, certainly," Dominic replied. "And I will go along with it if that is your wish. But leaving you like that is not one of the choices I wish to offer."

"What, then?" Leesa asked, confused now. She had thought she had but two choices: have Dominic train her, or send him away. She was glad to hear there might be a third option, whatever it was.

"One choice you already know—for me to stay and teach you how to use your powers. That road will be a long and difficult one, and a very dangerous one. Still, it is the path I hope you will choose. But I realize how much I am asking of you. I want to make sure you fully understand the dangers before you decide."

Leesa appreciated Dominic's honesty. She almost felt like he was trying to talk her out of choosing the path he wanted her to follow—which meant such a path must be very dangerous, indeed.

"What's my other choice?" she asked.

"If you wish, I can teach you to restrain your magic, to keep it locked inside you. You will not be able to use it, but it will not bother you the way it has been. Once I teach you that, I will go far from here, taking any danger with me."

Lock up her magic? Leesa had not realized that was a possibility—a possibility that sounded awfully good right now. She was tired of all this stuff, of nightmares disturbing her sleep and powers she could not control suddenly appearing out of nowhere. She had already done more than any young girl should be expected to do, helping to cure her mom and saving Bradley from Edwina. She just wanted to live happily with Rave and to enjoy her now healthy and happy family. Surely Dominic would understand if she chose to deny her powers, even if it messed up his big plan. Rave would understand, too, she knew. In fact, she thought Rave would probably prefer that choice.

"What do you think I should do, Rave?"

Rave looked uncomfortable, one of the very few times she had ever seen him like that. She wondered why.

"I'm torn," he said after a moment. "My first thought is a selfish one—that I want you safe and as far from danger as possible." He took both of Leesa's hands in his. "But you once told me you would never let me risk giving up my fire for you, because my fire is the essence of my nature. So how can I ask you to give up your magic, because like it or not, magic is part of your nature. This is a decision only you can make. Just know I will be by your side whichever path you choose."

Leesa realized Rave was right—no one could make this decision for her. Nor should they have to. She raised herself up on her toes and kissed Rave on the forehead, then turned to Dominic.

"I need time to think about this," she said. "It's a really big decision."

"Yes, it is indeed. I would never rush you into it. Please, take all the time you need."

"Let's continue our walk. You can tell me more about your

magic—our magic. Then I'll think about it tonight and try to have an answer for you in the morning. Okay?"

"Yes, certainly," Dominic said. "I'll tell you all I can about our powers, and then give you as much time as you need to come to a decision."

They had not gone far when Leesa suddenly stopped short. She grabbed Dominic's forearm.

"I just thought of something," she said. "How old are you?"

Dominic looked perplexed. "I have seen six century marks."

Leesa raised her eyebrows. She had known Dominic must be two hundred years old at least, but had not expected to hear he was three times that.

"When you passed your magic on to me, did the age thing come along with it?"

Dominic allowed himself a small smile as he realized where Leesa was heading.

"I'm not completely certain," he said, "but to some extent, yes. If you choose to forgo your magic, you will probably still live a bit longer than the average human. If you embrace the magic, it's possible you could see five centuries or more."

"Five centuries?" Leesa could not believe it.

"Provided you survive our enemies, of course, which is by no means certain," Dominic cautioned.

Suddenly, Leesa did not care about the danger. All she could think of was having five hundred years together with Rave. She wrapped her arm around his back and smiled. This was the easiest decision she had ever made.

"I'm in," she said to Dominic. "Teach me the magic."

BREATHLESS

Scott Prussing was born in New Jersey, but was smart enough to move to beautiful San Diego as soon as he received his Master's degree in psychology from Yale University. Scott is currently working on Fearless, the third book in the Blue Fire Saga. In addition to writing, Scott enjoys hiking, riding his bicycle near the beach, and golf. He is one of the few remaining people in the United States without a cell phone.

Contact Scott and learn all about his books at
www.scottprussing.com.

9351273R0

Made in the USA
Charleston, SC
04 September 2011